T0304837

the
drownings

Also by Hazel Barkworth

Heatstroke

the
drownings

hazel
barkworth

REVIEW

First published in 2024 by Headline Review
An imprint of HEADLINE PUBLISHING GROUP

1

Cataloguing in Publication Data is available from the British Library

Hardback ISBN 978 1 0354 0953 2

Typeset in Dante MT by CC Book Production
Printed and bound in Great Britain by Clays Ltd, Elcograf S.p.A.

Headline's policy is to use papers that are natural, renewable and
recyclable products and made from wood grown in well-managed forests
and other controlled sources. The logging and manufacturing processes are
expected to conform to the environmental regulations of the country of origin.

HEADLINE PUBLISHING GROUP
An Hachette UK Company
Carmelite House
50 Victoria Embankment
London EC4Y 0DZ

www.headline.co.uk
www.hachette.co.uk

To my parents, Linda and Glen

'. . . the years of hard swimming had packed muscles on my frame and made me very strong [. . .] strong enough to inflict heavy damage'

Esther Williams

'The water was closing around me'

Stevie Nicks, 'Crystal'

'Shelley said, mournfully, "Why can't I swim, it seems so very easy?"
    I answered, "Because you think you can't."'

Edward Trelawny, *Recollections of the Last Days of Shelley and Byron*

PART ONE

PART ONE

1

Darkness fell differently in that nook of the north, earlier in the year and earlier in the day. It made the mid-afternoon desolate. That northern campus was almost an island, with a swift tributary of the River Limn sweeping down one side, and raw coastline biting into the other. It should have soothed Serena to be surrounded by so much water, but this wasn't the water she knew. This water was brutal.

She focused on nothing but the footpath she trod, each clumsy step sending a jolt of pain through her knee. Her room was only minutes away, but those stretches of grass between buildings felt remote. The university campus didn't seem to exist on a map but as its own sequestered world, inaccessible except by invitation. Mist hung over the winding path like a headache, leaving only a few feet ahead clear as Serena walked. The screaming caws of seagulls sounded unearthly, and creatures of myth must surely live in that ether.

Everything around her writhed. Tree branches hid themselves, then silently clawed to tangle her hair. Tarmac twisted, the footpath slinking left or right when the whim seized it.

Then, something broke the fog. A solid shape moving closer. Serena felt the flash in her gut all women know. Was this it? Was this the moment of her great miscalculation? There was no one in earshot. Her crutches made running impossible, so instinct forced her hands into fists, gripping the handles, preparing them as weapons. Blood flooded her cheeks. Was it already too late to be out alone? She couldn't grasp back the advice she'd read. Was she supposed to meet his eyes? Should she cut across the damp grass to avoid him? By now, he was visible. Serena forced her head straight. He was no older than her, smiling as he emerged from the mist, lips pressed, eyebrows raised in greeting. Serena breathed.

He paused as they passed.

'You alright, love?' His accent was local. She'd barely spoken to a boy in the three weeks since she arrived there.

He clocked her plastered leg, the metal crutches.

'Yes, yeah, I'm going to . . .' Her lips were too cold to move easily.

'You sure?'

The ornate university buildings around them were indistinguishable, with no way to discern what happened behind each wall. Their honeyed stone loomed grey in the gloom.

'Yeah, thanks. I live over there.' Serena pointed to the nearest building. A library, perhaps, or a faculty. Without waiting for a response, she turned, pushing herself to hurry, mustering a clattering lurch. She wondered if he was watching.

The hospital, when she reached it, was as grey as the weather. Serena waited for blank minutes on a plastic chair. Her cast was cut by a saw. It wasn't what she'd expected, that shrieking serrated blade, a breath from her body. Whirring, it magically discerned what was plaster and what flesh, one slip away from gruesome. Fluff from the shredded material lingered in the air as the cast was halved and cracked like a nut. Her fractured patella was apparently healed enough to cope. The padding and stocking that had lived beneath the cast were snipped, and the material smelled so pungently human that Serena had to look away.

Her leg was whiter and smaller, withered from no weight on the muscle, no sun on the skin. Thick hairs had grown in those weeks, and the revealed calf was as furred as a hibernating creature. It felt cruel to expose a thing so vulnerable. It should be left it in its plaster burrow, to heal more, to ready itself for the outside world.

The walk back through campus from the bus stop was murky. Only the chemical glow of streetlamps broke through, at odds with the ancient architecture. Those vaunted walls were complex, no bricks but carved stone with coats of arms etched in their sides, arches pinched at the top, spires reaching to the sky. So many people, over so many years ago, had worked to create them. Serena's crutches clanked with every step, her knee still unable to take the strain. Each of those imposing buildings was studded with windows. Behind the glass of every one of them, behind their identical curtains, were people doing better than her, finding their feet after a couple of weeks. Serena couldn't settle, but there was no way back. She was bound to this place for three years.

She followed the river this time, rather than those tangled paths across the grass. It began at the northernmost edge of the campus and flowed down its east side, cutting off the rest of the county, before eventually reaching the sea. Serena had never looked at that river without dread. High brick walls hid portions of it, but other stretches opened to the churn below. She'd heard about the drowned students. Stories of them clogged any internet search for the university, their names were whispered in every fresher conversation. Signs along the wall warned of deep water, but that water held more than depth. A welcome letter had cautioned against walking this way in the dark, hinted at the fate of those unlucky under-graduates. They'd stumbled on the towpath after nights out, and their mottled, bloated bodies weren't found until days later. That water was unrelenting. It was a terrible way to die.

Something had drawn her to the river path, and Serena longed to dip a hand into the freezing water, to feel that con-nection again. It would be nothing like the warm chlorine she was used to, not clean or controlled or kept within strict lanes. This water was wild. It had flowed through that ground for centuries, long before the university was dreamed of. It had killed. Its cold on her fingers would be excruciating, but might give the same thrill she knew from the pool. Serena could never be rid of the water; it filled every cell to the brim. On dry land, she felt lost.

Sitting on a stump, Serena stared at the river. Behind her were trees that lined the whole stretch of water and, behind them, the scattered buildings of the campus, those clusters of rooms that were now her whole life. The sweatpants that had once clung to her cast were damp and loose now, her fleece jacket offering little protection from the October chill. Resorting to a primal impulse to keep itself warm, her body shuddered, muscles contracting and releasing outside her control. Her left knee seared. Every part of her was knee.

Despite the proximity, the rest of campus seemed distant. Thousands of people breathed within those same three hundred acres, but Serena felt alone. Hidden by the canopy of trees, with the river swallowing every other sound, she could be anywhere. Early evening had drained all colour. The river was the same grey as the sky, and Serena dissolved into it. Life on land was too harsh. She looked down at her shaking hands and imagined the fingers fusing, webbing with a fine membrane until they were no longer digits but a scoop that could speed her through the water. Gills could part at her neck, brilliant and obscene, able to gulp oxygen. Her legs could bind to form a thick tail, knee healing in seconds, skin shimmering. The muscles would grow powerful, letting her dive without a twinge. It might be simpler under there, but the river was cruel. Its ripples were dense with memories.

Serena closed her eyes, breathed the river's dank scent. When she opened them, the view was different. Through the dusk a girl was walking. She was unsteady, veering from one side of the towpath to the other. Her dress was vague in the half-light, snug around her hips and thighs, a dress for a nightclub. When the safety lights caught it, the material glittered, making her momentarily spectral. Serena blinked to make sure she was real.

She wore no coat in the stinging cold. Her steps wobbled as if in heels, but Serena could make out her shoes, straps hooked over two fingers. Picking her way across the frozen mud in bare feet, she seemed to dance, a strange sway to no music. As the girl staggered, air caught in Serena's lungs. Those other students had lost their footing on this same stretch of river. She could only stare at the girl. The complicated criss-cross of straps at her neck. The reel of her gait. The glisten of her dress. The girl glimmered in the phosphorescence for a moment. Then vanished. Nothing but grey was left where she'd once been.

THIRTEEN YEARS OLD

She'd sensed it immediately. His eyes. The prickle of his eyes on her wet skin. As she cut through the water, Serena became conscious of how her body moved. The pool was busy, but she wanted to be alone. The noise – the thwack of water, the whistles, the shriek of voices smashing against ceramic tile – calmed when her ears went beneath the surface. It wasn't muffled like a film, not that lumbering slow motion, but clear. With no air, the sounds went straight to her skull. Serena wished she could stay under and complete whole lengths in one breath, but every stroke forced her head up. Noise, then calm. Noise, then calm.

When she reached the end of the lane, he was waiting, squatted down, legs splayed so the thick muscles of his thighs showed. His trainers were inches from her eyes.

'Are you in a team?'

Serena lifted her goggles. His arms were tanned.

'A squad? Are you in a squad?'

The noise, now she hoisted herself onto the pool's gutter, was inescapable.

'You're a natural in the water. Completely instinctive. And you've got incredible form. I think you should train. I'm Niko, by the way.'

Serena became aware of her swimming costume. Faded raspberry pink, once her sister's. It felt insubstantial when he looked at her. No one had ever looked at her like that.

'You're a bit old to start out, but I reckon you can make up the difference.'

He bobbed on his heels, the white soles of his shoes nearly touching her fingers. Serena had never been called old. She'd turned thirteen the month before.

'What do you think?'

Niko's accent was odd to her, slow and drawn out, from somewhere far away. She wasn't sure what he was asking, but a thrill formed in her stomach, the water buoyed her higher. He thought she was special. Serena nodded.

The first thing Niko taught Serena to do was think. *Winning is about vision. If you can imagine it, it can happen.* On that first day of training, she didn't touch the water, though she longed for it. Sat by the side of the pool, he spoke, lips so near to her ear his voice was all she heard.

She closed her eyes, shutting out everything but him. That lulling Australian accent. Slow vowels and blurred consonants.

Like a spell. *You're walking up there.* Serena felt her muscles respond. Without conscious thought, her calves twitched in the walk he described, as if he spoke straight to her sinews. *You're standing on the block. Your feet are rooted down. You're primed.* Her toes pressed against the ground, massaging the bobbled tiles of the poolside. Her eyes stayed closed, but she could smell the chlorine and sweat of him. If she peeked, she'd see his forearms. *You dive perfectly, smoothly, barely ruffling the water.* There was a tattoo under the hair. A shark's jawbone, gaping and hideous. He was tanned in the depths of winter, as if he'd brought the Antipodes with him, baked into his skin.

You're powering through the water, slicing through it. Niko had been a champion. Serena knew before he'd told her. *Your muscles don't even ache.* He'd swum nationally and internationally. His hair was longer now but held the same bleached tips. *No one else is as fast as you; they're trailing behind. You know you're the best, and they know it too.* His voice tightened as the imagined race reached its climax. *You know you can do it. You push harder. Harder than they will. A few more strokes.* The pool sat beyond them. That perfect rectangle housing so much movement. *Your fingers reach the pads first.* Serena could sense the pool's sharp scent, feel its textures. Every detail was vivid. *You've done it.* His voice right into her brain. *You're powerful.* If you can imagine it, it can happen. *You're so powerful.*

The alarm's bleat should have been horrifying, so early it was still night, but Serena sat upright. There was magic to that dark morning. She'd be in the water soon. Moving silently, she wrestled herself into one of the new swimming costumes, damp from the previous afternoon. It stuck to her skin, cold and cloying, refusing to move despite her tugging.

Her mother stood in the light of the kitchen, coffee in hand, breakfast prepared at five-fifteen.

'It's high protein. Like Niko said.' Their voices were whispers, so as not to wake her father and sister.

When Niko had explained the schedules, her mother hadn't blinked. When he'd told Elizabeth what he thought her daughter could be capable of, she'd simply nodded, but Serena had seen the delight flicker around her mouth.

The car was cold and the roads empty, the whole world silent. For three mornings a week, that hushed journey was theirs. They sailed through roundabouts and waited at deserted red lights. When they pulled in, Serena kissed her mother's cheek – *Love you* – and left her in the car. As the leisure centre's automatic doors parted, the warm air and fluorescent lights smacked. From that point, it was hectic. She had to keep pace in the cramped, stifling changing rooms. Clothes off and stuffed in a locker, costume underneath, hair dampened, cap and goggles on. Those sessions had strict beats.

One wall of the pool was glass, and Serena watched the morning morph as she swam. In the brief pauses between sets, she charted the progress of the sky. Dark for several breaks, like it would never alter. Then – barely discernible – deep violet. After that, it sped. Reddish pink. A startling swing to blue, vivid at first, then softer with each break, until it settled on the dull lilac of morning. Serena recognised that colour: it was the sky everyone saw. In that water, she witnessed a world most people never knew. They woke after the wonder had faded.

Serena's first racing costume transformed her. Lycra compressed her breasts, hips and stomach to a hard thorax, flattening every curve so the water had nothing to cling to. It was too tight to wear for more than half an hour. Serena stared at herself in the changing-room mirrors. She wasn't a girl any more, with her hair hidden under a cap, her eyes distorted by goggles. She was formidable.

She lined up with others from around the region, exactly as Niko explained. They had the same firm stomachs and meaty shoulders, nothing about those bodies was soft. Serena found her mother in the stands, met her eyes and nodded. There was no doubt in the returned nod. *You're standing on the block. Your feet are rooted down.* Her toes pressed on the rubber mat. Every detail was as he'd described, as she'd imagined. Her name echoed around the poolside. *Serena Roberts.* Then the beep that made them crouch. She'd done it before in her mind. *You are primed.* She entered the water as they'd planned. *You dive perfectly.* Her limbs did what they already knew. It was instinctual. *You're powering through the water.* Niko had explained her body to her. She was lucky. When dry, she could be awkward – height too obvious, arms too long – but in water, she was ideal. *No one else is as fast as you; they're trailing behind.* She never had to fight her genes. Every part of her was as if it had been divined. The width of her shoulders, the span of her hands, the exact ratios of feet and calves.

At the end of each length, she tumbled, then drove forward. She couldn't see the other girls, but sensed clear space ahead. *You know you're the best, and they know it too.* The ache in her muscles started, like he'd told her it would, but only a length was left. She'd trained for less than a month. It came so easily it felt like magic. *You push harder. Harder than they will.* The end of the lane must be close, but each stroke brought more water. *Your fingers reach the pads.* Serena stretched as far as she could. Her hand smashed against the plastic so hard it hurt. She knew she'd been first. Everything Niko had told her was true. It worked. *You've done it.* What she'd imagined was real. Her mind had that power. Pulling off her goggles, Serena saw Niko pacing towards her. *You're powerful.* Her body was electric. *You're so powerful.*

Serena watched as her sister braided Zara's hair, lifting each thick piece, twisting it around, then gripping in place. Zara's hair was so abundant it took hours. Kelly cosseted their younger cousin, dressed her up like a doll, and Zara beamed from the attention.

The trip had been planned for months. Kelly had memorised the lyrics from a downloaded cast album, then played it all morning until Zara also knew them by heart. They sang two different parts. The girl with the green skin, Serena assumed, and the blonde who spoke into her ear on the poster.

Zara's singing voice was a whisper. She hid behind that mass of dark hair, skittish, eyes widening at the slightest clatter. Kelly could coax her out a little, but she seemed so much younger than eleven.

'She can miss this one session, Liz.' Zara's mother, Anoushka, had a voice that filled the house.

Serena's throat tensed at her aunt's words. It wasn't possible. She reached to grab her mother's wrist, but didn't need to.

'Absolutely not, I'm afraid. She has a race tomorrow. This practice is essential.'

Anoushka inhaled slowly, toying with one of the sparkled hairclips, pulling it wide open before snapping it shut.

It was only the second race Niko had prepped her for, but there was nothing more important. Serena needed to be back in the water; her skin grew tight on dry land.

'It matters a great deal to her.'

'Going into London to see a show with her cousins matters to Zara.' The glittered clip was stretched in Anoushka's hands to the point of breaking. 'It's all she's talked about for weeks. It's her birthday, for God's sake. You know she needs this.'

Elizabeth didn't move.

It began as a high wail, the loudest sound Serena had ever heard her cousin make. She didn't know Zara was in earshot. The sound deepened to a guttural cry of complete despair.

Anoushka sighed as she turned to her daughter, bent to stroke her back. The noise from behind that hair didn't cease.

Serena knew she should feel guilty, should join the others for a day of tiny ice-cream tubs and glossy programmes in the dark, should watch those rival witches performing sorcery in technicolour, but her head was already full. All she could think of were Niko's words.

By the second race, Serena was certain. Her name reverberated again around the pool. All five syllables. *Serena Roberts.* Every eye was on her for that precious moment. Other girls stretched and warmed their muscles. Rotating their arms in wide loops, forcing shoulder joints to all angles, tilting their heads as far as possible one way, then the other. They crouched to the pool to splash their costumes, making sure no pockets of air formed between Lycra and skin. Serena heard them murmur to themselves, incantations to drive them on.

'You've got this.'

'Focus.'

They jumped on the spot, pointing toes then flexing them, fixing their caps, licking the insides of goggles to prevent fogging, shaking their legs, slurping from water bottles. Serena remained still. *Your feet are rooted down. You're primed.* Those jittery rituals made no difference to their time. She'd already imagined it. Placing her hands on her hips, she looked at nothing but the water. Niko's words were calm in her head. She left the others to their jiggling and tugging.

Eventually, a voice. *Take your mark*. The crowd froze, and the swimmers bent, one foot angled above the other on the starting block. So many seconds passed before the bleep. Serena didn't wait for the noise or the light that flashed in her eyeline. She knew. She already knew. She could feel the electricity surge down the wires, sense the finger flex that pressed the button. It was exactly as she'd visualised. She hit the water first.

She fixed on that stream of tiles, black where the others were white, that ran the whole span of the pool. Thinking only of that stripe, hearing only Niko's words. *You're powering through the water, slicing through it.* She trusted her body and trusted the water was hers. The others were fools. They charged into that pool like it was a battle, saw the water as the enemy and thrashed against it. *They're trailing behind.* Serena let herself submit to it, become part of it. She let the water hold her however it wanted. You didn't win because of training: those morning hours of drills and practice were the sacrifices you made on its altar, simply proof of devotion. *You're so powerful.* The others would never understand.

2

Serena felt her hand hit her mouth. The girl hadn't been consumed by the air but had fallen to the only possible place. Standing sent a stab through Serena's knee that took her breath. She cantered across the towpath's mud, her steps wild and unbearable. That greyness made time stretch.

The girl was a real person, not a shimmering, dancing spectre. Real and solid and struggling in the black water of the river. The cold must be outrageous, but she didn't cry out. The only sound was the white noise of the water itself. Part of Serena's brain snapped to attention. She'd been trained in this. The girl would have been swallowed right down at first, deep into that freezing darkness – head covered, whole body enclosed – then spat back up. She was on the surface now, her arms and legs battling the current. This was good. If she was moving, she wasn't drowning. Drowning had an unexpected stillness. Water safety was taught in mandatory sessions at the pool and Serena remembered key phrases. *Speech is secondary to breathing.* Silence was necessary.

'Hey! Hello!' The girl didn't react. 'Can you see me?'

For a second, Serena lost her again to the fuzzy dark, then she was there, arms extended as if trying to press down against the water. As if trying to fly.

Every instinct in Serena pushed her to enter the river. Every muscle knew what to do. Grab the girl and swim across the current to the bank. It would take no time, but it was impossible. Her smashed knee made her whole body useless. Even with the cast gone, she couldn't kick, couldn't bend to clamber in.

Serena's breaths came too quickly. Each second that passed became more dangerous. Leaning as far as possible, arm looped around a tree trunk, she held out one crutch, its grey tip wobbling in the gloom.

'Can you reach?'

It was far from the girl's grip, out of her sight. She'd stumbled down that towpath under the influence of something. Something that muddled her thoughts, dimmed her eyes, stopped her from reaching out. All she could do was churn her legs and arms, and that energy wouldn't last.

Scanning the bank, Serena urged her eyes to drink in more light. Behind the trees, the campus might as well be a world away. With no time to call for help, it was on her. A branch had fallen into the bracken on the far side of the towpath. It might be long enough to reach. Serena rushed to it and grabbed at the damp bark, felt it slip under her fingers. The girl needed to keep moving. That glittering dress would be growing heavy, its complex tangle of straps yanking at her neck. The river was remorseless. Its reeds would grab at her like hands, claim her as its own.

The branch wouldn't budge. Serena was tentative, afraid of the pain, but she had no choice. Tightening her grip on the slimy bark, she pulled. Arms had always been her powerhouse. As she wrenched it from the undergrowth, her hands were slashed by whatever twigs hid in that dense darkness.

The girl was there, but slowing. Her eyes would be turning glassy. Yanking the branch into place, Serena let it rip across her cheek, but couldn't get close enough. The water would engulf her. There was no way to stop it. Serena would be dry and useless on the bank, watching as a young woman died in front of her. Nothing she'd learned was helpful when her body was so feeble.

'Help.' Serena's voice rasped in her throat.

'Help! Please!' There was no one to hear.

The river kept flowing, the trees swayed. They didn't care.

In the dimness, only details were visible. The slick of the girl's hair. The faint light of her eyes when they reflected the streetlamps. The gap of her open mouth.

'Come closer. Come towards me.'

No matter how intently Serena focused, she couldn't make that other body stir. Instead, she stared at the water. It wasn't water she knew. This water hadn't earned her trust. It wanted to pull the girl under, to drag her out to the sea, smash her in its white foam. Serena spoke to herself, feeling the shape of the words in her mouth. *Bring her closer. Bring her closer.* It had to still be possible. Her muscles were tight with desperation.

Nothing was clear in the growing dark but – for a fraction of a second – the water didn't tug the girl, just held her. The current paused. Serena didn't let her breath out. Barely a blink, but enough time for the girl to gasp, fill her lungs, send oxygen to her extremities. It was hardly perceptible, but everything had changed. The girl could lift her left arm to smack the surface. Her legs kicked once, twice. It was enough. She drifted closer.

Serena leapt at the chance, holding the branch out as far as she could. Her feet slid on the mud, her knee screaming. The pain was savage but irrelevant. Stretching with all she had, she locked eyes with the girl.

'You can reach it. Please, grab it.'

Serena felt a tug, an extra weight on the branch.

'Yes!'

With every heave the girl drew nearer. Serena reached, feeling cold air, then, all at once, the firm warmth of the girl's flesh, a hand in her own. Now to pull her from the water. Serena couldn't fail now, but the body she once relied upon felt pathetic. The girl's hands were slipping, inching her back into the lethal depths.

Then, other hands. Another person.

'Stay there. I can help.' A voice.

A figure stepping boldly down the bank, one leg in the water, one leveraged against the mud. A woman, her face firm, her body moving in ways Serena's couldn't. She grasped the girl and hoisted. The river water reached her thigh, even so close to the bank.

'Do you have her?' The voice was calm and clear.

Serena couldn't reply but heaved as best she could, the girl rising from the water, but not far enough.

'Keep going.'

It took several attempts, their bodies swinging forwards then back, their muscles straining together until Serena tumbled onto the mud, the girl in her arms. The force of it landed the woman on her knees. For a moment, they were a tangle. The woman's breath was warm on Serena's neck, prickling the hairs of her nape. Their arms were tight around each other as they righted themselves. She held this stranger back through instinct. They'd done it. The girl was on land. Serena's nose on the woman's neck, gripped in a hug as adrenalin whipped through them. She smelled of woodsmoke, some memory of heat in all that cold. Holding each other, they were safe. They were victorious.

The girl stayed where she'd landed, that sodden dress scarcely covering her rump. Breaking apart from the woman, Serena knew to check the girl's breathing, that her heart pulsed its blood fast enough. Her wrist was icy, but the flutter under its skin was strong. It was impossible. The river should have taken her like it took the other students, but there she was, convulsing with cold, her whole body jerking and alive. Serena wrapped her fleece around the girl as a blanket.

The woman unwound the scarf from her neck and crouched down, her head level with Serena's. Their clothes were soaked, thick with mud.

'Are you okay?' It felt strange to look at her face for the first time. Grey eyes, dry lips, no make-up. 'You must be freezing.'

'So must you.'

'I'm fine. You were incredible.'

Serena's breaths were still ragged. It shouldn't have been possible. That moment the river paused. Without it, the girl would be gone.

'Thank you so much. I couldn't have done it by myself.'

The woman shook her head. 'No, it was all you. I heard you when I was heading to my office. I'm Jane.' Those shouts had reached someone.

'Serena.'

Jane stood. 'She wouldn't have stood a chance without you.' Straightening, she pulled out her phone. 'We're on the bank of the River Limn, down from the university's Bowland Gate.' She paced as she spoke, composed despite it all, her face sharp in the dark.

Serena tightened her grip of the girl, let the spangled dress soak into her own clothes, her own skin.

3

The metal dial was devious. Its numbers bore no relation to the temperature of shower water that flowed. Serena needed warmth. The mud had washed off in minutes, but the cold persisted. Her knee hadn't been exposed to water for weeks. She dragged a razor over the dark hairs, leaving her skin bald and bright. The shower spray did little to ease the ache. Clambering on that muddy bank had taken too much, and tablets didn't reach the edges of her pain.

In the heat of the cubicle, Serena's hands throbbed. Shots darted up and down her fingers as they burned their way to warmth. She tried to ball them into fists, rub them against each other, but they wouldn't flex. They'd done something remarkable. She could still feel the grip of the girl's hands on her own, the woman's arms around her. Jane. Those unknown women were the closest Serena had been to anyone in the three weeks since term began.

She knew what she should be doing. Finding her people. Every website trilled out the same platitudes. *Put yourself out there and talk to everyone.* Vloggers stared right down the lens as they gave their advice. *Everyone's as nervous as you are. Keep your door open.* Not one of those suggestions was possible. Those magnificent buildings were so full of people she didn't know. *Hang out in communal areas.* Even light felt intrusive. *Invite your hall mates to join you for a cup of coffee.* Serena turned her lamps off and watched her cousin's early weeks at university play out in real time. They'd never planned to arrive at the same campus – Zara straight from sixth form, Serena after a couple of years' hiatus – but some glitch of fate sent them along the same motorway, so far from where either grew up.

Zara's social media feeds became Serena's portal to everything beyond her room. Those blurred videos, jagging left and right as Zara danced. Clips strung together, a couple of seconds of footage each, a bricolage of light and movement, lips and cheeks. Serena didn't swipe past, but watched the images tumble over and over. Zara gluing eyelashes to her lids. Paint streaking Zara's arms into a tiger, face contorted in a growl. Zara eating from a polystyrene container of chips. She was always laughing.

Serena's own days passed in a fog of forced smiles and cafeteria lunches. By night, she sipped tea in the dark, listened to the girls in her corridor singing. *One: don't pick up the phone.* They clattered into walls and doors in their excitement. She smelled those girls as they gathered. Hairspray and eau de toilette, the same potions as on Zara's posts. *Fenty, Glossier, NYX, Isle of Paradise.*

They'd knocked for her at first. She'd answered a few times, explaining how tricky her crutches made things, then ignored their knuckles against the wood, tapping in the rhythm of the songs they sang, twice as fast as a human heartbeat. She'd held her breath until they'd gone, knowing the isolation that lurked in crowds. Other girls found it so easy: the right words landed on their tongues, their clothes fitted, their limbs were never cumbersome. Serena watched from her window as they stumbled into the courtyard. Tight dresses and hooped earrings, dancing as they walked, a loose happiness to their movements, something childlike Serena could hardly recall. She was two years older than those girls, already twenty. She'd spent seven years underwater. Seven years she was cramming to catch up on.

Tiny snatches of joy from their nights were captured. Serena traced them across campus, from room to bar to party. Every video blared music. She downloaded an app that grabbed songs from the air, a graphic circle bulging to locate the tune. When the names and artists appeared, Serena memorised them. Zooming into the images, she clocked every detail of location and outfit. Exhilarated captions were scrawled over videos. *Getting chaotic. Haute mess. Madness.* Serena spoke the typed words out loud to her empty room. One click triggered another, and she was always awake hours later when their footsteps made her look outside. Everything beyond that window was grey. Gravel, stone and mist. It was always dark there, always raining. She had paid thousands to hide away in that beautiful, bleak campus.

Serena looked down at her wet thighs, stomach, breasts in the shower, so different from the body she'd once known. That body had triumphed. She poured bleach straight from the bottle. A lavish stream that caught the light like oil. She hadn't bought that bottle but had stolen it from the communal toilets, sneaking it back to her room in the folds of a sweatshirt like treasure. She poured directly onto the plastic base of the cubicle, then breathed hard, drinking the air's new texture. There it was. That delicious prickle in her eyes, that grip at the back of her throat. As the vapour rose, Serena took full gulps. The smell had dimension, time as well as space. It cast her back, plunged her underwater, sent a tremor of power through her muscles, energy with nowhere to go.

Reaching behind, she found the metal dial. Without looking, she turned it to the right, in increments, then bolder. The skin of her shoulders sensed it first, the water hotter and hotter until it hurt. The cubicle filled with toxic steam, clouding her eyes. She didn't let herself flinch.

The fire alarm felt like Serena's pain made aural. This siren was collective; every other head in the halls of residence would ache with its wail. It was three a.m., but Serena woke swiftly, nowhere near deep sleep. She'd drowsed in snatches for weeks, her mind never fully settled, never fully awake. The judder in her veins didn't leave. Pulling on a jumper and trainers took less than a minute, even with the hindrance of her knee. Serena paused by the door. Could she stay in that room still lined with piles of boxes? There was no option. Making her way down the corridor, every door opened and every face she didn't know blinked into the light.

Stairs were treacherous. Others skipped down two at a time, or one by one so swiftly their feet were a blur. With plodding steps and the clatter of crutches, Serena felt bovine. She didn't want to meet other eyes. Then, a voice from behind.

'Toast.'

Serena didn't stop her descent but glanced backwards.

'It's bound to be. Post-club toast. Classic. Inevitable, really.' The girl slowed to match Serena's gait.

'I'm Keira.' She stuck her hand out across Serena's body. 'We've actually met, but it seems so long ago. I live next door to you.'

'Serena.' Trapping one crutch under her elbow, Serena shook Keira's hand, as she assumed she was expected to.

Despite their pace, Keira never stopped moving, fingers working through her hair, coaxing the curls of her short afro to uniform buoyancy.

'It was always going to happen, but three in the morning is lethal.' This girl's energy was luminous, her voice and features animated despite the time.

Pulling a make-up compact from her bag, Keira dabbed a sponge across her nose. As she snapped it shut, she waved to a group congregated just outside the foyer. Serena didn't recognise them. When they walked through the main doors of the building, the temperature was a shock.

'Jesus Christ, its freezing.' Keira's shriek was so high everyone turned.

Serena knew she needed to speak. 'I suppose we came too far north to complain about the cold.'

Keira's laugh was immediate. 'You've got me there – we brought this on ourselves. What are you doing?'

Serena stopped short. What invisible boundary had she crossed?

'Subject, I mean.'

Her breath returned. 'History.' It had been her strongest A level.

'I knew it!' Keira stamped the ground to warm herself. Serena winced. 'I've seen you in lectures.'

The cold smashed against Serena's left knee and it was hard to keep smiling.

'I do take your point, but fuck me, it's Baltic here. And is it ever actual daylight? Leysham is so creepy. Did you hear about that girl? Tanya something. Fell in the river like those stories you hear. Like those kids that died last year. She was pulled out, but even so, must have been hideous.'

Serena swallowed. 'Hideous.' Tanya. Her name was Tanya.

'Totally.' Keira nodded. 'The beach here is meant to be an absolute death trap too. So, it's not just a balmy choice to come to Leysham, but an entirely safe one.' Her head jinked. 'We do share lectures, right? I'm usually face down in a coffee, to be honest.' She clutched Serena's hand. 'Sit by me tomorrow. Which is, of course, today.'

The feel of other skin on her own made Serena ache.

The centre of campus was startling. Serena wasn't used to those ancient buildings gazing out to the sea. She'd visited castles and stately homes as a child, but had never imagined wandering casually through one, living among turrets and quadrangles. It unnerved her to see students resting grubby trainers on ornamental balustrades, eating lunch perched on a carved windowsill. Her application to Leysham had not been for its prestige, but she'd known it was renowned. When people thought of universities, it was these grand towers – with their vaults and arches and lavish stained glass – they envisioned. The honey-yellow stones had been blackened by time, but that only deepened their resonance. Ghosts of long-dead footsteps seemed to echo through every hall. Serena had heard others complain about the disparity between the prospectus architecture and the grey blocks most of them lived in, but she didn't mind. It wouldn't feel possible to relax in bricks so ornate.

On the way to her lecture, Serena passed Carnforth Hall, the ceremonial building where graduations took place, where people formed processions in black gowns with Leysham's distinctive purple hoods, where words were whispered in Latin and honours gravely bestowed. Dotted around its walls, tucked into doorway arches and along crenellations, were faces. Human faces. Where other buildings from the same period sported fantastical gargoyles, Leysham had the faces of women, carved smoothly and staring out over the quad.

Carnforth Hall's grandeur was completed by an elaborate flight of stairs and, at the heart of a gravel courtyard, a fountain. The statue in its centre was a man with a rippling torso, his oblique muscles bulging. Serena knew bodies like that from the pool. In one hand he brandished a three-pronged trident. He was Poseidon, king of the sea, god of freshwater and the ocean. His other hand was held aloft, majestic above his head, water flowing from the palm. Serena reached out to break one of the streams, splashing it in all directions. As she licked her wet fingers, there was none of the chlorine she'd expected.

A bright rectangle at the base of the fountain caught her eye: a poster stuck to the stone. Its colours were vibrant, blaring out from the gloom. The paper was laminated to protect it from the rain. *Join us to stand up. Students have the right to feel safe.* Serena couldn't tell what it referred to. The danger of that thrashing river? Did it evoke the night she'd pulled Tanya from the cold? A pink handwritten font screamed across the bottom. @zarakarmic. Her username, as if it had been autographed.

Serena hadn't seen Zara since they arrived on campus, and yet she'd seen so much of Zara. Zara's body was public. She shared it widely, revealing all but a crucial few inches to the world. Serena had followed her cousin's social media feeds for a month, and already knew that body better than her own. The flesh that held one eighth of the same DNA. She knew Zara's body in static images and short videos. Zara, arms flung wide, dressed in a bikini. Zara lying on a rumpled bed, a mountain range formed by the flow of her hips. The warm, wide squash of Zara's belly. Her content stacked in neat grids, in a wash of rich pastels – gold, teal, peach – like a perpetual sunset. Every square was deliberate, and Serena had scrolled through metres of them. It felt too intimate to stare. A dress cupping Zara's cleavage. Lingerie letting her skin peek through. Zara eyeballing the camera, making it confrontational. The deep dimple of her navel.

Over two hundred thousand people followed her. She was a beacon of the body positivity movement, and the content she uploaded chimed with nearly a quarter of a million people. They clicked to see everything she posted. Serena had tried to visualise that many bodies: the crush and breath of them. More than twice the capacity of Wembley Stadium. So many people felt vertiginous in person: a terrifying weight of human flesh. It was as if Zara stood on that London stage, clothes removed so they could see everything. They could read every uplifting quote she digitally scrawled. *My darling, you are made of stardust.* Their eyes were on her constantly. *I hereby refuse to treat my body like a thing I hate.* The population of a major town or small city. Swindon. Aberdeen. *Have you thanked your body today?* They each owned a tiny piece of her. *This body is your home. You are safe here.* And those eyes were lucrative. Zara could apparently earn thousands from a single post that allowed a company to sneak a hashtag after her affirmations. *You are magical.*

@zarakarmic • 207k followers

As you know, I've been here at Leysham a few weeks. They've been every bit as daunting and as extraordinary as I'd hoped.

I'm getting used to my new habitat, I've had more fun than is probably advisable, and I've worn every single costume I brought with me.

You can see here that I've got my productivity zone set up. I've got my succulents that, who knows, even I might not be able to kill, and enough rose quartz to fend off all imaginable stress.

Starting anything new is always overwhelming, but I'm certain this experience will nourish me, not diminish me.

I'm just going to be me. I want you all to remember, no one else is you, and that is your power. That is always your power.

4

Serena's eyelids weighed heavy. The lecture hall felt too warm after the freezing outside. She still woke every day at five. Her body didn't understand; the energy it had once expended each morning was now an anxious fidget that dogged her constantly. Hours had vanished as she'd stared at her laptop screen, willing herself to write the term's first assignment. Every sentence had crawled, their letters tangling. She'd cobbled together no more than five hundred words in three days, and each one had robbed her. Discipline had once come easily – school-work had been a satisfying way to fill time on dry land – but university days were baggy. Time was hard to corral and the tablets she took every four hours muddied her mind.

Every other student filing into the hall seemed to have the same slick, silver MacBook, the same colourful metal water bottle. Serena's Dell looked clunky, her bottle of Evian crass. The room grew full as she watched for Keira. At other lectures she'd lingered outside until the last minute, slipping into a seat near the back for a droning incantation she'd barely felt present for, fingers poised over laptop keys, grasping nothing to capture.

'Heya.' Keira's bag dropped into the seat next to Serena. She'd chosen ones halfway down the room and hoped they were suitable. Wriggling out of her puffy coat, Keira seemed content. She dug in her bag for a pack of pink chewing gum and offered Serena a pellet.

'She's meant to be brilliant.' Keira nodded towards the woman walking to the front of the room. Serena watched as she placed her bag on the floor, removed a grey scarf, positioned a folder on the wooden lectern.

'She's new here this term, but I've heard people rave about her.'

It wasn't until she straightened that Serena saw the woman's face. Her mouth grew dry as the room fell silent.

'Good morning. I'm Dr Jane Sinclair, Lecturer in the Department of History. Thank you for coming today.'

It was Jane. Jane whose arms had held her so firmly. Whose breath had felt warm and damp on her neck. Jane who'd saved a life with her. The decisive voice Serena had heard in the dark now reverberated around the hall.

'I'd like to begin my autumn lecture series on Disobedient Women with the history of the place we live in.' Every syllable was crisp, she was as calm as she'd been by the water. 'Institutions can be treated as homogenous, but you didn't choose to spend three years on the south coast, or in some major city known for its nightlife. Something lured you to this particular landscape, with its particular stories, and you should know them.'

When Serena turned to look, Keira was smiling widely.

'The land you're living upon was once important in the worst possible way. In 1603, Queen Elizabeth died and her greatest rival's son, James, took the throne of England as well as Scotland. But you know that.'

Previous lecturers had shone their name and topic onto the screen behind them, giving long preambles, introducing themselves and their work. Jane hadn't touched the computer. She simply stared out at her audience, one hand resting on the other, twisting a silver ring in methodical circles around her finger.

'In the years prior to this, James had become concerned with the threat of witches. He grew obsessed with the North Berwick trials, which reported a mystical summoning of storms to the North Sea that had endangered his own life and that of his new bride. He came to believe this had been instigated by witches who met with Satan himself. These trials played no small part in the creation of *Daemonologie*, which he wrote in 1597, and I'm sure you've heard of. It covers what he deemed the black arts, discussing not only witches, but demons, werewolves, vampires.'

Jane seemed to taste the words as she spoke. She wasn't dressed like a lecturer. Her wide-fitting trousers looked sleek, a draped top left her arms revealed. The outfit was sculptural, unlike anything Serena would be able to recreate. Had Jane been wearing something similarly immaculate when she'd waded into the water without a second thought?

'It's witches, though, that capture his imagination. He cites a line from the Bible, Exodus 22:18: "Thou shall not suffer a witch to live." The translation of this has been hotly disputed. In the Knox version, the verse reads "Sorcerers must not be allowed to live", and the Hebrew word in question – *mekhashepha* – can roughly be translated to "enchanter" or "magician". Its roots relate to "mutterings" and can refer to anything from the cutting of herbs to poisoning.' She paused. 'But James went with "witch".'

Lectures so far had been punctuated by the incessant flicking of PowerPoint slides showing blurred images from the period, faded sources, links to the work of recent scholars. Jane's eyes didn't leave the seats in front of her. She didn't pace but stood firmly in the centre of the raised stage. She didn't glance at a single note. Serena remembered how that kind of focus felt.

'And this interpretation does not rest with James. It seeps beyond and affects the wider populace. It grows.'

Jane let the silence hang. That took confidence. She knew there would be no clatters, no whispers in that room. She knew they were listening. Her actions were as certain as her steps into the river.

'James believed it fell to him to use his power to defeat this evil. He posited himself as a spiritual warrior, God's represent-ative on earth, able to fight the legions of Satan for his people. He was consumed by a notion that the devil desired personal vengeance against him. It made him savage. Witchcraft Acts had been passed by both Henry and Elizabeth, focused on condemning the Catholic faith, but James upped the stakes considerably. His actions were far crueller.'

Her voice resonated in that vast room. No one looked away. Serena could hear Keira breathing next to her.

'The Witchcraft Act of 1604 expanded the previous Acts to bring the penalty of death to anyone who invoked or com-muned with "evil spirits". This kind of language has power. Real power. James's convictions had a tangible influence on the views of the general population. They believed him. And that belief sat behind the horrors that followed.'

Jane's hands were rigid. Serena could see how the words she spoke affected her. They held something more than aca-demic interest.

'For my current monograph project, I've been unearthing contemporaneous sermons from churches around this area. Churches you can reach within a short walk. They make for alarming reading. Women – and, as you can imagine, it was almost always women – who had contravened the most minor of social codes were accused. It was usually petty squabbles, the result of the bitterly impoverished lives people endured. James Stuart himself concedes in *Daemonologie* that events were driven by the "greedy appetite of fear caused through great poverty". But the clergy clutched the chance with both hands. It was clear ammunition against any woman. Within a few years, a full-blown frenzy had taken hold. The feeblest of reasons was enough: if anyone made a speedy recovery from illness, if possessions went missing, if crops didn't grow as expected. When anything was unexplained, the answer was witchcraft.'

Her voice toughened; something darker creeping in. There was only a trace of accent, but Serena wondered if it came from north of that border a hundred miles away.

'Individual congregations were governed by local ministers who, as learned men, held significant influence. Surviving sermons from the period show how frequently they were preaching about these supposed moral transgressions. And they didn't stay vague. They went into graphic detail of witches' sabbats, where they were thought to engage in acts as wild as cannibalism, sexual unions with demons, the ritual sacrifice of unbaptised infants. The women accused were sometimes established members of the community, but they were often young. Young women who were deemed trouble-some or wayward. Their bodies were described in lurid ways, their imagined carnal encounters dwelt upon in depth. Many were barely out of their teens.'

Serena didn't move. Women no older than her had been accused. She wanted to drink in everything Jane knew. Those lectures she'd attended so far had been no different to school: dispassionate accounts of the actions of monarchs and admi-rals. Men she didn't care about. This felt alive.

'Polemical discourse can shift culture, and the words of these sermons changed how people understood the world around them. This vilifying rhetoric of the clergy became dominant. People were scared. They feared the devil had genuinely infiltrated their communities and they were eager for punishments to be meted out. They fully supported them.'

Jane spoke so quickly it was hypnotic. The muscles in her exposed arms were taut.

'And these punishments were as harsh as it gets. The women were deemed to be denying God's sovereignty. If they refused to admit their guilt, they were declared to have succumbed to evil. The clergymen insisted there was a divine necessity for convicting these women, and that their offence to God was worthy of death. Not simply death either, but agony for thousands of years, until their blood was free of the stain.'

Every syllable ended sharply. The strength of Jane's feeling was palpable to Serena, anger and disgust restrained in her crisp consonants.

'James personally supervised the methods used in these trials and executions. He believed water was so pure it repelled the guilty. If the accused survived, it was because the water had rejected them. They were convicted. Ponds weren't used in this part of the country; instead, they relied on the river we walk by every day. If the women drowned, they were simply let go of, for the current to steer their bodies to the sea, innocent but destroyed. They'd be held under for minutes at a time. Anyone would have to inhale before then.'

Serena's body ran cold in the packed lecture theatre. They would time each other at the pool, stopwatches in hand, calculating how long they could remain beneath the surface. Anything over two minutes garnered respect. The sensation was visceral: head under the water, willing her lungs to hold out, counting slowly. It was about resisting the urge, withstanding the diaphragm's burn.

'If, by some miracle, the women survived the first dunking, they'd be thrown further out into the water, arms and legs swung by the largest men of the village, left to the mercy of the rocks and current and, further downstream, the waves.'

There was such terror in those last moment before pushing upwards: the shadows of other heads looming, the disoriented sense that the surface was no longer above, the flash of horror that you might be held down.

'This is the history of the ground we walk on at Leysham. It's what makes this place unique. The stretch of river where the wall stops by the Bowland Gate – where students have been lost every year since records began, where they have been allowed to die, where one was saved only days ago – is exactly where the trials were held.'

Serena had known it from the moment Jane began speaking. The water she'd battled was the water that killed those women. The water that tried to take Tanya. The water she could still smell in her own hair. That was why Jane hadn't hesitated, why she'd entered the water with no fear when she saw a woman struggling.

'These stories are baked into this ground. There is a reason this place appealed to you.' Jane surveyed the seats in front of her and the mood of the room grew heavier. 'But it's not understood. It's not respected. Many of you will attend a party in the next week known as the Gilly Sampson Bash. I'm told it's usually fancy dress and I'm sure it will be incredibly entertaining for all involved. But how many people question that name?' She paused, her cool stare accusing them. 'Almost none. It washes over us, like so many traditions. It's existed for years: other generations have accepted it, so why should we challenge? Around here, Gilly Sampson is a ghost story.'

Jane laughed in one exhale, but there was no joy. The hard *g* of Gilly's name sounded sharp in her mouth. 'Gilly Sampson was a woman. She was a woman who died in the river on this campus several centuries ago. A woman who died and is recalled today only in the spirit of irony.'

Every eye in the room seemed to look down.

'Something drew you to this place.' Jane held the pause until it was uncomfortable. 'It's worth considering.'

At the close of the lecture, backpacks around the room were stuffed with laptops, but Serena lingered.

'I'll catch you up.' She nodded to Keira.

Serena walked slowly down the stairs to the lectern as Jane gathered her belongings. Her arms must be cold, exposed to the air of the room while everyone else huddled in jumpers. The chill of that muddy bank hadn't left Serena's bones. She fought the urge to turn and follow the others. What happened at the river was too important to leave unspoken.

The room scuffled to quiet as it emptied of bodies. Serena didn't have the gall to make herself known, so she transferred her weight from foot to foot, feeling the pang in her left knee with every shift. Eventually, Jane's gaze landed on her, but didn't settle. Did she recognise her under those fluorescent lights? Did she know it was Serena she'd gripped in triumph?

'Hi.' Serena's voice was quiet, but echoed around the panelled walls.

'Hello.' Jane was brisk.

'I wanted to . . .' As the words formed, they felt wrong. What had happened was too dark for that bright room. Now the words of Jane's lecture had ended, the spell was broken. It suddenly seemed inappropriate, a foolish overstepping. Serena swallowed. 'I enjoyed the lecture.'

A neat smile flashed across Jane's lips. 'Thank you. I hope to see you at the rest of the series.'

Serena bit down on the soft inside of her cheeks.

Then, as Jane headed towards the door, her bare arm glanced Serena's fleece coat. No more than a second. The faintest pressure on her elbow. There was enough room that it must have been deliberate. Everything about Jane was deliberate. She'd brushed against the coat she'd held so tightly, the coat that had been thick with mud from the riverbank, that had wrapped around a woman who would be dead if it weren't for them.

@zarakarmic • 211k followers

I know this is a bit different to what I usually talk about, but I think it's vital and I'm sure you'll agree.

I live on a campus, and it seems obvious that students should feel safe here, but this isn't the case. We're exposed to real dangers every day.

If you're at Leysham then join me on the field near Bowland tomorrow at six to have our voices heard.

If not, please give your support digitally. Add a comment here or a reaction video. I want to see your views and share them.

Always remember, we are strong. And we are strongest when we stand together.

FOURTEEN YEARS OLD

Of all strokes, breaststroke creates the most resistance. Serena admired it for being the slowest but the most instinctive. When infants are placed in the water, their limbs intuit its form immediately. It was the stroke that fitted Serena's body, and that she swam exclusively from her first year of training. Breaststroke is ancient, Niko told her; people have taken thousands of years to master it. Other strokes are about brute power or technical prowess. This is about connecting with the water.

Niko explained how breaststroke races were won in the spaces between strokes. Serena longed for those instants. There were eight or nine in a length, and each was delicious. You had to slip beneath the water, understanding it so fully your calibrations were perfect. To get the ideal streamline, you had to be a fraction under the surface, body fully extended, back flat, legs together. Serena would feel the invisible line Niko described, from her fingertips to her skull to torso to waist to knees to toes. *You're an arrow shot through the water. There is a steel plate from your palms to your shoulders.* Ribcage tight, head in line with spine, staring resolutely at the black line on the bottom of the pool. In those brief moments of glide, Serena became part of the water.

Serena expected the wax to be hot, but as the beautician smeared it on her leg with a wooden spatula she sensed nothing. A strip of material was placed over the green paste, smoothed down, then ripped off in one swift stroke. Serena didn't blink. At fourteen, she was used to far more pain. *If it doesn't hurt, you're not swimming hard enough.* Strip after strip was applied and removed. Her mother stood close, observing every stage. The process of transformation was essential. Breaststroke was wasteful, keeping the body under the water, forcing it to heave out to breathe. Everything Serena did was to conjure back seconds. Not only her technique, but all aspects of her body were honed to its will. She grew her nails long for extra grip.

Her mother frowned, leaning in to inspect the waxed patch of calf. Running her finger across the reddened skin, she pressed her lips together. She didn't trust it. The risk was too great, and waxing could never be thorough, would always leave stray hairs. Serena didn't mind going back to those long minutes in the shower, shaving every inch – arms as well as legs before a race – so no strip of bristle would snag. She revelled in the ritual of it, making sure she was slick as a fish, perfect for the water.

The printout was already damp. Nothing stayed dry in that clammy poolside air, and the schedule was limp by the time Niko lifted it from his red clipboard. That day it was two sides long. It varied, some days inexplicably more intense. Serena turned it over, scanning the lines. That piece of paper mapped out thousands of metres of warm-ups, skill sets, main sets and warm-downs. Every moment of the three-hour session was charted.

Serena began as she always did: stretches by the side of the pool, then a few lengths to get the feel of the water. Chlorine woke her, like a daily baptism. As she swam, she imagined how the session would go, Niko's words in her mind. *You slice through the water.* Niko watched her constantly. Other girls giggled about him in the showers: his lips, his eyes, those thickly haired arms, dreaming about what lay beneath his shirt. It seemed absurd. Niko was Serena's guide, the way she could swim faster. Eight lengths into her main set, he signalled for her to stop.

'You're not trying.' His face was unusually still.

'I'm doing everything on the plan.' Serena pointed at the paper, not grasping his severity.

'You're going through the motions.'

'Are my length times up?'

'Your times are fine, but you're not fully here.' He pressed on his own temple. 'If you're not serious, why show up?'

Serena looked at the water, cheeks flaming in outrage. She'd done everything possible, chanting his words in her mind as she swam, to the tempo of the stroke. Others sang songs to themselves, but Serena knew that was a distraction.

Niko stared down at her. 'You can't afford to miss a beat.' He didn't blink. 'You can't let up.'

'I didn't . . .' Serena hoisted herself further out of the water, scrambling to think of a way to convince him.

Niko's silver necklace dangled as he leaned towards her. A silver Saint Sebastian, the patron saint of athletes, his naked body studded and bloodied with arrows, bowed in rapturous pain. He was offered as inspiration for endurance, his extraordinary stamina withstanding endless agony.

'You've got to think of those other girls.' Serena didn't stop thinking of them. 'They're fierce. Those girls in the ranks above you. Some are younger than you.' Serena tensed. 'They give it everything. When you're relaxing, when you think it's okay to curl up and watch Netflix, do you know what they're doing? Swimming. And if the pool is closed, they're not chilling out, they're stretching and lifting and doing anything they can to get better.'

Serena could sense them out there, muscles flexing.

'They don't sit and drink hot chocolate with their friends.' Serena had waved to Niko from the sports centre café the day before. She cringed at the memory. 'They're training. And do you know why?'

Serena didn't move.

'They want it more.'

The table was enormous. Serena had never been upstairs in the sports centre, never seen the conference rooms. Her mother passed a plastic cup of water from the dispenser, so flimsy it bent beneath her fingers. The three of them sat on office chairs. Between Niko and Elizabeth was a flipchart. They spoke as if Serena wasn't there.

'She's fourteen, and we've got some big choices to make. If we want to go all in, it starts now.'

'I think we're very clear we want that. We know she has what it takes; we know she can be world class.' Her mother glanced across the table. Serena felt the swell in her chest, the air expanding at Elizabeth's pride.

'It's going to take quite literally everything we've got. It means extreme dedication.'

Squeezing the sides of her cup until they pressed together, Serena forced water to the brim. Thrill mixed with a flare of dread, a plunge in her gut. It would be her body's responsibility to realise their ambitions.

'We know.' Her mother tapped a marker pen against the table.

'Other girls have represented Britain. Other girls her age.

Serena missed those youth squads, but that doesn't mean she can't catch up.'

'I think she's proved beyond doubt she can. It's pointless to dwell upon what she did or didn't do three years ago.'

Serena wished she could grab her younger self, force her into the water where she belonged.

Niko stood and ripped away the first flipchart page, revealing a blank one behind. The noise startled Serena. He scrunched the torn sheet, dropping it to the carpet tiles.

He drew a rectangle in red pen. 'The first goal is getting to the Nationals. The Summer Championships.' NATIONALS in capital letters inside the box. 'If she nails it there, she'll get noticed. If she can get to that podium, it's elite squad.' Another box. ELITE in green. 'It would cement her in the top rank of her age group.'

Elizabeth nodded, as if it was straightforward. 'And beyond that?'

'Training camps, international competitions, eyes on the 2018 Commonwealths, if that's not too soon, the 2020 Olympics, 2022 Commonwealths, and then 2024.'

The flipchart's thin paper ruckled as Niko drew five rings in the top right-hand corner. The page didn't go any further.

'She'll be seventeen the first time we can try out for the Olympic team, twenty-one for the next.' He inhaled. 'Older than ideal, but it's possible.'

Serena couldn't imagine seventeen, but she could imagine the Olympics. She'd watched all the previous summer. Niko had never talked her through that particular visualisation, but it arrived as complete as a dream. He'd coached two other girls to Olympics trials, and she knew he thought she was stronger.

The ceremony everyone gasped at had bored Serena. The supermodel strutting through the stadium, colourful samba dancing, an imagined rainforest. For her, the spectacle was all in the water. She'd watched every moment, waking earlier than ever to catch up on events from overnight. Adam Peaty, fierce and golden, breaking his own world record in the heats, then again in the final. Impossibly composed in a blood-red cap, allowing himself to lean back in the water, luxuriating in success, for only a second. Serena had imagined herself in his mind, in his body. She'd watched Katie Ledecky smash the pads eleven seconds faster than her next competitor. Serena had tracked Ledecky's career backwards, becoming transfixed with the previous Olympics. August 2012, when she'd first tasted victory, forcing Rebecca Adlington to bronze. Serena had wept imagining the emotions coursing through Adlington's phenomenal body. That twenty-three-year-old body four whole seconds behind the fifteen-year-old American. Fifteen. One year older than Serena.

Serena imagined those sketched-out years vanishing. She'd be seventeen, limbering up for victory, *GB* etched on her costume. She'd be good enough; her life would contain something so massive. The red and blue and green lines on the flipchart paper pointed upwards and those pen marks blazed in her brain. She could be in that top corner. Serena knew in that moment how much she'd sacrifice at the altar of this one goal. She'd wipe her life clear. Losing wasn't an option. Serena squeezed the plastic cup in her hand so hard its rim shattered and water spilled across the table.

Barack Obama apparently wore the same outfit every day. A whole wardrobe of identical shirts, trousers, ties, jackets. It made perfect sense. The space in his brain for decisions was left clear. Pure open space to focus. Serena's own prep leaned on the same principle.

The same bag was packed the night before every race. Two race suits and two practice suits, same brand, same style, same colour. Board and pull buoy for kick sets or drill work. Hand paddles, blade fins. Inside the black duffel was a smaller mesh bag of vital items she took to the lane. Two pairs of goggles, adjusted to fit snugly. Silicone earplugs. Nose clip. Two caps emblazoned with the squad name. Water bottle. Protein bar for after the race. Microfibre towel. Her hand hit the same items whenever it reached in. Other girls chose bright colours, patterns and slogans, tags from previous competitions hooked onto the zip to slap together as they moved. Serena avoided distraction.

That day was no different. She glanced inside the bag as a final check before they got into the car. It took no more than a cleft of her brain. It always saw what it always saw. But that day it was wrong. As she reached in, something jarred. It wasn't obvious at first what was missing, but Serena's throat clenched.

Her mother sensed the tension. 'Okay, superstar?'

Serena shook her head. 'Goggles.'

It was all she needed to say. Her mother took the bag and rummaged. It was useless: no other hands could find them. Both pairs, safe from scratches in their own cases, were gone.

'Where can they be?' She didn't ask if Serena had left them upstairs or at the pool. That wasn't possible.

'Has anyone seen Serena's goggles?' Her voiced echoed through every room of the house.

They were all going to the race: Anoushka and Zara as well as her parents and sister. Their whole day was focused on her efforts. Elizabeth's tone made the urgency clear, and everyone leaped to action, looking under chairs, running hands along the tops of shelves. Serena stood in the hallway, jaw tight. They never left her bag.

Standing in the chaos of five other bodies moving, she kept her mind clear, her blood calm. The race was ninety minutes away. Her father's footsteps, her mother slamming objects aside, Zara and Kelly whispering. Eventually, an exclamation. Serena rushed to the noise. Her cousin, eyes wide, two black shell cases in her hands. Serena stopped herself from snatching them.

'They were down here. They must have fallen, or someone must have grabbed them from the side.' Statements sounded like questions in that quiet voice.

Those cases were never grabbed. That mesh wasn't opened. Serena couldn't utter the accusation. There was no reason

Zara would want to disrupt her day. She couldn't know how important it was. Serena gripped the cases, her fingers white with the pressure. Zara couldn't know. There was no space in Serena's mind to contemplate it. Her arms and legs were tense, the muscles far from warm. Her joints sat wrong. Her mouth wanted to scream.

The box looked like it might hold jewellery, but as Serena ripped the paper off, she realised her fifteenth-birthday present was a Fitbit. It felt like a slur. No machines were needed to monitor her dedication. She didn't stick to those rituals for the numbers.

That rubber bangle on her right wrist tracked every length she pounded in the empty pool before the rest of the squad got there. She'd been given a set of keys to the complex, so she didn't have to wait. Breaking the surface of the water was vital, swimming before anyone else sullied it. Twelve times a week she trained, not counting land training and competitions. It was never enough.

The hours between sessions were barren, the bangle's graph running flat. Serena experienced it as sludge building in her stagnant muscles. Nothing that happened in those hours improved her; no teacher's words could make her swim better. She concentrated on lessons out of habit, because doing well was all she'd ever known. It irritated classmates that her grades stayed high despite the constant training, but they didn't understand. It was all drills to her. Every portion of time was charted and useful. Twice during the school day she'd take two Nurofen, an hour after the nagging in her shoulders and knees began. Swallowing those perfect white tablets felt like her most productive moments.

Niko had plugged his flipchart scribbles into an Excel sheet, cells charting every key date, every competition heat, every qualifying race, every pot of funding to apply for. Serena knew the details without looking. She imagined herself in miniature, clambering up each spreadsheet box. The Nationals, and her chance for the elite team, were less than four months away. Without that, her career would be over. Her mother might never again look at her with such fierce joy.

Other girls were monitored too, bangles on their wrists like fashion accessories. Those rubber bracelets were aspirational because Natasha wore one. Natasha was four years older than Serena, a mainstay of the elite squad, a star in butterfly, and idolised by all. Niko called her Sasha, and she was his clear favourite. A full-colour butterfly tattoo sat on the flat of her hip that racing costumes revealed. For three years running, she'd bagged silver in the Nationals.

Serena had never wanted to be like anyone more. She'd stare at the impressive lat muscles that ran from Natasha's spine to her shoulders, the broad expanse of her back. At the end of every training session, Natasha crouched by the benches at the side of the pool, counting out raisins from Tupperware. No one was more regimented. She'd allow herself twenty, which Serena knew was a little over thirty calories.

Numbers punctuated Serena's days. Swimming had long ago swept everything else away, forcing her to turn down invitations, miss family events, stop pursuing school friendships. It didn't feel like sacrifice. There was never a time she wouldn't rather be in the pool. She had a chance to do something almost no one could. She had the chance to be extraordinary.

The Fitbit never caught up. She'd already imagined every mouthful. The perfect quantities of protein, of carbohydrates. Wholemeal pasta. Chicken breasts. Nut butter on plain crackers. A handful of unsalted cashews. The tiny spy on her wrist recorded every action. Serena watched the numbers flicker throughout the day, certain they'd be immaculate.

5

The trees that lined the river were vivid in Serena's mind. They haunted her. Those trees she'd struggled behind, the branch she'd wrenched free. From the campus side, they looked like ordinary trees, almost bare of leaves and bowed from the October wind. On that side, they bordered a small field marked with lines of white paint, where lads who'd played in their schools' first fifteens charged at each other on Wednesday afternoons, mud-streaked and muscle-bound. The field was full now, so different from that night a week before.

Clutches of people gathered around, groups of four or five filling the grass, facing a makeshift stage. Word had clearly spread through the paths of the campus, across Zara's various platforms. All these people had seen the luscious folds of her stomach, the soft ripple of her thighs, the glossy pelt under her arms.

Keira walked ahead, steering them towards the front of the

crowd, glaring at anyone who got in Serena's way. With her crutches jolting against the hard ground, Serena struggled to keep up. The field was transformed. An event like this took effort: permission forms and strings of emails with the facilities office, microphones and speakers borrowed from a nearby department, tables dragged across ancient stone steps from the cafeteria. Everything here was signed for and sanctioned. It was impressive.

A message had arrived earlier that day from Zara. *Would be great to see you at the rally. We need to raise our voices and get things changed!* Serena had imagined the same words pulsing the phone of every one of Zara's contacts.

Lights popped, illuminating the stage, taking the field from dusk to noon. There she was. Everyone else was braced against the cold in scarves and zipped coats, but Zara wore a dress that left her arms, chest and thighs exposed. Serena recalled another girl's freezing limbs fighting the water only metres away. The dress was a mustard yellow that would drain a duller face, but Zara glowed as if she had stolen its pigment.

'Thank you so much for coming out on this freezing night!' The microphone took Zara's words and sent them echoing. 'A week ago, a woman was walking along this riverbank. At about this time. It would have been this cold, this dark.'

The two nights were nothing alike. Stage lights stopped the dusk from shrouding them now. Dozens of people added their noise and warmth and colour. The smell of the bank's deep sludge didn't reach through the trees.

'She was alone, but she should have been safe. She was just walking home. She's one of us. And she's not a statistic, she's Tanya Evans from Sheffield, a second-year studying Biology.' The spotlights made sure Zara was all anyone looked at.

'But Tanya wasn't safe. First, because this towpath is insanely dangerous.' Zara waved in the vague direction of the river behind the trees.

Serena hadn't been back since that night, hadn't seen the mud her feet had flailed on, hadn't watched that dark water flowing. She couldn't bear to imagine what had very nearly happened. Tanya wasn't yet safe. She was in hospital with a lingering head injury. Everyone had heard by now. The impact of her fall hadn't eased, as fluid still pressed on vital parts of her brain.

'We know how many other students have fallen to their deaths in this river over the past few years. Everyone talks about it, but nothing changes. All the university has done is put up some signs and added a few weak safety lights. This places the onus on us as Leysham students and essentially blames the victims.'

Serena turned to scan the crowd, shifting her weight onto her left crutch. Dozens of faces were tilted upwards, taking in Zara's words. She didn't recognise anyone except Keira beside her. Then, Jane. A jab of adrenalin. Of course Jane was there. Jane would remember what Serena remembered. It might live in her thoughts just as clearly, creeping upon her in the dark.

Jane wore a white scarf over a sleek navy-blue coat, as though the mud could never again touch her. She stared at Zara, as transfixed as everyone else.

'This campus is where we live, and we should feel able to walk around it without risk. We should feel safe.'

Unhooking the microphone from its stand, Zara moved towards the front of the stage. 'But the river is not the main reason Tanya was in danger.'

Serena felt her forehead tense.

'Tanya was in danger because someone actively put her in danger. We know a drink she bought in the club she visited had been tampered with. It was deliberate. A flavourless, scentless liquid was dropped into her glass, with the distinct aim of making her easier to attack.'

Serena froze. She'd had no idea. She remembered Tanya's unfocused eyes, her flimsy limbs. Someone had intentionally drugged her; it wasn't only alcohol. She hadn't stood a chance in that water.

'Her friends didn't see her leave the club,' Zara continued. 'Fortunately, it appears that the cretin who spiked her didn't either, or this could have been far worse. We don't know who he is, but I have no doubt his intentions were grim.'

Zara strode out as far as the tiny stage allowed, a field of people gripped by her words.

'And this wasn't a one-off. There've been a spate of similar incidents. Women have gone on perfectly normal nights out – like we all do – and have been left not knowing what's happened to them. Spikings are becoming rife in clubs around here and the university is doing nothing.'

She was lit by three beams, but didn't need them. Zara was her own light source.

'We come here for three years and we deserve to feel safe.' She stopped. 'Actually, that's bullshit. We don't deserve to feel safe. We deserve to *be* safe. We deserve to be protected. The women carved into Carnforth Hall are treated better than the real, living women on this campus!'

Growing applause, a few whoops. Next to Serena, Keira clapped, her hands raised above her face. Serena gripped the grey plastic of her crutches, thinking of the impassive stone faces in Carnforth Quad.

'We need the university to act. They need to publicly condemn the spiking and take the proper steps to work with local bars and clubs to end it. They need to make sure the police do their jobs and protect us from harm. As they don't seem willing to do it unprompted, we need to make demands!'

The crowd had grown. More voices joined the assent. More hands smacked against each other. Serena felt nauseous, overwhelmed by the bleak awfulness of that night a week ago. The cold, the impossibility, the dark earth working against her. Now, a man with poison in his hand, blanking Tanya's mind. Serena had seen a person grappling frantically with death in the same merciless water that had drowned those students, that had killed those women hundreds of years before. A man had tried to make a woman weak enough to attack. Applause was appalling. Practical steps weren't enough; they seemed almost flippant. Nobody else here had seen how the water tried to rip that girl away. Nobody but Jane. They didn't know what this place was like. They should be tearing up the mud.

'I invite you to stand with me. To rise up and demand more!'

Zara's voice was triumphant. Serena disagreed with nothing she said, but could only see the horror she'd diminished.

Lights dimmed, casting the field deeper into night as people dispersed. Two boys, who'd nodded vehemently as Zara spoke, lingered on the grass. One was broad and taller than Serena, with a beard so black it was nearly blue, the other slight and pale. They walked closer. Jane's scarf was a beacon in the dark as she headed in the same direction.

Before they could speak, Zara was upon them. 'You guys are so amazing for coming tonight. Keira!' She kissed her cheek. 'Luke! Dean!' Zara waved. She already knew everyone on that campus. 'My lovely cousin! It's been too long. How have I not seen you yet?' Zara's cheeks and breasts and neck were marble-cold as she pressed against Serena. Her fragrance was so strong Serena could taste it in the air.

As she pulled away, Serena's eyes met Jane's. The recognition on her face was unmistakable this time. Jane knew who Serena was. Perhaps she looked more familiar in the half-light, so close to the water. Serena remembered breath on the hairs of her neck. The intensity of Jane's gaze was startling, and neither looked away.

'I'm Zara.' Her cousin switched on the full beam of her smile.

'Jane Sinclair, pleased to meet you.' A gloved hand was held out to be shaken.

'Thank you for being here tonight.' Zara's voice was unusually quiet. The tiny blue stone in her nose winked in the remaining lights. She'd had it pierced the previous summer, the resulting photograph gathering over twenty thousand likes.

'I think what you're saying is vital, Zara. This has been going on far too long.'

Jane's words seemed as composed as ever, but Serena knew what burned beneath that calm. She didn't listen to their conversation, instead watching Jane's fingers twirl the ring beneath her glove. Jane spent her days reading about brutally murdered women. Serena had heard that vehemence.

Zara's hair caught in the freezing wind. Her lips must be purple under their red gloss. She stared at Serena with a strange expression. 'Sorry?' She turned back to Jane.

Jane's voice was even. 'I said it was Serena who saved Tanya.'

'What?' Keira's head tilted in question.

'It was Serena who saw Tanya in the water. Who rescued her.'

Silence thickened as the fact landed with the group, as Zara turned to Serena, her mouth slack.

Keira's squeal broke it. 'Are you fucking kidding me?' Her pitch rose further. 'That's incredible. You saved her? Why didn't you say? That's nuts!' She grabbed Serena in a hug, forcing her face against the puffed purple nylon of her coat. 'You absolute goddess. I knew you were amazing.'

Serena saw the boy called Luke smile as she was released from Keira's grip. Dean nodded at her, mouth downturned beneath his beard.

Zara's own smile was wide now. 'I had no idea.'

The invitation, lurid and glossy, had sat in Serena's pigeon-hole for weeks. She could no longer ignore it now that Keira insisted on meeting her there. Serena didn't know about parties like this, didn't know how bright the room would be or what songs would play. She didn't know if her knee would let her dance, or what that should look like. She could imagine the pink of other girls' lips, the sweet tang of their hairspray, but didn't know how to recreate it. Weighing on it all, Jane's words in the lecture hall made going to the Gilly Sampson Bash smack of betrayal.

Her costume was from Amazon. The theme was Disney heroes and villains, and only one option felt right, but when it arrived, that dress didn't fit. She'd clicked to buy in dimensions she'd once known, forgetting how substantially her body had altered. The purple bodice was savage, a vice across her ribcage that made breathing laborious. The turquoise skirt tugged with every step, bunching around her thighs.

When Serena reached the Student Union, after a slow trek across campus, the room was hot and loud and dark. She paused in the stone doorway, its solid wooden door hooked open. With pointed arches and carved flowers, the building fitted the night's theme, resembling the castle an animated princess might long to escape. There was no sign of Keira. Th bar was so packed with bodies, Serena couldn't see where the walls ended, and the music's dense thumps seemed to block her entrance. Her knee throbbed. Leaving the crutches behind had been a mistake.

The room raged. Elbows and shoulders, and glasses held in the air, laughter reaching a note that jagged her ears. Serena couldn't cross it without other legs smashing into her own. As she stood, faces loomed from the darkness, grotesque with paint. She pressed a hand to her cheek. The tablets still fogged her head. She was too hot, and her costume was all wrong. It was clearly supposed to have been constructed from offcuts of whatever you had lying around. A boy with a brush and smudges on his face, a girl in a long, white coat who'd talcum-powered one half of her hair. Several blonde girls in blue dresses and stapled-on capes. It was meant to be haphazard, not fresh out of cellophane. Sweating in tight rayon, Serena wanted to hide. There were so many faces, none of them familiar. Then, out of the darkness, the one she knew. Above the others, dancing on a chair, was Zara.

Zara was also dressed as Ariel. Serena bit her tongue. She'd chosen the one princess who lived in water, the only Disney character that ever resonated with her. Zara knew that. The heat of the room pulsed. Zara's mermaid wasn't a plastic replica; hers looked authentic, like she'd morphed into a sea creature for the night. The glittered top fitted her like skin, and green chiffon scraps floated around her legs as if she was underwater, buoyed by the darkness and breathing in brine. She didn't see Serena. She didn't see Serena's ugly costume. Zara gestured to someone across the room, arms flung upwards and outwards. She drew attention to herself, to the broad curves of her body, twirling and shimmying on the chair, the tendrils dancing as she moved. Could Serena ever steal some of that sheen?

Rooms far larger than this had reverberated with Serena's name. She'd triumphed over so many others. Now she was hollow. No one cared how fast she could swim and, in that dry room, she could barely walk. Saving Tanya didn't matter here. This was Zara's domain. Staring at her cousin, something stirred inside Serena; some deep, anxious thrum buzzed her bones. She needed to be far away from that room, from that party with its glib name.

As Serena turned, she smacked into a boy nearly as tall as her, who'd already found his clan. They wore the ragged waistcoats and fur hats of Peter Pan's Lost Boys, with matching purple cravats around their necks. He reeled from the knock. Serena panicked: he was too close, his naked chest against the bare skin of her arms, his aftershave sour in her lungs. He steadied himself, his hands on her shoulders, sending a shot of pain to Serena's knee. She shook herself free of his grip, shoved with both hands. *Get off. Get off me*. She heard the venom in her words. As he walked away, shaking his head, muttering to his friends – *Massive fucking psycho, mate* – Serena felt dazed. She looked straight ahead, unable to check if anyone had seen, and walked as fast as she could back to her room.

The first mouthful was easy. Sugar hit like medicine. Light sponge dissolved as it reached saliva and whole inches of the cake vanished. Icing was more difficult, sharp on her teeth, but Serena persisted, crushing it into a paste against the roof of her mouth. She forced herself to swallow. The campus shop had been open and the cake, in its cardboard packaging, cheap.

She sat on the floor of her room, back against the bedside table. Boxes were still stacked against the wall. Wedged into a pint glass was a bouquet of flowers. *To my incredible heroic cousin xxx.* They'd arrived that morning, their fuchsia petals jarring in the near-empty room.

With no forks in sight, Serena ripped chunks from the whole. The round slab had been a neat handspan wide but was now cratered and ravaged. She didn't use a plate, just let the base of the box pucker under the force. Battling another few inches, she imagined the cake's constituent parts. It had been made in a factory; no hands had beaten that butter and sugar to peaks, no human had forced the flour through a sieve. Swallowing had lost its power. Serena was crammed from nose to tonsils. The gorge rose, and she breathed deeply, driving that vanilla sludge down. Saliva sprang, but she wouldn't let herself vomit. That cake had to stay inside.

Something so forbidden must hold power. She'd never before have permitted herself a slice with so little nutritional value. A substance denied for so long might summon some magic. Her body might become more like Zara's. Serena could grow glossy and plump, no longer taut but lush. People might notice her. Sugar could invade her cells and alter something fundamental, pushing her genes closer to her cousin's. It could give her some of Zara's ease, some of her sparkle. Serena slumped on the gritty carpet tiles. Nearly half of the cake remained, inches high and thick with frosting. It could make her significant again.

@zarakarmic • 215k followers

I know, I know, I should accept I'm more Ursula than Ariel, but I'm going to the legendary Gilly Sampson Bash tonight and who doesn't want to be a mermaid for the night?

Before I head out, I wanted to talk to you about my body. My body is my own, and it is completely glorious. And crucially, I make the choices about what happens to it.

What I love about Joni Razors – who I've worked with before – is that they don't prey on women's insecurities, they don't urge us all to look the same, but they celebrate our diverse and gorgeous bodies exactly as they are.

Sometimes I shave my armpits, sometimes I'd rather they grew free. That's my choice. And that's your choice.

Whatever makes you feel good is always the right thing to do.

6

'We missed you last night, lovely.'

The social science café was a cluster of heavy wooden tables. Keira threw her rucksack on one to claim ownership. It was wildly beautiful for a functional building: the floor chequered with black and white tiles, windows intricately leaded, roof reaching to absurd heights. More a cathedral than a faculty. Every time Serena thought she was getting used to Leysham, she'd be struck afresh by some dazzling symmetry or impossible curve. She'd grown up amid the concrete cubes of modern school design, the blank glass of the leisure centre. So much here snagged her gaze, made her feel small.

'Sorry, yeah. I felt awful not to go, but the headache was blinding.'

'That honestly sucks. You didn't miss loads, but it would've been more fun if you'd made it. It was essentially a slutty prince-slash-princess party. You'll be delighted to hear that my microscopic Tinker Bell costume went down an absolute treat. I know the party's name is crass as hell, but I don't think even Gilly herself would begrudge me getting with that hot second-year, do you?'

Keira broke off half of her brownie and put it on a napkin. 'Is your head okay now? You need this as medicine.' Serena couldn't look at it, her mouth thick with last night's sweetness.

The others arrived, some blurred with fading hangovers. Dean and Luke, a few girls whose names Serena hadn't caught. Ordering coffee and muffins, they talked over each other. Snatches reached Serena.

'Seriously, though, they need something radical. It's infuriating. I don't think anyone else has a suitable vision for that society.'

'Alright, Kanye, cool it.' One of the girls punched Dean lightly on the arm.

Serena hugged her coat tighter.

'Luke, is Gressingham Hall as wild as rumour reports?'

'Wilder. A non-stop rave we only leave to attend lectures so the rest of you don't feel bad.'

Serena recoiled from their conversation. There were so many codes, so many words to translate, tones to strike. It was too intricate, too fragile. The others were younger than Serena, but sped ahead whenever they spoke, tapping into some buzzing frequency she couldn't access. They all wore the same chunky white Nikes, but knew exactly who they were.

Serena smelled Zara before she saw her. That rich floral sweetness. Zara strode to the counter to fill her KeepCup. Her face showed no sign of fatigue despite the night of dancing.

As soon as she sat, she addressed the group. Serena struggled to tune in.

'So, I've got some experience in bringing people together around a cause, but I need your input.' Serena watched her cousin's hands draw elaborate shapes in the air as she spoke. 'You might not know, but I have a decent number of followers online. I talk mainly about body image there, and I've managed to connect with a lot of people. Basically, I've been taught to feel utterly crap about myself, and I wanted to call that out.'

They'd spent so much time in the same rooms – shared a grandmother neither was born in time to meet – but Zara felt like a stranger to Serena. How could someone who possessed her body so fully feel bad about it? No longer a timid child, every eye was now on her, with thousands of fans primed to click their devotion each time she uploaded a selfie.

'I'm not sure I'd call it activism as such, but I've chosen to show my body so other people might feel better about theirs, to stand against things that are exploitative. I refuse to sign with a management company, so I can say whatever I want. I know a bit about getting energy behind an issue. People seemed pretty engaged the other night.'

Every expression of Zara's was extreme, joy and despair both thorough, the membrane between them so fine.

'But I'd love to know what you guys think, and gather some ideas about what to do next.'

Keira began. 'What happened to Tanya was terrifying because it could happen to any of us. We've all done exactly what she did. It was so fucking vicious that she was targeted. Apparently, she's had to go home to recover and miss this entire year, which is totally crap, but she could have died if it wasn't for Serena.'

Tanya's eyes in the dark. Her hair lost to the water. Her whole life pitched on its axis.

'And no attempt has been made to make us any safer. They're so lax it's absurd.' Keira's energy was bright, even when she was furious.

Dean rose to his full stature in his chair. 'Yeah, and it's not the first time stuff like this has gone on. Leysham has form. I'm not sure how much you guys know about what happened here last year. You're all first-years, right?'

Everyone except Luke nodded.

'So, Luke and I were on the rowing team.'

'I was clearly the cox.' Luke gestured, smiling, to indicate his height.

'I rowed at bow.' Dean looked over his shoulder. 'Oh, hi.'

Jane appeared behind him. She moved an empty chair closer to the group, making no sound. There was a stillness to her that kept Serena looking. Everyone around fidgeted, arms folding, knees jiggling. Jane was calm. She seemed pristine, her clothes newly pressed, her skin fresh from the shower.

She bought nothing from the counter, but sipped from a plain black Thermos. Serena wished she knew what was inside it.

Dean tried to find his thread. 'There was this, ah, crew night out – men's and women's crews together – dinner then a club, you know the sort of thing, a lot of drinking, and in the club one of the girls was assaulted. Let's just say touched inappropriately on the dance floor. Like, really inappropriately.' His voice boomed around the café, clanging to the vaults of the ceiling. 'And there were witnesses.'

Luke leaned forward, cutting over him softly. 'We were nowhere near what happened, but a lot of the others were. It was a member of the men's crew, we know that, but have no concrete proof.'

'We could give it a good guess.' Dean looked around. 'Other lads saw what happened, but no one came forward. The girl didn't know exactly who it was, so the whole thing was hushed up.'

Luke nodded. 'The punishment for the crew was to miss one race.'

Keira jerked in her chair, oak screeching against floor tiles. 'Fucking hell! This place!'

'It was an important race, in fairness, but still a race.'

'The whole thing was so horrible, like a conspiracy of silence.' Luke steepled his fingers. 'Most of the guys in the rowing team are very privileged. Their families are the ones that donate. I think only me and Dean came from schools where rowing wasn't an option.' He paused. 'It felt deliberate. If they kept it quiet, it didn't happen. No one needed to do anything, and the uni's reputation was safe. The girl involved was devastated, of course. We've been in touch with friends of hers.'

Jane cleared her throat and Serena glanced up at her.

Another woman in this place hadn't been safe. Another woman had been hunted.

'Luke and I spoke up, of course. We complained that whoever it was effectively got away with it, and it basically got us chucked off the team.' Dean addressed Jane directly.

'Not in so many words, but they made it clear. When we heard you were gathering people to speak out about a similar issue, we wanted to get involved.' Luke placed his stretched hands on the table, and Serena resisted the urge to do the same. Her span was wider than his.

Zara nodded. 'I'm delighted you did.'

'It's fucking hideous. To think shit like that gets glossed over.' Keira's feet tapped the floor in a galloping beat. 'This stuff goes on around us and everyone looks the other way. It makes me livid.'

'You have every right to be angry.' They all gave Jane's words space to land. 'It's the only reasonable response.'

Zara flicked her phone to life. 'I think I can use my social channels to drum up attention. My demographic is chiefly uni age, and pretty switched on to social issues.' Without looking at the screen, she found her feeds and displayed them to the group. 'My engagement rates are consistently high.'

She scrolled so that colourful boxes fled across the surface, weeks and months of her life in seconds. Serena knew no one so in tune with technology. That device wasn't a separate entity but part of Zara's body, a machine grown from her flesh, meshed until they were one, until her cells melded with the plastic, linked with its chips.

'I think they'll get behind this, and we can launch something big.'

Dean coughed a short bark. 'I don't mean to step on anyone's toes. This is clearly your thing, and that looks very impressive, but your channels seem mainly focused on aesthetics. Will we reach the right people?'

'My followers are interested in practising self-care, but are you implying that's somehow flimsy?' Zara's hands filled the air in front of her.

'No, not at all. I'm not doubting its gravitas, more its focus. Should we have a space where people can gather behind this particular issue?'

'I see your point, but publicity is oxygen to causes like this, and I have nearly a quarter of a million people ready to listen. It's crazy not to use them.'

'Your followers can't possibly be from this campus, though. You've been here a month.'

Zara frowned. 'We could always think beyond our own backyard?'

Luke spoke over them. 'Maybe it would be good to have something grassroots, you know? Something specific to Leysham, at least for a while?'

'Totally.' Keira nodded. 'A place women can share stories about what's happened here. Where it can't be hushed up.'

'It isn't only women suffering, though. Two of the students who died in the river last year were guys, and we can't ignore the problem of violence against men.'

Keira's voice rose to meet Dean's. 'But that violence is almost always perpetrated by men. You can't possibly think it's the same thing. Do you understand how scared we are? Do you? Do you know how we weigh the odds of our safety doing things you barely consider? Every dark alleyway, every short cut, every date, for fuck's sake. Women have to be vigilant to the point of exhaustion. We're constantly reminded of our own vulnerability. We're meant to be empowered, and so many people have fought valiantly for our liberation, but really, we're just knackered. It's endless, and it's boring. I'm sorry, but men simply aren't as frightened as we are.'

Serena pressed her knee against Keira's under the table to show her solidarity.

'I understand . . . honestly, I try to understand, but the statistics don't really bear it out.'

Luke's hand rested on Dean's elbow, a subtle signal to quieten his friend. 'Why don't we ask people to share their experiences first? Truth be told, we won't know what we're dealing with until we see the extent and nature of the issue. We can expand at a later stage.'

Dean tilted his head. 'What do you think, Jane?'

Jane paused as they turned to her. 'I think a focus on

Leysham experiences could be very effective at first.' She looked to Zara. 'Your extensive reach will be invaluable when you take things further.'

'Okay.' Zara beamed at the praise. 'I'm happy with that if you guys are.'

Jane's words were supportive, but Serena sensed they were masking something. She might agree with Serena's assessment. That this sounded logical and reasonable – a measured, mature response to a terrible situation – but nowhere near enough. The river never left Serena's mind for long, as if she carried part of it with her, its dank water lodged in some hidden place. The group's plans didn't grasp the reality of that night. The sense that the earth itself was against them, the water hellbent on destruction. The horror soaked into the land, the stories of women that came before. Nothing about what she'd experienced that night was safe or sensible. They needed something that matched its enormity.

Serena opened her mouth to speak.

'We want—' Dean began.

'Sorry, Serena, were you going to say something?' Luke stopped him, one finger raised.

Serena breathed, but no words arrived. Nothing of what she thought could be translated. She shook her head.

Dean jumped in. 'We want to be the best possible allies, and to make this place better for everyone.' The others nodded. 'We can chat further over a drink, if anyone fancies the SU? Jane?'

'Not tonight, but thank you.' Her face barely moved as she spoke.

As Dean reached down to his rucksack, Serena saw the tips of his ears grow pinker.

On the walk home, Serena reached Carnforth Quad and paused, perching on the fountain's cold stone rim. People gathered around the main arch of the hall, pushing pennies into the mouth of the carved faces there. Serena knew what they were doing. The custom was legendary. Freshers were told if they fed the Carnforth women's parted lips on any given Sunday of autumn term, they'd gain luck for their full three years. Rumours circled that it increased romantic prowess, and first-years saved their shiniest coppers.

The phone's buzz in her pocket startled Serena. Another message from her mother. They arrived every few days, updating her on a life she could no longer live.

Pool closed for filter cleaning. Niko furious at the disturbance.

Her mother still went to the pool and sat on those benches, coffee cup in hand, staring out at that tank of water.

Thea was at training today. She needs to work on her line to stay in elite.

Her eyes would be red from the chlorine. That bleach was vicious, ravaging the hair of those who swam in it, so blondes bore a greenish tinge and brunettes grew brassy. The distinct detergent smell lingered on skin for days.

Niko pushed them today. Tough drills. No one with your times.

The messages seemed like deliberate cruelty. Elizabeth had leotards from the gymnastic prowess of her youth tucked away in a drawer. She knew what it was to have potential. Her notes never asked about Serena's knee. When it could perform, her daughter's body had been Elizabeth's chief concern. She'd still wake at five, Serena was sure, still drive that same route in the hushed darkness, ignoring the empty passenger seat.

She'd sit by the side of the pool as the sky changed colour, assessing the competition. In every race of Serena's, she'd held the stat sheets, knowing each swimmer's split time to the hundredth of a second. It would be too soon to give up. Elizabeth would sit and watch those other bodies now, judging their form and dedication, noting their strengths and flaws, nodding as Niko gave his advice, all the time knowing her daughter had failed.

@zarakarmic • 218k followers

I want to talk today about relationships. My relationship with myself is – and always will be – the most significant love affair of my life.

Bodies like mine are so often treated as second rate. There is a shedload of money to be made by making us feel shit about ourselves. By making us buy into diets that starve us or punish us. By selling us creams that promise to erase the dimples on our lovely thighs.

I know how that stuff sticks, how it buries itself deep and eats away. We've been trained to loathe our own bodies, but I refuse. I adore my stomach and my thighs, and all the puckers and wobbles of my skin.

This body is perfect. I wish we could say it together. All our bodies are perfect.

FIFTEEN YEARS OLD

It always hurt. Not immediately, but always. No matter how hard Serena focused, her muscles could only last so long. Every race held the moment it stopped being bearable.

With the Nationals weeks away, training became savage. Niko's schedules were designed with precision but could never simulate the agony of competition. That pain was canny; it intuited when the stakes were high. All Serena could do in practice was push herself to the moment she wanted to stop. She always continued. That's what made her better. At that threshold, she kept going. Others would collapse, puffing into the gutter. It hurt more when you lost. *Swim to the wall.* That's what Niko repeated into her ear. *Swim to the wall. This wall. You don't have to think about the next one.* Some girls carried water bottles with slogans. *Embrace the pain.* Natasha used to scrawl in Sharpie on the inside of her wrist. *Keep going.* Pain had to be their ally.

Serena knew what it was, that fire in her lungs and legs. Visualising didn't quash its power. Lactic acid. It felt sentient, an enemy inside her, swamping her tendons and gnawing away. Her body eating itself from the inside out. If Serena let up, it would take over, weakening her strokes. If it took over, she'd already lost. The girl next to her would withstand more. The mind always gives up before the body.

Some part of that pain was pure. *Pain is the fire in which you forge yourself.* Niko's voice was rigid. *If you can come out the other end, you'll be golden.* Serena tried. She tried to embrace the sensation, but her brain grasped it as nothing but threat. She looked at the end of the lane. *Swim to the wall.* If she won that race, she'd be in the elite squad. If she won, it wouldn't hurt.

The coach journey to the Nationals took three hours. For the first forty minutes, the others played music and sang along. *We dipping in the powder blue.* Serena rested her head against the window. The roads were dark and her face flashed orange in the motorway streetlamps, lit to a dramatic shine, then gone. Lit, then gone. Then gone. Then gone. She knew the silence would drop eventually; there was too much at stake for camaraderie to last. Serena knew everyone on that coach, had trained with some of them for years. They wore the same purple hoodie with a black marlin sewn onto the back. The fastest fish in the sea, apparently, reports of its speed reaching mythical heights. Serena knew those swimmers well, their quirks, nicknames, in-jokes, but more than anything, she knew their times. When they'd chat over snacks, she'd think of the 0.65 of a second that had stretched between them at trials. It's impossible to set a record in training. They needed each other, needed the opposition, but that made it no easier. No time was ever good enough. They all chased the same shimmering dream.

When the noise calmed on the coach, the others pushed in earphones. Serena watched the same video as always. The eight and a half minutes of the 2012 eight hundred metres freestyle Olympic final. She knew every beat. Adlington holding her own for the first few lengths, then faltering and finishing clear seconds behind Ledecky. The screen shone in the dark. Serena's heart sped every time she watched those final seconds. Adlington grabbing Ledecky in a hug as soon as the results landed, then wiping her hand down her own wet face. Serena paused the video. She didn't know if she had it in her to embrace her defeater. Adlington might love the sport more than her own success, might have been delighted that her world record had held. She might simply have been strong enough not to let the pain show. That's why she had two golds at home.

Others longed for the moment of victory – the air punch at the end of the lane, smacking the water in jubilation – but Serena was spurred on by fear. She began to dread losing more than she craved the win. There were thirty of them on the bus. They all knew what the next forty-eight hours would bring. Two slots for each age group, and competitors pouring in from around the country. Most of them wouldn't sing on the journey home.

Natasha wasn't on that coach. It was Serena's first major event without her at the helm, without hearing her group sing the loudest. Her absence didn't need to be explained. It wasn't age, not the natural decline they all knew was coming. This had been rapid. Where there had once been muscles, thicker and more magnificent than any other girl in the pool, there had suddenly been ribs. They all kept their weight low – it was vital to be streamlined – but their frames were packed with might. Natasha's had diminished entirely. Three weeks away from the pool were all it had taken, a brief recovery from a sprained metatarsal. Lycra costumes left nowhere to hide and, as Natasha had walked along the bobbled tiles on her return, Serena had heard the murmurs. People had always looked at her, but never in concern until then. Serena had braced herself for Niko's shock, his distress, the lectures they'd have to sit through. He'd protect his Sasha at all costs. She'd watched as he'd clocked Natasha's faded limbs, his eyes scanning her visible bones. She'd watched as he turned away, crouched to the water and talked intently to the freestyle relay team.

The others went for pizza, but Serena refused. Everyone else somehow managed to be both: vowed rivals and a close team, grasping any opportunity to socialise, with make-up on their tight skin, their hair made soft. They didn't miss out. Other girls flirted, borrowing the enormous purple hoodies of the boys they liked best. Serena found it impossible. She needed the solace of her tiny Travelodge room. The others longed to think about anything that wasn't swimming, but it consumed her. Lifting pink plastic hand weights, she completed the routine Niko had taught her. As her muscles expanded and contracted, she imagined herself in the water. Her intensity was becoming known. Images on social media, shared by teammates, showed her lethal focus on the starting blocks. Their hashtags indicated admiration. #gogetitgirl #eyesontheprize #siren. Serena never clicked her approval, had no channel where she added her own pictures. She preferred the images that showed her swimming: rising out of the water, mouth gasping, hands together in what looked like prayer. That looked closer to how it felt.

Serena filled the bath and lay flat. She visualised the following morning's race: every beat, every stroke, every moment she'd want to give up. *You slice through the water.* She needed to experience it. *You push through the pain, so much stronger than the others.* She wouldn't allow herself not to win. *Your hand hits the pad first.* It was unthinkable. There was no space for the distractions the others loved: the oozing mozzarella, the squeals of joy, the gossip. Serena lay in the water until it was cold. She imagined the minutes of that race twenty times before she got out.

They trained in a full-size pool, but this one looked longer.

It stretched into nowhere as Serena walked to the starting blocks. *Serena!* Her name shouted, loud and urgent. *Serena!* Stopping, she scanned the seating area. So many bodies were crushed into those stands. Her mother or Niko would never distract her at this point. Other swimmers wore headphones as they walked out, but Serena didn't struggle to focus. The shout came from people she hardly knew. A mother and daughter she'd seen at the sports centre. They waved as they raised their sign higher. They'd drawn out all six letters, coloured each with a different paint and covered the whole thing in glitter. *S-E-R-E-N-A*. They'd driven so many miles to see her swim.

Serena turned back to the pool, to drill her mind into it alone. Another noise jarred her ears. The smack of plastic against tiles. An object dropped. She couldn't help but look. Her competitors lined up, but Serena scanned the crowd again. Zara sitting next to Elizabeth, pink t-shirt, sparkled necklace. Serena had no idea she'd be there. Across the pool, Zara pushed her hair back and made a face of exaggerated apology to the people who'd turned. Serena had seen her playing games on that pearlescent pink console so often, creating houses and lives for miniature people, dictating their behaviour. She was always plugged into some technology. Zara reached to pick up the plastic slab with a flourish, practically curtseying. She met Serena's eyes across the room and smiled. Serena's legs hollowed. The laugh that rang out from Zara was rich and confident. This was not the timid girl she knew. This girl had distracted her deliberately. For a plunging second, she knew it to be true. Zara sat back down, and Serena saw her mother lean over to inspect the complex console for damage. Serena's cheeks burned. Her mother's attention should be on her. This was her room. Let the computer's innards smash to nothing.

Serena's eyes went back to the pool, but her mind was on Zara.

As soon as she entered the water, it was wrong. The water didn't hold her. The connection had weakened. Her dive created too big a splash, she rose too slowly to the surface. The first strokes were clumsy. It didn't usually hurt yet. Her muscles weren't sore so much as raw. It made no sense; she'd limbered up, iced her knee the night before, imagined every second. Zara had cut through her focus. Serena wanted to root her feet to the bottom and call out to Niko, but she only had his words. *Swim to the wall.* The pain usually gripped with a length to go, but this seared within the first seconds. Every kick sent rips further along her legs. Each stroke mauled her shoulders.

Serena focused on the black line. *Pain is the fire in which you forge yourself.* This pain wasn't pure but messy. As she exhaled, Serena let herself scream, short guttural shouts, with each stroke. It gave a moment of relief, but there were so many more to go. *Swim to the wall.* There was always another wall. Serena forced every pull through the water. Her muscles must be tattered. She continued in nothing but an act of will. *The mind always gives up before the body.* With no idea where the other girls were, she just had to finish the race. *Please let this be over*. Chanting to herself through each stroke, an incantation. *Let this be over. Let this be over.*

Her hand reached the pad, and Serena slumped onto the lane rope. The water didn't buoy her. Yells and claps from the crowd, but through the fog of pain, Serena couldn't grasp who it was for. The girl in the next lane caught her around the neck. Taking her goggles off, she tried to concentrate. The crowd cleared, and she saw her mother's teeth bared, Niko looking to the sky. She'd won. Despite it all, she'd claimed the victory. Niko and Elizabeth were elated at her agony. Her pain had bought their joy. Zara was still seated, still smiling.

7

'We need to know the truth.'

Dean's voice carried across the field. A bigger field this time, in the heart of the campus, away from the river and the trees. The university's buildings were scattered with careful irregularity across the land, as if positioned by whims of topography or ancient flows, rather than centuries of design. It created the feel of a village, with stretches of grass easing between each man-made structure.

'And to know the truth, we must expose the truth.'

The density of the assembled crowd gave the event the atmosphere of a gig. What felt like hundreds of people stood in huddles, holding plastic beer glasses. If Zara's rally had been organised, this was slick. Trestle tables were laden with piles of leaflets. Serena walked over to pick one up, more confident now without her crutches. The paper was glossy and unrippable, and she knew the bright words splashed across it had been printed professionally. They'd sought quotes from three companies before selecting the most cost-effective.

'Universities are expected to provide a duty of care over their students, but statistics show that campuses are one of the least safe places to live.'

A wide arch of balloons soared over Dean's head in the same shades as those that filled Zara's feed, those rich, sunset pastels. Gold, teal, mauve, peach, lilac. Signs and banners covered the sides of the stage, the arranged tables. Written across everything were the words *Rise Up* and the website address they'd bought the week before.

'Data demonstrates university students are more at risk of crime and mental ill health than the rest of the population. It's estimated over a third of UK students become a victim of crime during their studies. And stories of assault are perennial. With every academic year, new reports emerge, but nothing meaningful is done to stop it.'

Dean looked out to the crowd as his words rumbled through the pole-mounted speaker system. It had taken hours to rig up.

'A BBC investigation revealed UK universities received more than seven hundred allegations of sexual misconduct in one academic year. Sixty-two percent of UK students report that they've experienced sexual violence at university. But only two percent say they are satisfied with how their institution handled it.'

He paused after each statistic, letting it steep.

'This has already become endemic. We need to detail and document what's happened to those of us who live and work here. It might be tough to share, but we need to know the facts to call for real change. Universities, including Leysham, claim to have a zero-tolerance approach to misconduct, but there's simply no evidence of this.'

Dean's beanie hat was pulled so low it almost reached his beard. His right hand slashed forwards with each point made.

'Essentially, these institutions are not held accountable in any way. It leaves students unsupported and unsafe.'

Zara's hand was on the microphone before Dean's sentence ended.

'Dean, thank you. Thank you. That was both illuminating and horrifying. Really important stuff.'

As Dean left the stage, Zara walked closer to its front edge.

'I want to say a few things before I invite some friends up here to tell their stories.'

At the side of the raised platform, Dean gestured with as much force as when he'd been talking to the crowd, clearly riled by Zara's actions. Luke's hands patted the air as if to soothe it.

'I've shared my struggles with disempowerment openly.' Zara paused. 'I've been candid about the fact that having a body like mine makes everything so much harder. You're told things aren't for you. This outfit. This activity. This way of being. The world becomes a smaller place if you live in a bigger body.'

Serena saw everything Zara posted, but the words seemed harsher in person. Despite the confidence, something in her tone was taut.

'Bodies like mine are seen as wrong, immoral even, and we internalise that shame. I was bullied.'

She looked out to the gathered people as if down the lens of her camera. The same intensity, the same intimacy.

'I was bullied mercilessly as a child. Called every name you can imagine, because of my body size. It's always been the weapon used against me. My own body. A lazy weapon wielded by every single person in my life.'

Serena remembered that quiet, pudgy child, too shy to look from under her dark mass of hair. Had Anoushka made sharp comments? Had Serena herself judged that body, so unlike her own?

'But I've been lucky. I've learned that speaking out can make it easier. Knowing your words are being heard, that they resonate with others, it helps. It lightens the individual load and adds force to our collective message. The more I've talked to people, the more I've realised everyone has some story to share. And that's why we're here today. We know terrible things have happened and we're getting rightly angry about it. So, we need to tell our truths. We need to hear from you.'

Jane had arrived late, and stood by the side of the stage, close enough that Serena could see the dents in her lobes where holes were pierced but no earrings had been pushed through. Serena inhaled but couldn't catch the smoky scent she'd breathed by the river.

A girl who'd been in the café was on the stage now, her words barely audible, even through the microphone.

'I study Engineering. I'm in my second year, and it's been horrific, to be honest. It started with comments, oh-so-ironic, because they couldn't possibly be sexist. But they still said them. About a woman's place. About how I can't do certain calculations, can't set up certain apparatus by myself.'

Her accent was from a little further down the coast, where the beachside was lit for six glittering, hectic miles.

'I laughed along at first, because what choice do you have? But it does make me worry I shouldn't be here. Like I'm a way of bumping the numbers, giving them better ratios or something. I get higher grades than most of the lads in that lab, but I'm still made to think I don't deserve it.'

Serena felt Keira breathe deeply next to her, then head towards the stage. Jane touched Keira's back as she walked past. A silver chain around Jane's neck had tangled in the loose strands of her pale hair. She never wore make-up on her face. Nothing about Jane was overstated, but that simplicity felt somehow luxurious. Serena looked away, certain she'd been staring.

Keira had reached the platform. 'I want to share something I haven't spoken about before.'

She coughed and glanced at Serena, readying herself. 'When I was in the sixth form, a picture was taken of me, passed out at a party. It was late; I'd drunk too much. Someone pushed my skirt right up over my thighs so you could see my underwear. That picture hit every phone in my school before I woke up.'

As she paused, the field fell quiet. Serena's breath shook.

'No one who was there stopped them, and no one ever admitted who did it. My friends were in that room, but not a single one came forward. I complained to my head of year, but they tried to wriggle out of it, saying it wasn't on school property. My body had been shown without my permission, and I was told to shut up.' Her voice grew stronger. 'I know the colour of my skin was a factor. I'm not stupid. The angry black women trope is alive and well, and it lets people get away with so much shit. I was made out to be the aggressor when I was the victim. I was told I shouldn't have put myself in that position, shouldn't have drunk so much. I was basically told I asked for it.' She swallowed. 'I was sixteen. I felt like my body had been stolen from me in those pictures. It's taken years to get my confidence back, but now I intend to be exactly as loud and aggressive as I fucking choose.'

Serena gripped Keira's hand when they stood together again, willing the pressure of her skin to indicate the force of her support.

Zara called another girl to the microphone.

'I'm a fresher, so I've only been at Leysham for a few months. In the first few weeks, something happened that's made it hard to relax here. I went to a party, a drinks thing for a society I was thinking of joining.' Her voice wobbled. 'After an hour or so, the door crashed open and a group of boys stormed in. They had purple scarves, and their hands were stained with purple ink. They started leaving marks on everything. Some of them shoved their hands against people's faces, others went for our clothes, touching anywhere, hips, boobs, the lot. We yelled at them to go, and they did, but not before a lot of clothes were ruined, a lot of people upset. I assumed we'd go to the Proctors to complain, but everyone said it wasn't worth it.'

Serena watched Jane pull a tube of balm from her pocket and press it slowly to her lips. The boy at the Gilly Sampson Bash had worn a purple cravat around his neck.

The girl continued. 'It was an initiation thing, apparently. A group that call themselves the Carnforth Club. I don't know much about them, but I know they felt entitled enough to barge in, to touch us without permission, to make us feel like shit.'

Serena frowned. She hadn't heard of them.

Jane whirled around, her eyes landing on Serena, the sheen of her mouth reflecting the stage lights. Her voice was no louder than a whisper, but flinty. 'This has gone too far.' A crease deepened between her eyebrows. Serena nodded back, radiant with the knowledge she'd been Jane's confidante, even for a moment.

Something began to itch in Serena's throat. The stories told on stage resonated. For those years in the water, had she been made vulnerable? She wasn't sure which words would form, but wanted to say them. She wanted Jane to hear her. The way they'd looked at her body, scrutinising each inch, hunting out changes, commenting on ounces of weight gained or muscle mass lost. The way majestic Natasha had been robbed of her power. The way their bodies had not been their own. Eyes on parts of themselves they couldn't even see. The cleft of their backs. The creases where their thighs became buttock. The way they'd been trained to think, brains rewired to see competition everywhere. Their teens distorted to fit the water. Serena wanted to speak the words aloud. She wanted to tell her own story.

Serena imagined the steps it would take to reach the raised platform, felt the muscles of her calves tense at the idea. Without realising she was walking, she'd reached the top of the metal staircase. She expected Zara to pass the microphone, as she had for the others. Zara turned, but rather than beckon Serena forward, she raised an outstretched hand. Head tilting, she mouthed, *Sorry* – then returned to the crowd.

'We all have our stories to tell, and the more we hear, the more we understand the problems around us.'

Serena froze on the flimsy metal steps. The words she wanted to speak filled her mouth, pushed down into her gullet.

'We've chosen to use a website because it's a permanent space where we can keep things completely anonymous. The address is here.' Zara held a bright flyer. 'It's a place you can share your experiences. We hope it's a way of giving some relief, but also a way these stories can come together and show the truth. Please join us and rise up!'

Applause thundered across the field.

@zarakarmic • 226k followers

Today has been massive. I've been so taken aback by your support. You are all utterly incredible. The messages and comments you've sent have given me real hope.

We should be genuinely empowered to demand more, to rise up. It starts here.

Well, okay, it starts after we've rested and gathered our strength. For now, it's date night; me, myself and my homeboys, Ben and Jerry. And, no, this is not a sponsored post, just an obsession.

Do whatever you need to recuperate. Never forget that self-care is a radical act.

8

'Sorry, sorry, I'm struggling!'

Zara was laden. As the pink Kanken rucksack manoeuvred from her shoulders, it knocked the desk lamp, nudged Serena's chest of drawers. No one other than Keira had visited Serena's room. A Sunday ritual had formed between them, gathering to watch the films Keira was dumbstruck Serena had never seen. Everything made more sense now she knew who wore pink on Wednesdays. Those sweet, streamed movies gave a glimpse of the years Serena had excluded herself from: ill-advised fancy dress, crushes, squabbles. Keira could quote along with the actors, pace out the dance routines, but for Serena it was new. She saved all week to buy the pizza they ate lying on the bed, her twenty-year-old hands feeding the fifteen-year-old who'd denied herself so much.

'I brought everything I thought you might need.'

It was the first time they'd been alone together that term.

Serena hadn't invited Zara, still stung by the hand blocking her way at the rally, but Zara must have sensed the dread that rippled through her cousin when a celebratory night out was suggested. As she emptied products onto the duvet, the room grew thick with that smell of so many flowers condensed.

'It's not actually perfume, you know, just a few drops of ylang-ylang oil. It's strong, but it's meant to be calming. The name means "wilderness" – isn't that lovely?'

Serena's bare room didn't know how to cope with Zara, her voice loud, her colours vibrant. The bed was piled with bright cardboard constructions holding bottles and jars.

'I know it's a lot.' Zara gestured as if to brush them all away. 'I know why they send things, but it's crazy one person gets this. I try to recycle or gift most of it.'

Serena knew why they sent them too. Zara had the power to persuade people to buy things – to do things – they didn't know they wanted. Stadiums-worth of people looked to her for inspiration. On the bed, so many shades and shapes competed for attention, spilling over each other like the contents of a magazine poured out. Hundreds of pounds – possibly thousands – filled the duvet, a significant chunk of the student loan that had landed in Serena's account the month before. Other girls would have wept at the treasure.

'Sit there.' Zara stood over her.

The make-up felt oily on Serena's face. She left the decisions to Zara. Deciphering those balms and unctions would have taken too long, and Zara spoke their language.

'Close your eyes.'

She obeyed as Zara's fingers massaged her cheeks. The creams all smelled like coconut. She resisted the urge to wipe their cloying sweetness from her face.

'Keep your lips still.'

Pressure on Serena's skin made her uneasy. No one had touched her face for so long. She might never have been this close to her cousin. Zara's fingers were gentle but never stopped stroking.

'Thanks, Rena. No one ever lets me do this!' Zara's laugh usually clanged but now was only a rush of air against Serena's eyelids. She was softer than Serena had ever known her.

'You'll have fun tonight, I promise.'

Each layer of serum, of cream, of primer sat on Serena's skin, Zara describing each as she applied them. They were surely supposed to sink in.

'Make-up now. A bit of foundation. You're so pale, I won't use too much.'

'Pasty, more like.' Serena scrunched her nose under Zara's fingertips.

'No, it's lovely. Like our mums.' Zara didn't share the other women's pallid cheeks. Her own were darker, and flushed so often with what seemed like joy. She dabbed something warm over Serena's temples. The ylang-ylang from her wrists was overwhelming.

'They must have done this all the time.' An enormous brush

flicked across Serena's forehead, chin, cheeks. The powder was a relief, soaking up some of the oil. Serena's sister, Kelly, had spent hours with Zara when they were young, daubing each other's faces with nubs of lipstick and half-empty eyeshadows from their mothers' stashes until they looked ridiculous. Serena had never had time to join in.

'Open your mouth for me.' Zara worked a mascara wand through Serena's eyelashes. 'It stops you from blinking. I've no idea how.'

Serena flinched as Zara nudged her knee.

'Oh, God, sorry.' Zara's hand on her shoulder. 'Are you okay now? That must have been awful.'

They'd never discussed it. So little had been said about the injury, the surgery, what it meant for Serena's life. She couldn't face the enormity of that conversation, not with Zara's face so close.

'Yeah, much better, thanks.'

Zara moved Serena towards the mirror on the wall. Serena was prepared to look unfamiliar, to see a garish rendering of her features. But, when she opened her eyes, her face was simply in sharper focus. Zara's ministrations had made a more vivid version of herself.

The geometry of the clothing changed her. The starchy rectangles Serena lived in were replaced by softness, fabric draping in ways she'd never known before. The dress expected Zara's body and missed those dimensions, bagging in places usually full. Only her shoulders gave it stretch. Serena couldn't look away from the new shape she formed in the mirror.

Zara snapped a shot before they left, her arm around Serena.

'You look hot, you know.' Serena tried to wriggle free, but Zara gripped. 'You really do.'

She knew the image would be online in moments, to live there eternally. Sitting high on her thighs and low on her breastbone, the dress covered little. Far more of her body had been on display in the pool, when she'd held no qualms about bending over until her hands hit the bobbled tiles. This felt different. The body that swam had been purposeful. This body was to be looked at.

They stayed on campus, wary of who might lurk in the town's clubs. Serena wasn't sure why they assumed Leysham was safer. The Student Union bar shone with purple lights, its archways and flamboyant stone foliage forming dramatic shadows. Serena walked through the door this time, let them stamp her hand with ink. It was a week into November, but the bar still celebrated Halloween: green, orange and black streamers, cobwebs in every corner. University was a constant costume parade, with no occasion left unthemed.

'Is Jane coming?' Serena heard the words Dean aimed at Zara's ears.

'I shouldn't think so, Dean.'

'Yeah, mate, she's totally buzzed to join a bunch of undergrads at an SU Halloween party.' Keira joined them. Her top sparkled with stars and half-moons, so sheer you could see the bra beneath.

Serena had envied before. Envied the upper arms of a competitor, cursed the way they propelled her through the water. Now, she stared at these people she nearly knew, marvelling at their ease. They knew how to operate in a room like this. Zara was dancing already, wiggling as they chatted, red dress matching the horns on her hairband. People stared – clocking her curves, her eyelashes, the waves of her hair – and she basked in their gaze.

Keira balanced a tray from the bar on one upturned hand like a cocktail waitress. It twinkled with tiny glasses. They each picked one between thumb and forefinger, gulping it back, seemingly confident the drinks were safe. Serena did the same. The contents of the glass were startling chartreuse. They tasted of sweets, then, in a rush, a bitterness that coated Serena's mouth and couldn't be swallowed away. She stiffened her face so no reaction revealed it to be her first ever shot. Alcohol had never been an option: the sugar alone ruled it out. She'd been told it was poison and, as she felt the warm flow of ethanol through her body, realised why. It reached her head and made it lighter.

The others shrieked in joyful disgust.

Serena had once been able to calibrate her body to a millimetre, but this reaction was new. That lime-green liquid eased the pain in her knee. Her weight on that joint no longer jabbed, even in Zara's ridiculous shoes. She knew the alcohol would mix with the painkillers she still took daily, forming a toxic muddle to smash through her veins, but didn't care. As they headed to the centre of the room, she could dance. She closed her eyes and let her body move.

Keira pulled her into a hug. 'You look bloody stunning, lady!'

A pack of boys by the bar came into focus. Their eyes traced the women dancing, up, then down. Serena stiffened at the abrasive gaze as one of them scanned her limbs, her borrowed dress. His assessment was immediate; eyes lengthening to vulpine intent. No one had ever looked at her like that. The desire in his stare was palpable. Her body had once triumphed in competition but had never held this different ability.

Turning away, she reached an arm around Keira's neck and danced with the group. She was one of them. Night after night had passed in that purpose-built bedroom, slumped on the mottled carpet, imagining how many feet had trodden it before. The room was thick with other people's memories. Greasy smudges dotted one wall, where Blu-tack had held someone else's photographs, club flyers, sports schedules. A rich seam of experience had sat beyond her reach. This was it.

She danced for hours. Another tray of shots arrived, maybe more. She danced until the music made sense. The songs that played were all rhythm, nothing to complicate but a pounding beat that spurred her body on, synching with her core like it came from the earth. Serena didn't have to mimic; her bones knew when to move. She didn't need Niko's words in her ear. There would be no winner here.

The girls – Keira, Zara, some of the others from the rally –

posed for photos, iPhone at arm's length, huddling into shot. Their faces drained of wit for those seconds. Serena dulled her expression along with them, slanted her head to the same angle. Once released, they laughed again. Glitter had been smeared onto their faces so eyelids and lips shimmered. Serena could smell their hair, their skin. They danced with pure joy, mouthing the words of songs as if the lyrics were written for them. Their glow came from make-up, but it looked like sorcery. Serena had missed so much; only overhearing those years of lipstick and band logos and swigs of vodka, arriving at the end of her teens blank. Impossibly, her face in the phone's screen matched theirs. Zara had brushed sheen onto her cheeks and the end of her nose, combed cream into her hair to erase the chlorine's damage. A red trickle – added by Zara as a flourish as they left her room – flowed from one corner of her mouth, down her neck, ending in a smudge at her cleavage. It was Halloween, and she was fully disguised.

So much human warmth filled that dance floor, so much sweat and flesh. The air was lit like water and Serena felt it as bliss. Drinks lifted, splashing shoulders with sticky liquid. Zara held Serena's arms above their heads, trailed hands to her waist, leaned over to kiss her cheek. The boys danced with them now. Dean holding his pint, leading with the shoulders. Luke moving without self-consciousness, as if he genuinely liked the song. He wore a black jumper painted with white skeleton bones that must be too warm. A piece of blue string was tied around his wrist. Every time Serena glanced up, their eyes locked. He was looking at her. Not Zara. Not the others. He was watching Serena's face.

In the group's small circle, she was steps from him. Her breath became ragged. She'd never done this before. Could the twist of her hips have the power to lure him closer? Flashing lights made every movement robotic. He was staring. Each time the lights flickered, he was a pace nearer, until Serena sensed a new warmth. His jumper against her dress, against her bare skin.

'Having a good night?' Had he ever spoken to her directly before? The vapour from his breath prickled the down of Serena's cheeks.

He was a handful of inches shorter than her. She leaned to reply.

'Yeah, great.' She let her nose nudge his jaw before pulling away.

He danced so close she could smell him. So close the only way to move was together. Stomachs nearly touching. Saliva flooded Serena's mouth. His hand skimmed her thighs. One song blurred into the next and the small of her back grew damp from his palm. He stepped back and alarm flashed through her. Had her power waned? But he didn't walk away. He stood, pulsing in the lights, gesturing, a clawed hand tilting. Serena translated. *A drink?* She nodded.

He returned with two plastic cups – one clear, one dark – for her to choose between. For a second, an unknown drink felt treacherous. Tanya had sipped from a drink that nearly destroyed her. But Serena knew Luke. Lifting the dark cup from his hand, she sipped. Cola with an unknown spirit, its fizz bursting against the roof of her mouth.

'I hope you like it.' His breath was sharp with alcohol.

Those plastic cups prompted a gear change. Moving her around, he pushed his front against her back, his hands between them, slipping under the hem of her dress. Her legs might crumple beneath her.

A flash. The girl from the rowing team, touched on a dance floor by unwanted hands.

Serena did want this. She was sure. She was sure of the shudder that ripped across her body. A male hand inched its way higher than any male hand had inched before. His fingers on her underwear, the one scrap of her outfit she owned. Blood rushed to the parts he grazed. Sweat on the back of her neck. They hadn't even kissed. Luke turned her round to face him, her body reacting to his will. He moved against her in a steady rhythm, then his mouth was on hers, colder than she'd expected. Softer than she'd expected. She'd hardly spoken to him, but some primal force pushed her hips forwards. The music sped, and they moved to meet it. The thump of its bass line filled the cavity of Serena's chest, her whole body juddering. His body around hers. She was subsumed.

9

His room was almost identical to hers. The bed, the desk, the drawers in the same places. Serena nearly knew it. Plants grew in pots along his windowsill. A furred cactus, a fern with fronds that stretched like fingers, something with waxy leaves that flattened when she pressed them. Plants he must feed with water each week. He didn't ask, but handed her a cup of coffee, pale with milk. He sat on the bed with his own.

'I hope that's okay. I've run out of ground, so I'm afraid it's instant.'

The Ikea mugs they drank from matched. Their hands bore the same ink stamp. They'd walked into the cold together. Taking the ticket from her hand, he'd conjured her coat into his arms. Serena wasn't sure how they'd arrived back at his room. Had they taken the dark path by the river? Had she heard the rush of that water, smelled its dank earthiness? She wrapped her hands around the warmth of the mug. In her own room, the radiator was cranked up full.

The coffee tasted acrid, but she sipped. Caffeine might help, might stop her eyes from blurring. She'd tasted so many drinks that night, each one pushing her further from her body. Her memory was patchy, her vision erratic. Had something in those drinks done something terrible? Was it the same toxin that had made Tanya's steps wobble? Or was it just what alcohol did? She'd drunk more in those hours than her body had ever known.

Luke folded one leg beneath him. He was talking too quickly. Was he trying to impress her? The prickle in the air was either awkward or wonderful. In the light of his lamp, she could see him. She'd never looked properly before. This was Luke. His hair curled slightly, his skin was pale. That gentle prettiness made him look like he enjoyed difficult music, like he understood poems. Luke's bones were delicate, didn't stretch as far as her own. He'd coxed the rowing boat, tucked at the stern, taking up as little space as possible.

Leaning over to his bedside table, he picked up a filmy green pouch, *Golden Virginia* on the side. He lifted a wad of tobacco, settled a filter in place, and rolled the paper strip tightly. It was an intricate process. Some of the brown filaments escaped and flecked the bedcovers, but he didn't brush them away. His tongue flicked the edge before sealing it. The message in black on the side of the tobacco pack was enormous. *Smoking seriously harms you and others around you.* Luke noticed her reading.

'Fortunately, I only smoke flippantly.'

Her laugh came seconds too late. Halls of residence rooms had smoke detectors wired above every door, so Luke opened his window as far as it would go, letting cold air in. He lit the cigarette, sucking as he held it over a silver lighter, then exhaled, leaning his head back so far his Adam's apple bulged. The cigarette's tip was a tiny fire in the air. Serena picked up the lighter. It was heavy, the old-fashioned metal kind with a lid that swung open and snapped closed. On the back was a swirling inscription. *To Sarah.*

'I should make up a story, say it's from a grandparent or some famous person I met, but I actually found it on a pavement and kept it.'

'That's a good enough story.'

Its smooth planes were cool against her palms.

'Sorry, would you like some?'

Serena felt her head nod. She'd never smoked anything before. Her lungs had needed to be pure. The cigarette was damp where his lips had been. She sucked the end, like he had, filling her mouth, then tried to breathe the trapped smoke. The heat was a shock, a visceral pain that scorched her mouth and chest. Her throat clamped shut and she spluttered.

Luke laughed, but not cruelly. 'Oh no, sorry. I didn't know . . . You have these tiny hairs all the way down the back of your throat, and you have to burn them away before you can enjoy it. About a million of yours just got annihilated.'

Gulping from her coffee cup offered little relief. Luke smiled. Serena didn't know what they were supposed to do next. As she sat on his desk chair, her cheeks were numb from alcohol, her larynx ragged. Then, Luke's mug on the bedside table, his face above hers. She hadn't kissed a boy until that night. But Luke wanted to kiss her. Leaning in, his fingers in her hair, her head forced backwards. His mouth on hers, tobacco sweet on his tongue, and her mouth knew what to do. Some muscles don't need training. In one motion they were on the bed, lips wet on her neck, hands on her thighs. Her chest raced, throbbing with something new. Did the same thing pulse through him?

His jumper was on the floor. Serena could see his flesh. His was not the sort of body she was used to. Those muscles had never strained or stretched, never been rubbed with vigour. They were lazy. His body had never won anything, never pushed itself to the point of pain. His stomach was barely a ripple.

She was both taller and broader. Serena didn't know if it bothered him. Did he feel diminished? He wouldn't grasp why her shoulders were so meaty, or what the wingspan of those arms could do. He'd never seen that body cut through water. Did he wish she was soft and lush, small enough to tuck under his arm?

When he looked at her body, he didn't admire its speed or strength. He looked at her skin and wanted to touch it. His own body responded. Serena wanted to glory in the sensation, but she was suddenly beneath him on the bed, with no idea how they'd changed places. In a beat, her body wasn't her own.

His door was closed, and she couldn't recall if he'd locked

it. There might be no swift exit from that room. His face was visible only when he loomed over her. A flash in Serena's mind, and he morphed. Stubble suddenly bristle, coarse and terrifying. A second later, soft again. She blinked. His teeth were fangs gleaming, then shyly smiling. Even this gentle boy could trigger fear. Did men like him lurk behind those statistics? Something in his maleness tasted like threat. Did he carry that history, that brutality, with him? Serena could overpower him. She was sure. If it came to it, she could twist his arm behind his back, smack upwards into his nose so hard it shattered. Did other girls weigh this up? They wouldn't have her shoulders.

His hands were rougher than they looked, abrasive on her skin, but she couldn't ask him to stop. The words it took were too far from her mouth, and she wasn't certain she wanted to say them. She couldn't face the risk he might not obey.

Serena knew she was too still, too silent. His face in focus, he paused for a moment, eyebrows asking the question. She should nod, kiss him, show her assent, but didn't know how. Should she say his name in a false, purring voice? Look him dead in the eye and demand he fuck her? Bite him, slap his flesh until he cried out, urge him to pull her hair, tighten his hands around her throat? She'd seen it play out on the screen of her phone. Other girls knew how to behave. Zara would know what to do if it was her bra on his floor, her hair over his pillow. Serena knew how Zara would move.

Without Niko's words in her ear, she had to fathom for herself. Luke pushed closer, their tongues now frantic. This was the moment. The mythologised second when one thing becomes another for ever. It was now. Now. Now, and then gone. Serena's eyes widened. She could never go back. It wasn't pain she felt but outrage. Her mouth gaped at it. Outrage that this involved him getting right to her core. Not intimate so much as intrusive. Nothing of him was breached.

He kept moving, and the sensation drew her in. She let herself respond as he weighed down, let herself move. Looking up at Luke's face, he seemed so much more at its mercy. A third entity had entered the room, something neither of them had the reins of. Before Serena could focus on it, grasp it, get a sense of its shape, its heft, it was gone.

Serena woke to a blurred head. Alcohol remained active in her blood. The sole light came from Luke's alarm clock. 3:55. Serena used the green glow to make faint shadows on the wall, hands forming krakens, terrifying creatures from deep in the ocean. Luke didn't stir. His arm was flung backwards, his wrist all she could clearly see. The wrist without the tied string, his skin so pale that blue veins showed through. Serena felt between her legs but found only sweat; her body had pushed itself so hard in the water for so many years that no membrane could possibly have remained intact.

As she crept from the bed, Luke didn't flicker. His skeleton jumper lay over her bag and shoes. Serena couldn't recall him taking it off. It smelled of fabric conditioner as she lifted it to his desk chair. After those hours in a clammy club, it felt freshly washed. He must have emitted nothing as they'd danced.

The bag held her keys, her wallet and her phone. Her phone. Serena turned it over in her hand. Three percent battery and eight messages. One from Keira. *You'd better be having a blast, but if you need me, call.* Six from Zara. *Have you left the union?* They'd danced. *Let me know where you are, darling.* Zara's face close to her own, kissing her cheek. *Please call me when you see this.* The heavy scent of Zara. *I'm worried about you.*

The campus was empty. It was before five. Months earlier, Serena's alarm clock would have been primed to bleat. Rain started minutes after she left Luke's room, and cold air jarred her lungs, dragging on the charred tendrils there. As she walked, Serena imagined eyes on her, predatory eyes hidden in the under-growth, lurking around corners, waiting for the moment she let her guard down. The stories that seeped from the ancient stones of those buildings created threat in every shadow. The memo-ries of so many others lingered there: feet that had worn down steps until they sagged in the middle, hands that had trailed over bannisters until they shone. Memories of women screaming to their deaths. The ghosts of these places were not always kind.

If Serena looked away from the buildings, it could be almost any time in history. Trees and rain and wet grass. So many people had walked that dark, feeling just as unsafe, just as exhilarated. That earth could do such terrible, wonderful things. The throb between Serena's legs connected her to it. That sensation, new to her, must be universal. The women that came before her would have felt the same.

She lifted her face to the rain, hair dripping by the time she reached the crest of another hill. The false blood Zara had smeared on her chest ran down her skin. If anyone saw her, she'd look like a woman risen from the grave, come to wreak her revenge. The rain might cleanse her. Might take away the stench of sex from her armpits, her thighs. The sweat shed in bed. If she let it, it might rinse the ink stamp from her hands, the shimmer from her cheeks, the stain from her lips. It could ease the alcohol from her veins, the smoke that tugged her chest. It could cleanse, but Serena didn't want absolution. She wanted something of that night to stick.

@zarakarmic • 224k followers

I want to share this stunning new shadow palette from Stella Cosmetics today.

I've worked with them for a while, and there's nothing more satisfying than when a brand aligns with my values.

It is such a profound delight to paint myself with these gorgeous, right-on rainbows, some shimmering, some matte.

I used this palette to create my Halloween look this year because, let's face it, sometimes you have to remind yourself that you are an outright treat!

SIXTEEN YEARS OLD

There was a distinct second a race fell apart. A breath of time, and it was gone. Serena feared it more than anything. The race was in Exeter, another deafening room with triangular flags rippling in no breeze, another race she had to win to keep progressing. It was hotter than usual, and a headache had nagged at her all morning. She lined up with a group of girls, facing the pool, all hoping for the same outcome. *You slice through the water.* Serena wasn't unique. *Your hands hit the pad first.* They'd all envisioned how it would go. It struck her for the first time, as they crouched, that seven of them were wrong.

The first few strokes were straightforward, but then – in that single, dreadful beat – her limbs were cumbersome. Her mind snagged on what the other girls were doing. She tried counting, tried staring at the line, singing a song to herself, but couldn't keep the thoughts quiet.

The water turned on her. It morphed from fluid to viscous, glooping between her fingers. *You're powering through the water.* She was pulling the water, throwing it behind her. *You're powering through the water.* Digging, not swimming. *You're powering through the water.* As Serena thrashed, she was terrified. It was all so fragile, could be shattered by one failure. Each of those races carried so much. You couldn't be world class with setbacks; the journey must be flawless. Her arms strained and Serena knew. She knew it was over. *You push harder.* This isn't what Niko had described. She'd imagined too weakly, severed that connection. *You push harder.* The Excel document marking out her mythical route to success would be defunct without this win. The next round of heats would be ruled out, the Tokyo Olympics would vanish. She'd be stuck in the box of her last success, powerless to clamber to the next.

By the time they hit the pads, her hands felt like lead. She knew Niko was in the crowd, knew her mother would be looking at that screen. They'd be shattered. All that work would crumble to nothing. Serena's body shook. No tremble, but convulsions so hard her teeth smashed together, as if taken over by a malevolent force. The results flickered. Before the digits settled, she knew it was disastrous. Her name was usually so near the top, it took no scanning. Now she had to skim the whole board. Air couldn't get to her lungs. Serena's eyes blurred and the letters jumbled to nothing. She'd come sixth, her name uncanny so far down. *Serena Roberts.* Five names weighed upon her own. She tried to swallow. Her mother would sigh; Niko's face wouldn't move. Her fans would lower their hand-drawn banners.

Victories in the pool were always noisy, and she heard the yell of a girl a few lanes away, saw her hand hit the water, face tense with glee. Serena knew how that face felt from the inside. The girl was fifteen, an entire school year below her. Getting out of the pool was humiliating, legs wobbling too much to walk straight. She nearly lost her footing on the slippery tiles, staggering towards the changing rooms, desperate to be alone. Turning the corner into the shower block, Serena felt herself crumple.

When her eyes opened, Serena saw the white tiles of the communal shower. Her left cheek lay against its floor. She could feel the grooves between the ceramic. The tiles looked brighter from that angle. Her body had flopped as if she'd been punched in the stomach. Faces loomed towards her, hands helping her up. None of it was connected. The bleached tips of Niko's hair, her mother's fingernails. As Serena's feet found the floor, her stomach bucked. She'd eaten the prescribed amount of porridge exactly two hours before the race. Her middle lurched and forced it out. After the porridge was gone, her body dug deep for anything to expel; strings of bile heaving from her, washed away by the shower's spray. She had lost. Next year's trials were out. Serena's eyes and nose streamed. She had failed. Other girls had swum better. They'd tried harder, imagined more vividly. She remained bent over. It wasn't the loss that hurt, but the months and years of fearing that loss, rushing all at once and slamming into her. It felt physically painful. Serena stayed hunched, watching pale, yellow liquid circle the drain.

10

Serena would rather have gone anywhere else. By the following evening, the Student Union bar was well lit and unrecognisable. She could still taste those sickly green shots, still feel the music thud her ribcage. The room was packed, but Keira found two stools and claimed them.

Serena would rather have curled snug on Keira's bed, bolstered by her mound of cushions and stuffed toys. Their rooms, so close they might as well be adjoining, had become a haven from the rest of campus, a space no one could infiltrate. When deadlines pressed or the rain was too insistent, they huddled in Serena's black marlin hoodies and laid low in their soft sanctuary.

Keira nudged her way back from the bar, a pint glass in each hand. 'I forgot to ask what you wanted, but who turns down beer, right?'

The glass Serena took was slick with condensation, and

she struggled to grip as Keira clinked her own drink against it. She let the liquid wet her lips, flinching at the bitterness. Last night's alcohol still clawed her, leaving her stomach acidic, her head heavy.

Keira waited seconds. 'So?' Her eyes were eager. She'd seen them dancing together.

Serena blinked for too long, then nodded her head in a mimic of shame.

'No! You didn't?' Serena revelled for a moment in Keira's jubilant response to the gossip. 'You are a dark horse, Serena Roberts, a dark fucking horse!' Keira hadn't expected it of her. 'I didn't even know you liked him.'

Serena hadn't known either. 'Yeah.' It sounded weak.

'So, you went back to his, and . . .?'

So much was patchy. The thick, waxy leaves of his plant. A pouch of tobacco. Pale coffee. 'Yeah, I don't remember much, to be honest.'

Keira's head jolted, her brow darkening. 'Really?'

'No, it blurred together. I think I drank a bit much.'

Dragging her stool closer, Keira leaned so she could lower her voice. 'Okay.' The word stretched in her mouth. 'That's not ideal, lovely, that's not great. Are you alright about it?' She placed her hand on Serena's.

'Yeah. Yeah, I am. He wasn't pushy or anything.'

'Okay. But if you were drunk, you can't exactly have given full consent.'

'No, honestly. It's good. I was happy to. I just feel a bit

weird about it.' She couldn't explain to Keira how new it had all been.

Keira paused. 'As long as you're alright.' Their heads were close in the hectic room.

'I kind of left while he was asleep, though, and I think I should message him. It's been hours.'

'That is a truly callous action, bitch!' Keira laughed, nodding in approval. 'What do you want to say?'

'I don't know. Something a bit flirty, but not too much.' He would have rinsed those coffee mugs that morning, lifted his clothes from the floor. He might already be regretful.

Keira gestured to Serena's phone. 'Okay. It's a tricky one, because you guys know each other, and can't avoid hanging out. You need to sound spur of the moment. Send out casual vibes.'

'And how do I translate that into actual words?'

'I'll do it.' Keira grabbed the phone. 'Be pithy. Nothing too intense.' She typed as she spoke, fingers flying, not looking down at the screen. 'Your initial makes the sign off look kind of filthy. That's useful.'

She passed the phone back, warm from her fingers. *Sorry I left you dreaming. I love an early morning stroll. Sx*

The following day's lecture arrived with a jolt. Keira saved Serena a seat, which she slid into late. They couldn't speak, but her widened eyes asked the question. Serena shook her head. Although two blue ticks sat next to her message, he hadn't replied.

Serena had spent the rest of the night scrolling Luke's profiles, fingers tensed so not to tap a like. She'd flicked through the few pictures he'd uploaded. Luke resting a beer bottle on top of his guitar. Luke in a crowd with a handmade placard above his head. Luke's record player with a vinyl album facing outwards. Its title wasn't clear. Serena had grabbed a screenshot, cropped, then reverse-image searched. She needed to gather everything about him. The results had shown a curly-haired man holding a bottle cap over one eye, face scrunched and smiling, the sky behind him golden. Google had informed her the album was *Goodbye and Hello* by Tim Buckley. Serena had found it on Spotify and listened three times. While its rich, wistful songs played, she'd looked up the singer, reading about his broken fingers, his death at twenty-eight, his son who drowned when he wasn't much older. Could she glean anything of Luke from those lyrics?

He hadn't replied, but she wanted to risk trying again. Keira's message could have sounded dismissive. Her phone under her coat, Serena went with her gut. She remembered the red liquid Zara had smeared across her breastbone. *I hope your bed wasn't too horrific. Fake blood is a bitch to wash off. Sx.* It took a small action, a flick of the thumb of one hand. Keira might approve. He'd think of her wet and naked, but he might be unsettled. Serena didn't have time to fret. Seconds later, her phone beeped, the noise ricocheting around the lecture theatre. Everyone else knew to switch theirs to silent. Serena heard Keira laugh before she saw the message. *Mildly distressing, but nothing I couldn't handle. Luke x.* He'd added a kiss.

★   ★   ★

Luke's next message came before Serena had replied to his first. Keira had instructed her to leave it at least a day. As she brushed her teeth that night, a little before eleven, the phone buzzed. Although no one could see her, she tried to pick it up nonchalantly.

Hey. You still up?

Serena knew it was a cliché. Despite her submerged years, she'd picked up on that euphemism.

Now was not the time to stall. *Yeah.* There was nothing else she could think to say. She needed to be pithy. He wanted to see her.

Wanna come over for a bit? His casualness sounded as forced as hers.

Sure. I'm at a bar, but can be there in about an hour. Serena typed the lie without thinking. It sounded the right amount of interested.

Perfect x. The kiss was back.

Toothpaste foamed Serena's mouth and she was in her pyjamas. His room was a twenty-minute walk across campus, so there was time to make it look like she'd been out. Jeans and a strappy top she'd never worn. Make-up from the pile Zara had left, smudged with the heel of her hand. Her night's alleged antics would have blurred the edges. She poured wine from an untouched bottle on her shelf, and drank a beaker in three gulps, let it trace a sharp tang down her gullet. Brushing her hair upside down meant it fell messily. She wished there was a cigarette she could light, let its scent infiltrate her pores and the fabric of her clothes. He wanted to see her.

The distance was shorter than Serena recalled. She'd never walked it sober, and adrenalin must have sped her legs. He wanted to see her again. This might be the first of many meetings. Luke gave her possibility, a life on land that might be real and clear. A life of joy, not the dregs of a dead dream. It could be so easy. She could learn to hold that fragile body close. Learn to push her face into the sparse hair of his chest. Someone would be there to answer every call she made, to rest his limbs on hers as they watched films from a laptop screen. To order food from an app and eat it from cardboard containers. To drink whisky from coffee mugs. To fall asleep while the computer whirred, subtitles flickering over their silent, tangled bodies. It was a life she'd gauged from the fringes of other people's social media feeds. A life of red wine and red lipstick and live music and framed artwork and cigarettes she'd learn to smoke. Of friends arriving unprompted and parties springing from nothing. Of late nights and candles stuck in toused spirit bottles. Of dancing in groups at festivals in faraway fields. With him, she could have a life other girls craved. With him, it could be straightforward.

Serena slowed as she reached the centre of campus. She couldn't be early, so paced Carnforth Quad. The fountain gushed steadily, Poseidon's muscles forever flexed. The women's faces stared blankly over the gravel. It wasn't Sunday, but might be worth a try. She fished her wallet out and found a penny. She chose a stone woman near the bottom of the arch, skin smooth, eyes lulling closed after so many years, carved hair piled onto her head. Serena stroked her temple, then slotted the penny into the gap of her mouth. It sat there, with so many others. Serena instantly wanted to take it back. The woman must judge her, sense her desperation through those cheeks full of coppers.

By the time Serena reached Luke's building, her phone digits had clicked past midnight. She pressed her fob against the security pad and the door beckoned her in. His room number was 317. She remembered that. Third floor. Walking down the corridor, her body stiffened. This could so easily go wrong. Her fist paused in the air. The knock needed to sound spontaneous. She opted for three taps, a haphazard rhythm. No answer. With eyes screwed, Serena tried again with more force. Nothing. She couldn't possibly call out his name, so would have to phone him. It took little scrolling to reach his number, and she didn't breathe as she touched the icon by his name. Silence. Maybe it pulsed with no noise. He might be searching for it, scrabbling around his room to find that throbbing slab.

His hands might find the phone, his face might appear, fingers through his hair as he apologised. Still nothing. Serena hung up and pushed her ear to the door, so that sounds didn't have to fight through air. A clatter at the end of the corridor, and three girls came towards her. They'd seen her pressed against the wood. As they walked, they laughed, gripping each other in a tumble of hair and lashes and expensive trainers. Serena avoided their eyes. The hall fell quiet again. He might be in there, breathing softly until she left. She couldn't bear to find out.

11

The scent hit Serena immediately. That dark smokiness reminded her of the river. Jane had suggested her office when they needed a sanctum, a space to discuss the overwhelming response to the Rise Up website. Other lecturers' rooms, in meetings or seminars, looked almost identical: wooden-panelled spaces with inlaid leather desks, muted oil paintings of animals or landscapes, walls filled with bookcases and the occasional rowing oar. Leysham's prestigious history was always tangible. Jane's didn't follow suit.

Serena had expected a space as pared back as Jane's clothes, simple and sparse, white walls and angled mid-century chairs. The room, when the door opened, was instead a riot of richness. Despite its immaculate layout, colours and textures battled for precedence. As well as dark upholstered armchairs with draped antimacassars, there was a wrought-iron daybed, plump with velvet throws. The others filled the floor with their rucksacks, greeting each other with hugs and quips, but Serena could only stare. Every pattern in that room seemed faded, as if Jane had owned the objects for centuries. A rug with complex swirls masked the municipal carpet. A wooden chest sat by the window. Jane's books were stripped of dust jackets so that their hardbacked colours showed: maroon, emerald, indigo, all with glinting gold letters. Six bodies in that ornate room filled it.

A fire crackling in the hearth made the room unbearably warm. Serena's coat was already on the back of a chair, and she had no layers left to remove. Jane clicked a kettle on, rapidly thickening the room with steam. She handed them each a china cup of tea with no milk. Serena inhaled. Earth and fire and salt. This was it, the smell she'd breathed that night.

Jane noticed everything. 'Lapsang souchong.'

Serena had scavenged scraps of information about Jane, hungry to understand more. Her year-long masters in a Belgian university, her secondment to a distinguished college in New England. The objects that filled Jane's office told of her cultural travels; was the draped lace Flemish, the embroidered pillow from Massachusetts? Was that strange earthy tea brought back in a folded brown bag from some distant conference?

As the others arranged themselves, Serena homed in on Luke's back, the only part of him she could see. Those blond straggles that needed a wash. The peacoat that was a little too big. He'd messaged her the morning after she'd knocked on his door. *I'm a complete dick. Fell asleep with my phone on silent.* It hadn't been deliberate. Serena had felt something close to relief, then read it again. No apology, no invitation to meet. She hadn't replied in the days that followed, couldn't bring herself to show Keira. He'd smiled as she'd brushed past him to enter Jane's room but said nothing. Serena had tightened her stomach muscles as a ballast against the silence. The blood vessels on her neck might still bear the marks of his mouth.

'We enabled the site so comments could be added via the submissions form, which explicitly asks for consent.' Dean faced Jane as they gathered around her desk. 'We didn't employ any kind of censorship. This is raw. I think that's best, don't you?'

Luke cleared his throat and adjusted tortoiseshell frames. 'I did actually wonder if we might want to vet things before we make them public, in case of legal issues with institutions or people being named?' Serena hadn't known he wore glasses. They both stood, leaning against bookcases, while the others sat.

Zara reclined on the daybed, her hair coiling onto its crimson throws. 'I'm actually with Dean on this one.' Dean lips stretched into a smile. 'I don't think it's our role to be any kind of gatekeeper. We're providing the space. Who are we to say what should and shouldn't be said?'

Did Luke's bed still smell of her, of the perfume she'd taken from Zara's pile of freebies? That light, sweet perfume a company had sent to a PO Box, hoping Zara would compliment it. Purple smudges sat beneath his eyes as if he hadn't slept. Serena wondered what he'd done in the few nights since he'd slept so soundly he'd missed her knocks on his door.

'You need to look at the site.' Jane tapped her computer to life.

That day, she wore a simple shift dress and leather flats, her hair held back by a single band. The plush leather opulence of her room made sense to Serena. The room reflected the inside of her. The intensity that raged behind that calm control.

Fire smoke and the deep earthiness of the tea combined to create a fug as they gathered to see Jane's screen. The website had taken Zara and Dean only hours to create from a basic template. It was bright turquoise, picked hastily from the colour options. The opening page gave a brief introduction and featured trigger warnings in a cerise box.

The testimonies ran from a handful of sentences to long paragraphs. They were chiefly, but not exclusively, written by women. Almost all from their university. One by one, they'd put forward their experiences. Most were uncomfortable encounters: muttered comments in classrooms, persistent suggestions, questionable jokes. They unveiled a bleak tapestry of unpleasantness at Leysham. Some told of far worse: serious sexual assaults, racist discrimination, transphobia, relentless bullying. Woven throughout, the name *Carnforth Club*.

'Those fucking Tesco Value Bullingdon twats!' Keira's words broke their silence.

'Carnforth? The drinking society?' Dean asked.

'Of course. The uni claims they've disbanded. They were known for the blandest kind of debauchery in the eighties and nineties – you know, fucking up local restaurants, burning fifty-quid notes in front of homeless people. Now, they're a bunch of private-school wannabes mimicking the behaviour of the worst people imaginable. They perform some grim initiation where they dunk new boys' heads under the water of the fountain in the quad to try and prove something.'

'Fucking hell!' Zara straightened in her seat.

Serena imagined their heads held under Poseidon's water until their limbs grew weak.

'Yeah.' Luke agreed. 'They're definitely wankers. I've got a few in my seminar group and they derail everything.'

'But it's worse than that,' Keira said. 'The whole point of Carnforth is that you don't talk about Carnforth. Nobody's officially in the club these days, so they get away with making life miserable for a lot of people.'

'And the university back it, or at least condone it,' Dean added. 'They protect them. They're basically allowed to do whatever they like.'

Jane scrolled steadily. There were so many stories. Scores of horrifying testimonials, more appearing every time Jane clicked her mouse. Serena gripped the bookcase. A wave of vertigo ripped through her, as if the room sped skyward. There was nowhere to turn on campus that wasn't dangerous. It seethed around them, oozing from the dark of the land. On Jane's advice, they'd listed the numbers for the university's peer support helplines, but it didn't feel enough. As the screen scrolled, Zara's colour scheme seemed increasingly crass.

'In a way, this is incredible.' Zara ran her hands through that dark hair. 'Rise Up has clearly hit a nerve.'

Dean rose from his seat. 'It's done exactly what we hoped – it's galvanised the student body and revealed problems the institution would rather keep hidden. It exposes the sheer weight of the issue.'

A cough escaped Serena's throat. Jane turned to look at her.

'It's . . .' Serena paused. 'It's so awful. So overwhelming. I don't know what we do with this.' She didn't know how else to put it.

Jane nodded. 'I agree.' Her legs were tucked beneath her on the office chair, her whole frame folded into the tiny space. 'We asked for them to be shared. These people are trusting us.'

Dean raised his hand in front of the screen, fingers splayed. 'I think we need to be concrete. We need to issue some real imperatives.'

'Yes.' Zara said. 'Something they can't squirm away from.'

Jane stood and gestured for Serena to take her seat. Without speaking, she left the room.

'You sit too, Luke.' Zara moved from her seat and, when Luke settled, positioned herself on his lap. Serena's pulse drummed in the roof of her mouth. Zara's thighs were on top of Luke's, the warmth of her on places Serena had touched only days before. He'd wanted to see her again. She couldn't look away. Then, Luke's hand on Zara's leg. To steady himself, or pull her closer? Zara shifted her weight, nestling in. 'Is this comfortable?' He nodded. Was he awkwardly enduring it, or eager for every moment? Zara smiled at Serena. They all knew. Gossip whipped around through phone bleeps in seconds. There was no way Zara hadn't heard what had happened. She'd seen them kiss on the dance floor. This was a deliberate marking of territory. Everything had to be hers.

Serena drank from her cup, focused on swallowing that deep, burnt darkness. It gave her hands and mouth something to do, gave her space to breathe. But breathing didn't dissipate the anger. It crackled through her like electricity. Zara knew what she was doing. Serena placed the cup down, scared her grip would damage it. She leaned forwards to hold Jane's desk. It was old, no plastic laminate but oak or cherry. Serena squeezed so hard the grain could splinter. If the others looked, the only outward sign would be the white and red beneath her nails.

Jane returned, an A4 binder in her arms. As she opened the door, Zara leapt up as if she'd been stung. She moved over to where Jane stood.

'Dean is right to say you need to make solid demands.' Jane's voice was deeper and firmer now. 'There's a risk this becomes a consciousness-raising exercise, a route to mild catharsis, but doesn't engender action. Institutions are adept at silencing.

This isn't some disembodied system you're up against but real people who make decisions and have bias. You need to be clear on what you want to expose and what impact you want that to have.'

The light in the room was low, with no ceiling fixtures but a series of lamps. A narrow window was built into the door, crosshatched with wire to make it unsmashable. Jane had covered it with an art gallery print. Serena stood up and stepped closer to the picture, away from the others as they debated. It looked like a pencil sketch, but darker, showing four naked women talking together. Their buttocks and stomachs and breasts bulged, with dimples on the base of their spines and the backs of their knees. While their hair was styled in complex braids, their flesh was free. Those women's bodies were starkly different to the honed muscles of the poolside, but the expanse of skin took Serena's mind to the water.

'It's impossible not to be drawn in, isn't it?' Serena hadn't known Jane was watching her.

'They're incredible. Who are they?'

'It's by Dürer, about 1500. An engraving. They call it *The Four Witches*, and it's essentially the first time witches had been shown as desirable women, not grotesque crones. They'd been shown as possessing wild sexuality before, but as hags. Their power had never been in seduction.'

Jane's small hands picked out the details of the image, her movements as controlled as her voice. 'Look at the poses, clearly referencing *The Three Graces* and, as well as the clearly erotic fleshiness, we have this orb resembling a pomegranate, a known symbol of fertility. Bear in mind, witchcraft is a punishable offence at this point, and men who engaged with them sexually were thought to be damned for ever. No one had depicted anything like this.'

Serena imagined a man carving out each line of those women's bodies, each ripple and curve, lingering on certain parts.

'He makes it so unequivocally alluring.' Jane's grey eyes were alight as she spoke on her treasured topic, her accent creeping stronger. 'This is about a hundred years before the height of the witch trials, but it is highly taboo. Dürer taps into dark, enticing qualities that were simply forbidden.'

Serena wanted to lift the picture from the door and examine it more closely. She wanted to ask Jane more about those women, but there was no time. The others were standing now, their teacups drained, their bags gathered. Plans had been made to reconvene in the new term. Serena followed the group, her mind on the picture. Luke walked away before they had the chance to speak, but in the pocket of her coat when she slipped it back on, she found a tightly rolled cigarette.

@zarakarmic • 220k followers

I don't know about you, but I'd love to talk to my younger self.

I used to fret so much. It would take me literally hours to get ready. I'd hunt out my most flattering clothes, my most flattering angles.

Now? I reject that toxic dynamic. I wear what makes me feel good. My body is not a problem to solve. It is a delight to enjoy.

I've had to do the work to break that pattern. I wish I'd healed the relationship with my body so much earlier. I've had to learn that self-compassion slowly.

But I'd love to tell that freaked-out, terrified girl how good she'd feel one day. Instead, I'll tell you all how good it can be.

SEVENTEEN YEARS OLD

'One more lap, we've got time.'

Despite their pace, her mother's voice bore no effects of exertion. Every stride thudded through Serena's body. The slippery tissue of her cartilage took the brunt it wasn't used to. There was no water to bear her weight and hadn't been for weeks.

It was rumoured the pools would open again by the end of summer, July or August ideally, but nothing had been clear since mid-March. Being wrenched from the water had felt like cruelty. They could barely process it. There wasn't time. While the rest of the world stumbled to adjust to new rules and circumstances, Serena couldn't miss a beat.

Niko's words were still there, spoken through headphones into her ear, joined by his face on Zoom sessions. They found ways to keep her fitness up. Cardio meant endless journeys to nowhere on the exercise bike they'd ordered that first week, as many laps around the park as Serena and her mother could fit into their allotted hour. Replacing the tens of thousands of metres swum each week was near-impossible. Serena's tendons and joints were resistant to adapting. They missed the ease of the pool.

Focusing on core training kept her posture, stabilised the spine. In water, she had to resist motion and sit-ups didn't cut it. Serena stayed in plank position until her eyes blurred, her muscles shook. She kept pushing, needing that surge again, but nothing on land felt right.

Schoolwork offered some structure, filling mornings with online A-level lessons, afternoons with tasks, but her classmates' fear and tedium seemed contagious. Serena was lured to ennui, beckoned to its delicious listlessness. She had to resist. *The mind always gives up before the body.* She knew how to withstand. *Pain is the fire in which you forge yourself.*

Universality should have offered comfort. Everyone faced this hindrance, lost these months. Serena was at no specific disadvantage, but the gnawing fear felt personal. The boxes of that Excel sheet taunted her. She was trapped within their borders. When outside time was legally sanctioned, Serena walked to the glass walls of the leisure centre, watched the water from the wrong side. It sat dormant, bored, waiting for her. Every part of her craved its chlorine.

As the weeks went on, Serena felt her muscles diminish, her lungs harden. Her body was losing its brilliance. She could sense it within her. Her sinews were growing stringy. Her muscles were no longer red and thriving, rich with oxygen and care, but withered, creeping grey around the edges. Her cartilage was becoming gristle. The lush, supple meat of her arms shrivelled, as if left out too long. Each day, her body was less extraordinary. The tautness of her stomach yielded as if her guts grew thick with inertia. Blood pulsed sluggishly around her veins, the oxygen limp by the time it reached organs. It felt like decay, like something growing rancid. Did she smell differently, without the daily cleansing, without the purity of discipline? She felt a new weakness: the crunch of her neck as it rotated, a jab in her chest as she breathed. In a handful of months, she was losing the one thing that made her special. This body wasn't hers any more.

It was as if the water had missed her. No lingering showers or ice baths could conjure its magic. That never-deviating temperature, those exact chemical components, were needed. The thwack of the water, the whistles, the shriek of voices smashing against ceramic tile. Serena could have wept when the heat and light of the leisure centre hit her again. When Niko grabbed her and pulled her against his chest, breaking every distancing rule. But there wasn't time.

The water felt like a blessing. Like in a deluge after a drought, the hard mud of her slowly softened. Each cell drank deeply, swelling with its nourishment. The frozen panic of so many months began to ease. There wasn't time. Training schedules needed to restart, more severe than ever. Pages and pages mapping out every session, thousands of metres of warm-ups, skill sets, main sets and warm-downs. Every moment was vital.

Serena tried to pick up where they'd left off. *You dive perfectly, smoothly, barely ruffling the water.* She could do it. She could be the same as before. *You're powering through the water.* She could still predict that water, intuit it, understand it so fully her calibrations were ideal.

She could still talk to her body. The body she'd fought to maintain. *You are powerful.* The body she needed to recreate. *You're so powerful.* She could talk, but lived in fear it would no longer listen.

12

Serena lay in the bath she'd splashed in as a child. The tub was thick with scented bubbles and the tendons of her neck unknotted for the first time in months. The bathwater was warm, not the ice she'd lowered herself into for fifteen gruelling minutes after training sessions. Her muscles no longer needed to recover. It felt like privilege to no longer endure that pain.

Her fingers wrinkled in the water, the flesh puckering as blood vessels beneath the skin contracted. A panic response that made things easier to grip. Her body assumed danger, that it needed to climb out, clutch rocks to heave itself to land. For so many years, it had been on high alert.

The bath was welcoming, but Serena's bedroom belonged to a stranger. Everything it had once held dear had vanished. Its bed was the bed she'd woken in before each practice, where she'd lain envisioning every success. Its mirror was the mirror she'd chanted affirmations to, looking into her own eyes. Its drawers were stuffed with technical fabrics, caps and swim-suits, ankle strappings, tangles of goggles. Serena didn't open any of them.

When she'd hugged her mother, their bones had pressed in a memory of those fierce poolside embraces. They hadn't seen each other for over two months. Afterwards, Elizabeth had held her daughter at arm's length, assessing her face. Serena had turned away. She was a different person to the champion in those Lycra costumes and didn't want to clock the disappoint-ment. The alterations in her mother's face were unexpected: deeper crinkles at the corner of her eyes, a thinning of her lips. It was nothing but the clarity of time, but it startled Serena.

She was back in a room filled with boxes. Term had rushed to a close. Late November had become early December, and her energy had been spent on piling deadlines. The days had faded. Hours had sped by with nothing to differentiate them but the force of the rain, until she was packing her belongings back into unbearably dry cardboard. Returning to that house had felt nothing like going home.

Anoushka's hands were pink with beetroot. She hadn't stopped to wipe them before adding cumin seeds to the pan. The seeds had started to pop.

'Wait. Don't move. I need to grab this.' Zara aimed her camera at the pan of oil and sputtering kernels.

Her mother shooed her away. 'Don't be ridiculous. That'll

never show onscreen! And it's the scent you'd want to capture, anyway.'

Zara and Anoushka usually dropped by on Boxing Day, but their plans to explore the Cornish coast had fallen through and Anoushka had announced they'd be staying for the whole week. They'd unpacked only hours before, but the energy of the house had already shifted. Mealtimes became rituals with them. Everything smelled deeper and richer. The subtle decorations Elizabeth had positioned – cut-out snowflake coasters, a dark green table runner, a tree with coordinated silver balls – felt at odds with their expansive energy.

Moving around the kitchen, Anoushka left pink fingerprints on the grey cabinets, turned the cookery book livid with burgundy. Elizabeth hovered in the doorway, clutching a tea towel. Serena's father, Martin, was preparing their annual fire, fastidiously avoiding getting coal dust on the carpet. Serena took a pomegranate seed from the bowl and held it to the light like a jewel. She pressed it, fat and glossy, between her thumb and forefinger until it burst.

Anoushka wafted over to her sister, tinkling with every step, bangles clattering, necklace clinking on the shards of mirror that adorned her smock. She'd been born Alice, but had changed it legally in her teens. Barefoot on their white kitchen tiles, she took the tea towel and whipped it at Elizabeth.

'Lizzy, stop fretting. Now, where do you keep your tahini?'

By the time the beetroot had roasted, the whole room was sweet and earthy. Sat in its dish, its colours were so sumptuous it was more ornament than sustenance. Zara made the family stop before a single portion could be served.

'Darling, it's going to get cold. Do your fans really need to know what you're having for dinner?'

Zara grabbed a clutch of pomegranate seeds, let them rain onto the beetroot as she held her phone. It took five handfuls to get the perfect shot.

Kelly arrived in a blur of hugs and soft jumpers. Serena inhaled the familiar bright, sharp scent of her sister. Jo Malone Lime, Basil & Mandarin. Kelly's own home was dotted with candles she saved for, metal lids and trimmed wicks. Serena didn't want to let go, wanted to stroke the soft flow of her sister's hair and pretend they were little again.

When they settled with cups of tea and the baklava Anoushka had made, Kelly pushed a rectangle of paper across the table towards Serena. A photograph. No smiling faces, but blackness with a blur of grey. Serena's eyes took a moment to register. The round of the skull disproportionately large, a neat little nose and pout, tiny fingers already grasping. Kelly's twenty-week scan. She'd announced her news the week Serena had left for university, when her head had been fogged by painkillers and trepidation. At that stage, three months hadn't passed; the smudge within Kelly had formed the shape of a baby as vaguely as a constellation. Serena calculated that she'd been pregnant on her wedding day that summer, the youngest of her friends to marry. While she'd walked down that aisle with their father, dressed in immaculate white, a plug of cells had multiplied unknown within her.

Serena stared at the shape on the page. That shadow was flesh. It would be a baby in only months. On the other side of the table, Kelly, Martin and Elizabeth talked in low tones about concerns raised at the scan. Blood pressure too high, flashing lights noticed in the dark. Unusual at her age and weight. Might be nothing.

Serena watched her mother's hand rest on Kelly's. The light was on Kelly now. That light Serena had stolen so often over so many years, waking her too early, mangling weekend plans with competitions and practices, all of which had come to nothing. Martin and Kelly had watched TV for years, after Serena's self-imposed bedtime, with the sound so low they could scarcely have followed the plot. Everyone's focus was on Kelly now, on what Kelly's body could do.

Zara lifted the picture from Serena's hands. She didn't hold it by the edges but stroked her fingers across the image, as if she could reach the foetus.

'This is amazing, Kell. Utterly amazing.'

She held it to her face, breath steaming the paper. Serena tensed. That picture was too precious to sully. She wanted to snatch it from Zara's hands, place it back in the clean white envelope where it could never be smeared.

'Could you take a few more standing on the bench?'

They'd been in the back garden for nearly an hour. Serena

huddled in her woollen coat, Zara wearing nothing but a wispy purple slip. She sat cross-legged in the long grass. The temperature had barely crept above freezing and the grass was white with frost.

It was nine o'clock, and the time concerned Zara. 'It's dark enough to be midnight, right? You'd believe this was midnight in a video.'

The camera was heavier than Serena expected, packed tight with expensive technology, and she was terrified of dropping it. Zara flowed through a series of movements, then froze. It was a strange, stilted dance she performed with herself; rising from the ground, nightgown flowing outward to reveal her thighs, arms lifting sinuously into the air. Then stopping and repeating, over and over. Serena was responsible for capturing a little of its magic.

Zara spoke as she moved. 'So, you and Luke, then?'

Through the camera's screen, in miniature, Zara didn't look real. In the dark garden, shrouded in mist and lit by the porch light, she shone like a spirit, as if emerging from the grass to take solid form.

Serena didn't know how to respond.

'He's a total sweetheart, isn't he?'

Serena bit the inside of her cheek, hoping the pain would keep her steady. She made herself nod.

'You guys would be adorable together.'

Serena didn't reply.

When enough versions of the footage were captured, Zara

lifted the camera to examine them. Serena took the chance to rub her hands, craving heat from the friction. Zara didn't shiver, but her flesh up close looked nothing like the glowing creature in the lens. She was bobbled with goosebumps and surely in discomfort as she clicked through those videos, working out which angle was most enthralling.

As she settled back on the grass, she pushed her thighs down, splaying them outward so their dimples were on show. 'I don't want to look smaller. My flesh has ripples when I move. That's vital. They need to see how I actually look. My real self and online self have to be the same.'

By the time Zara was happy, the camera held hundreds of almost identical clips.

To thaw her fingers, Serena clicked the kettle as soon as they were back inside. Zara perched on a kitchen stool, bent over the camera's screen. When she found a version she liked, she swiped through possible filters. Some sharpened the angles, the contrast, making the mood ominous; others softened the image, so the grass blurred into her skin.

'I never doctor my content, you know.' She noticed Serena watching. 'But it's okay to make things a little warmer; it doesn't make it less authentic.'

Eventually, she chose the right one.

When the tea had brewed, Serena sat behind her cousin as she typed into her phone.

At one with natu— She deleted the whole line.

Feeling close to— Again deleted.

Zara's fingers sped out words, then paused as she assessed them. So much effort went into one casual video reel, so much time and planning and duplicity. She scheduled the post to appear early the next morning, as if she'd been out in the dead of night, communing with the otherworldly. Thousands of people would jab their screens in approval.

Feeling the solstice energy through my— Deleted.

It had to be perfect; it had to seem easy.

She went back to her original idea. *At one with nature on this shortest day, this saturnalia as the solstice arrives. Let us beckon the light back in.*

EIGHTEEN YEARS OLD

Swimming World magazine arrived at their door once a month. Serena knew the interview was due in the March issue, so she snatched it from the doormat before her mother saw. Licking her fingers to flick faster, she found the 'Surfacing Talent' article. A picture of Niko, crouched by the side of the pool, arms firm and tanned.

The opening paragraph covered his own achievements, before turning to Serena. *She's the most instinctive swimmer I've ever trained. Her feel for the water is incredible. It goes deep with her.* The questions were hyped to add drama to the article. *What is it like to train an Olympic hope?* It was a cruel overstatement. She had one more chance at the Commonwealths, and they all knew what 2024 could hold. That year had always been Serena's focus, but as it came closer, it looked uglier. She began to dread the turn of each new year. 2020 had set her back significantly, cursing her to languish, to lose form she could never claw back. The spreadsheet of her imagined achievements far outpaced her now. Nothing could ever be perfect again. Not since the lockdowns, not since the race she'd lost before them. *What is it like to work with such a gifted swimmer?* She knew Niko wouldn't have paused. *She's technically gifted but, more than that, she has such belief. She imagines a race in intense detail. I've never known a girl with that kind of power.* He spoke about a person she used to be.

At the poolside, Niko's eyes saw what he'd always seen. He still looked at her like she was made of gold. He'd invested so much it might feel impossible to give up. After each race, he tended to her legs and shoulders as if they were precious. His massage was essential, a ritual to stir the circulation and ease the soreness, his palms cool on her back muscles, on the lengths of her thighs, the soft of her buttocks. His fingers on places no one else had been. Niko whispered as his hands moved, telling her which parts of the race had gone best. As he worked, the swelling reduced, the pain receded. His hands were so huge they made her body, for once, feel delicate. Serena was suffocated by the prospect of his disappointment.

She fed the magazine into the shredder next to their printer. Ripping pages from their staples, she coaxed each one into the whirring blades.

Zara looked taller. Her head only reached Serena's shoulder, but she carried herself differently. As they settled around the train table with their mothers, she seemed to take up more room. Serena barely recognised her. That unruly hair was wound into two thick buns, high on either side of her head. Her clothes were a clash of fashionable colours. A green silk bomber jacket with pink patches sewn on, some shimmering, others that looked strokable. A ribbon of velvet around her throat. There was no timidity now.

The train lurched towards Brighton. Kelly had stayed living in Sussex after university and planned to meet them for elaborate hot chocolates in her favourite café. It was a cel-ebration – after significant disruption, Zara had completed her GCSEs and Serena her A levels – but Serena couldn't muster any excitement. She'd worked hard enough to expect a clutch of decent grades and had applied to Leysham University because of its outstanding athletic facilities. Niko had explained how university affiliation could be valuable. She'd been surprised to receive a conditional offer, but had deferred her entry. For now, her time was empty and all that could fill it was water.

Zara held her phone with both hands. Its case was bright red-and-yellow plastic, shaped like a carton of McDonald's fries.

'Show them, Za.' Anoushka nudged her daughter.

'No!' Zara shook her head so the buns became a blur. 'It's so silly.'

'Show them.' Anoushka's voice grew louder. 'You should be proud.'

Zara sighed. 'You know Instagram? Well, I've been putting a few things on, not much, me doing my make-up and hair and stuff. It's daft, but I've somehow got about five thousand followers.'

Zara turned the phone. The grid of images flashed as she ran her finger up the screen.

'They've started to send stuff too, new products for me to keep, all for free.'

Elizabeth took the phone into her own hands to examine. She scrolled slowly through the pictures, then looked up. 'This is a great achievement, Zara.' Serena knew that tone. It was no artifice. Her mother was impressed by Zara's prowess.

Five thousand people. More than had ever filled the stands to see Serena swim, more than knew her name. They watched Zara apply lipstick and twist her hair into strange new shapes.

'You can follow me if you like, Auntie Liz. You don't need to post anything, you can lurk.'

Serena let her forehead rest against the train window, let the judder of wheels against track reverberate through her skull, let her teeth clatter together. Zara was excelling. That once-quiet girl was shining. Outshining her. Serena kept her eyes fixed on the hedgerows that rushed by. A-level Geography had taught her how politically charged those shrubs were, carving up the country into delineated property. Field after field sped past, some livid with yellow rapeseed, others dotted with cattle, each patch of land owned by somebody. Serena stared at the expanses. When she looked back, she knew Zara would have claimed more space as her own.

*   *   *

With exams over, Serena could focus entirely on training. She was one of the oldest in the elite squad, and the others watched her with respect. They'd seen what she could do. She'd set every record for her stroke at the club, but records exist to be erased. All bar two of Natasha's had been toppled. Thirteen-year-olds turned up looking lost in their new purple hoodies, and it felt cruel to race them, except they had the advantage. In that water, every year was a burden. Those younger girls had the chance of finding a few extra seconds in the coming months, wrung from their malleable muscles. Serena was growing brittle. She still visualised each race, but her mind was waning. The images were less vivid and didn't always become real. It wasn't unusual for swimmers to continue competing into their twenties, but only after significant success. Serena hadn't clocked up anything outstanding and the respect of the other girls tasted like iron.

Serena still won regularly, but felt nothing. She saw the faces of other girls when they triumphed and knew they weren't faking. She'd hadn't experienced that exaltation in years. Victories were never as good as she'd imagined.

Her mother sat in on training sessions, watching from the side of the pool during reps. Serena didn't know what Elizabeth was looking for. She'd come close to glory herself, as a gymnast in her teens. Did she watch Serena and see her own talent on the mat and bar? Serena's parents were funding her, far beyond the point they could afford, and guilt layered heavily on top of the perennial pressure. She trained until it was painful, until her lungs and muscles could take no more, forever berating herself for not pushing harder. The exhaustion was constant, gnawing at the edge of everything.

Serena stared at her teammates. In the wrong light, those girls looked wretched. Their eyes were bloodshot, ringed with red where goggles left their prints. Their sockets looked bruised, and welts sat on the tops of their cheeks. These were the wounds of devotion. Bodies allowed only prescribed nourishment, fat whittled away. Skin burned dry from the chemicals, hair frazzled. Pruney, puckered fingertips. They were chasing something terrible, and it depleted them all.

One race could mean everything. The days and months of training pressed upon those two and a half minutes. Serena threw up before all major competitions now, her body preparing itself for the worst. The water didn't always take her side. The connection was gone. She knew all of it – the drills, the weights, the meals, the gritting of teeth through pain – was a sacrifice for the second a medal might be placed over her head. A wet ribbon. Handshakes with people she didn't know. Flowers wrapped in cellophane. All because her body had moved faster.

The British Championship qualifiers were the biggest event of that year. Niko talked into her ear. *If you smash this, everything else unlocks.* His voice was lower than before. *You walk out there knowing you can win.* Serena's legs didn't twitch at his instructions. *You enter the water before the others and dominate by the first turn.* The image was usually clear. Serena usually felt every stroke. This time, at the side of the same pool, on the bench they always chose, she couldn't focus. His words kept going. *By the final turn, you have a strong lead, but you won't ease. You know the others will try to grab it back in those last fifty metres.* They were only words now. They landed in her ears but travelled no further through her body. *You storm it for the last length. You forget the pain and think about the glory.* Her whole life could be determined in those hundred and fifty seconds. Her ability felt increasingly like a curse placed upon her head.

13

'So, another Yule is upon us.' Anoushka's arms extended outwards, as if to encompass the whole family. 'It's such a perfect time to gather our thoughts and number our blessings, don't you think?' The dining table was lit with candles, laden with tiny bowls of food. 'What are you most grateful for?'

The complex recipes Zara and Anoushka tackled involved every pan in the kitchen, made the air rich with the bittersweet scent of crushed caraway seeds.

'Lizzy?'

Serena knew her mother would find the question intrusive. Elizabeth spoke quickly. 'Kelly's wedding, of course, that was lovely. And the baby news. It's been a big year, I suppose, and next year will be even bigger.'

Clapping her hands together, Anoushka exclaimed. 'What delight!' She didn't wait for any other response. 'I'd have to say that, in a deeply crazy year, I'm most thankful for my incredible daughter's unfettered spirit.' She placed her hand on Zara's arm. 'And now she's reaching out to help others. I couldn't be more thrilled.'

Standing up, Zara poured more wine. Serena had never drunk at mealtimes. The clock-clock-clock of air escaping the bottle filled the room. Zara's face was lit by flickering candles.

'Thank you, Mama. I'm hoping to have more time to make a proper difference. This term's been a bit of a wild one.' She looked at Serena. 'I don't know about you, Rena, but I'm knackered. I didn't know it was possible to pack so much into twelve weeks!'

Serena nodded, but her neck throbbed. Her year had been empty, a shell of what she'd once imagined. Zara spoke, but Serena heard the words only vaguely. *President of the Photography Club. Belly dancing. The Rise Up movement.* Serena fixed her face into what she hoped was a smile. Her calendar for the following year was supposed to have been studded with opportunity.

Elizabeth cleared her throat and Serena braced herself. But her father spoke instead.

'I'm incredibly proud of Serena's year too. She had to deal with exceptionally difficult setbacks and made some big decisions. I think she's coped admirably.'

Those weeks after the injury had seemed unreal. After the shock, the pain, there were choices. Serena had made them on a whim. All she could see was time stretching ahead. She'd phoned Leysham's admissions helpline, seeking to hasten her start date. It was a long shot at a prestigious university, but they were surprisingly amenable. It took less than an hour for her next three years to be set.

'You're so right, Martin.' Anoushka stroked Serena's hair. 'You've been brilliant, darling.' Her hand was heavy and Serena wanted to pull away. 'You should be so proud of yourself.'

Serena hadn't told her parents about Tanya, the girl she'd pulled from that black water, the life she'd saved. Zara hadn't chosen to share the news either.

Turning back to her daughter, Anoushka smiled. 'Did you bring it, Zaza? You should show them.'

Her meal half eaten, cutlery splayed across her plate, Zara stood. 'You think?' She darted out of the room, returning with her hands full.

'I wasn't going to say anything, but I got this.' She held a wooden trophy, shaped like a star, stripes of pastel colour across its middle. Zara's name was etched into the surface.

'It's from a make-up brand I've worked with. I'm one of their Rising Star Activists, which is insane, but amazing.' She smiled. 'It's for how I've empowered my followers.'

The words sounded rehearsed. Zara held the slab of wood in both hands, as if it had just been awarded, not carried in her suitcase across the country.

Anoushka grabbed her daughter in a kiss. 'You've done so well, my love. You've come so far.'

Serena remembered that little girl with the grave eyes who had rarely spoken the year her father left. She had few memories of her uncle, but his physical presence wasn't necessary to know his actions. Aidan was a musician who'd scored a hit record in the early nineties with his experimental electronica group, *Quisling*. Serena sometimes heard that distinctive bleeping intro while walking around a shop, recognised the thwacking bass beat behind the words of an advert. Zara must hear it too. They'd had no more than two charted songs, but their albums held a place on the shelves of earnest young men, and they were often cited as an influence. Aidan lived in Stockholm with his wife, Ines, and their twin sons. He played occasional gigs and hosted a popular podcast. His presence in Zara's life was scant.

The trophy was handed around the table. It was less substantial than Serena expected, not a chunk of oak, but something light and hollow. As she handed it back, her cousin smiled. That awkward child had become a thriving young woman. Eyelashes so long they couldn't be real, hair so thick it could house small creatures. The liquorice smell in the room grew dense, its sweet stickiness tarring Serena's nose. She felt faded next to Zara. Nothing she could do was impressive any more. It had once been Serena's awards passed around an awed dinner table, her own parents flushed with pride.

The film's flicker was all that lit the room. Zara had begged for it and sang along to the first few minutes with gusto – *a pair of mittens that were made by your mother* – before turning to her phone. From that point on, she didn't look up, curled into an armchair so far she was contorted, legs tucked, jumper – pink wool with *Je ne sais quoi* embroidered on the front – pulled over her knees. There was so much softness. Her body didn't contain a single straight line.

From her place on the sofa, Serena could see Zara's phone. She watched the colours blink, the kaleidoscope of Zara's online life. Her own phone occasionally lit with messages from Keira – pictures of her siblings, favourite memes, snacks – but little else. As the movie played, Zara's fingers never stopped. There were comments to add, likes to be tapped. That fan base didn't gather by accident; it had to be tended. A fire that always needed stoking. It wasn't a job or a hobby, but a constant state of being.

Serena watched her cousin rather than the creatures on television. Their high-pitched singing grated. Zara's face stayed focused. Which words formed from those lightening thumbs? Was Luke's face on that screen? Serena kept the small, rolled cigarette in the pocket of her jeans, smelling the tobacco occasionally. He'd sent a few messages since they left campus, enough to make her mouth dry. *Keeping warm, I hope.* Was his number snug inside Zara's phone, shining as his words arrived? Did Zara press the pad of her finger against a picture of him?

A sudden pressure in her chest made Serena sit upright. The jittery energy of her early university days flooded back. The open fire her father had constructed so meticulously was blazing, its heat stifling. Those flames robbed oxygen, made it impossible to breathe. Serena couldn't be in that room any longer. She was opening the door before she realised she'd stood.

Running up the stairs, Serena didn't care if her steps thumped through the house. No one would follow. She slammed her bedroom door, the way she never had as a teenager. That room mocked her. The bed she'd lain in and visualised success, the curtains she'd opened every day when it was still dark outside. The one wall not stacked with boxes held her medals. That ridiculous display rack she'd been gifted for her fourteenth birthday. Grained wood and her full name – *Serena Roberts* – carved like it was a name that mattered. Twenty fat gold hooks were hammered in, and several medals hung from each. So many that some meant nothing. Her head had bowed for them all. She reached out to hold one of the metal discs. Their different-coloured ribbons still smelled faintly of chlorine.

She pulled the metal as hard as she could, but the ribbon held strong. She tugged again. Every one of those circles embodied success. Niko's voice in her ear for each. Successes she'd visualised and realised. *You're powering through the water, slicing through it. No one else is as fast as you; they're trailing behind. Your fingers reach the pads first. You're so powerful.* Serena pulled harder. Each one was cheap, coated metal, made to look precious. If she bit like an Olympic winner, she'd taste nothing. Some had her name etched on, others bore depictions of goggles, pool lanes, swimmers bent in preparation.

She grabbed a clutch and yanked downwards. With more leverage, several hooks bent. Medals rained to the carpet. Serena ripped the remaining ones. Her hands gained power, and ribbons tore along their seams. Every yank released more fury. Fury at the years she'd lost. Fury at the adults who'd pushed her to do things that could only end badly. At the talent useless on dry land, the life she'd given up. The brain trained to see winning as all she could do, all she could be. Those medals also held memories of the races she hadn't won, bore the scars of every failure she'd ever endured.

Fury seared through her. Outrage at the decisions that had left her in that freezing campus, struggling to be ordinary. At her inability to speak out. The feebleness that meant she couldn't push their polite activism further. At her sheer, pathetic lack of power.

Serena threw handfuls of medals down. One after another, a frenzy of red and blue ribbons, metal discs smashing together. Stamping on them, she willed them to crush, as if her socked feet could have impact. She wished the metal would melt, disintegrate, turn to ashes. Wrenching the rack from its roots, adrenalin lent her hands a lethal grip. Screws flew loose as she pulled, dust from holes in the wall powdering the air. She threw the rack onto the carpet. Those races should never have happened. Serena wished she'd never imagined any of them. Without them, she might know who she was.

*　　*　　*

It was nearly midnight and firmly below zero. Colder than it had been all year. Serena stood in the church, her mother on one side, her father on the other, their coats pressed against hers. Their breath clouded and rose as they sang. *Earth stood hard as iron, water like a stone.* Serena mouthed the words. She could hardly read the hymn sheet, her mind still skittish.

Zara somehow suited the church. Bundled in a fake-fur coat, her voice was clear, louder than anyone else's, lifting to the wooden roof. *Snow on snow.* She sang like she meant it. Like she could feel the chill of that stable, sense the presence of the infant godhead. *Cherubim and seraphim thronged the air.* No sound could fight through the block in Serena's throat.

As the hymn trudged forward, verse after verse, Serena twisted her neck to the stained glass looming over them. The lavishness of the building took her mind back to campus. From that angle, she could see the image of Jesus, formed by so many shards. Thin and pale, metres above their heads. The song ended, and they sat as the vicar spoke, his high-flown words focused on John's gospel, on stepping from true darkness into newly created light. That glass rendering of Jesus felt familiar. Exposed hipbones, shoulder blades that pressed through his skin, visible ribs. Serena had been close to a body like that. She knew how it felt, how it tasted. She could remember little of her night with Luke, but everything she recalled was sensory. The skin of his chest and stomach and thighs. Her upper lip prickled. The image towered above them, beautiful and furious, not the meek child they sang about.

The vicar's words buzzed in the background. Serena didn't tune in, but thought instead of those other sermons that Jane studied in such depth, that told of horrific things, that led to the murder of women. Those ugly, powerful words came from such pulpits.

When Serena turned forwards, Zara's hair was so close it touched her face. That dark hair she spread out in every photograph, so thick it couldn't be tamed. There was nowhere to turn that wasn't full of Zara. She was in every part of Serena's life, dominating every room, breathing all the air. She'd somehow sneak a picture of this moment and broadcast it to the world. Serena felt tangled in Zara's hair, choked by her floral scent. That jangling energy filled her again. She struggled to keep her face calm while the thoughts behind it burned. Closing her eyes, she let the energy course through her. When it abated, she could see. The sermon was over, and the congregation shifted position. Moonlight through the stained-glass Jesus sent glints of ruby and cobalt and jade onto their coats and hair. Serena held out one hand and caught a diamond of red in the centre of her gloved palm.

Sitting on that pew, with red light resting on her hand, Serena could think. Her mind allowed a chink of clarity for the first time in months. It might be possible again. The gift she'd assumed was lost for ever. She could think there, in the candlelit silence, and thought of only one thing. Zara's trophy. That wooden star with its pastel colours and etched words. Big enough to fill two hands, but oddly light. Serena could see it as clearly as looking.

Finally, in that calm, cavernous church, her mind was sharp. She could sense dust motes in the air, the rustle of flimsy Bible pages, the thick, sweet smell of communion wine. She could feel it all. The image in her mind was perfect. Heat was suddenly in her fingers, pulsing up her arms and down her spine. Serena knew that burn.

The trophy had been placed on the living-room mantelpiece, like a festive star. In Serena's mind, it trembled. *The base is not secure, and the plaque wobbles from side to side.* She visualised a slight quiver that built. Heat flowed through her. *It rocks more and more until it reaches the edge of the mantel.* Serena focused tightly on the bulk of it, its shape and the sound it made. *It teeters for a moment, seeming to hover in the air, then falls.* In her mind, Serena watched the smack of it against the marble hearth, behind the fire screen. She jumped on her pew at the imagined impact. She watched that star settle too close to the fire, watched its rainbow paint buckle and blister in the heat. She watched the thin wood set light.

When they arrived home, there was a flurry of coats being hung and boots crashing together in the porch. Serena headed straight for the living room. The plaque was still in its position, whole and perfect, with Zara's name carved into it.

The others made cups of tea and opened wine, relit the fire, then settled onto sofas and armchairs with mince pies. Serena stayed standing, so close to the mantel she could reach out to touch it. *The base is not secure.* She played it over a few more times, rapidly now, narrowing her vision to a pinprick. *The plaque wobbles from side to side.* The image was sharper than reality, its angles brighter, its colours glaring. Warmth coursed through Serena's hand, arm, chest, legs. Zara poured cream over her pie, lifting the jug so it flowed extravagantly.

It was faster than Serena had imagined, but otherwise identical. The trophy teetered. It wasn't obvious what caused the disruption, but something knocked it off balance. No one noticed. It wobbled, each rock gaining momentum until it toppled from the edge of the mantel. The clatter against the hearth was unfeasibly loud. The wood fell behind the fire screen and didn't rest, but seemed to bounce. Zara rushed towards the fallen trophy. Everyone stood. *Be careful!*

The fire beat Zara to it, licking the paintwork before she could salvage anything. The hollow wood offered little resistance and flames easily took hold. Zara reached in regardless. She yelped as the fire lashed out. Stepping back, she let the trophy burn. Serena stood silently, fingertips tingling.

NINETEEN YEARS OLD

Niko's words no longer held any power. Even with the qualifiers looming, in their adjusted track to success, his images couldn't permeate Serena's mind. Instead, she heard her own. It wasn't his accent in her head, but hers. She didn't want him there any more. *Your knee has always been fragile.* Her words spelled out a different result. *It's a weak spot for breaststroke swimmers. It is worn ragged.* If she could no longer be the best, Serena didn't want to be there at all. Losing was too terrible. *You've ground it down through daily practice.* She imagined the same images over and over, training her brain to accept them.

As the details grew clearer, Serena felt a heat rising within her. That had never happened with Niko's words. The strange warmth vibrated through her hands and up her wrists and arms, prickling her neck and head. It followed her line in the water. Fingertips to skull to torso to waist to knees to toes.

The words took over her whole body. She'd wrested control from Niko and the power lived within her.

It wasn't wear and tear she imagined, but catastrophe. *Your patella is a bone curved like a seashell. It could fit in the palm of your hand.* Every detail was in crisp focus. She wasn't going to win for much longer. A few more races might go well, but victory would soon be replaced by bitter loss, over and over, until she staggered away from the sport. *You can feel it under the skin. It protects the knee joint, but is fragile, prone to injury.* They'd never let her quit.

Your patella is a bone curved like a seashell. It could fit in the palm of your hand. You can feel it under the skin. It protects the knee joint, but is fragile, prone to injury. A direct trauma can shatter it. The impact will be disastrous. The bone will smash, and you won't be able to move. Walking will be difficult for months. Swimming will be impossible.

Serena was calm before the race. Her birthday had come and gone. Weeks and months of training had fled by, heat still tingling through her, and she was calm. It was her second chance at the British Championship qualifier, the race everything weighed upon. She needed to come in the top three of her event. Without a triumph here, the dream of 2024 would vanish and her career would go from lagging to lifeless. Before her own words had formed, anxiety had dragged at her veins. In those line-ups she'd felt something close to fear. She'd thrown up before so many heats she's easily won. Waiting for this race, though, Serena was composed. She knew what would happen.

The stands were full, and eyes were on her. Walking to the starting block, her back was straight. Other girls stretched and bent and jogged on the spot. They were all tense. They'd all given everything for this. Serena stayed still. Hands on her hips, she looked at nothing but the far end of the pool. Her name was read aloud, echoing to the roof and back. *Serena Roberts.* Applause, the usual roar.

The lined-up girls took their marks, each crouched with one foot angled above the other. The crowd froze. Serena knew before the beep, before the light flashed in her eyeline. She could still intuit it. She hit the water first, possessing it before the others. Each stroke felt slow, but she revelled in it. It was languorous, not the usual frenzied rush. She watched the line on the bottom of the pool, black where the others were white. The water held her like its own. Every stroke forced her head up. Noise, then calm. Noise, then calm. The moments of streamline between strokes seemed to last for minutes. Each one was delicious. The pain she'd grown so used to never came. Lengths passed easily. Serena had no sense of the other swimmers. Her fingers hit the pad when they were ready.

Serena knew what was coming. It had burned through her. She pulled herself out of the water and heard the squeals of delight, but didn't check her name on that digital list. She walked towards the showers. The bobbled floor tiles around the pool gave way to smoother ones near the changing rooms.

One step was all it took. One badly placed foot, one odd angle. *The impact will be disastrous.* She fell immediately. There was no time to reach out as her feet skidded backwards. No one could have saved her. The impact was every bit as hard as she'd pictured, but the pain was worse. *The bone will smash, and you won't be able to move.* She landed on her left knee, her whole weight multiplied by gravity on one pinpoint of bone. *Walking will be difficult for months after.* The pain was a pure, unexpected agony. *Swimming will be impossible.* From her position on the ground, pressed against those tiles, Serena breathed. *Swimming will be impossible.* The pain meant she'd succeeded.

PART TWO

14

Rise up, wise up, open your fucking eyes up.

The chant began at the back of the crowd and surged forward. Someone conjured the rhyme, and every other voice instinctively repeated. It wasn't long before drums joined. Their thuds resonated in Serena's bones.

Nothing about the campus looked familiar on that frozen January afternoon. It was speckled with a fine coating of hardened snow. Serena had first noticed the snowfall as clumps by the side of the motorway, a few cars on the opposite carriageway with thickly iced roofs. That journey north always led to a different world. She couldn't catch her bearings as they marched through the university grounds. The paths that criss-crossed were as white as the grass, leaving the expanse featureless. Every nook and crenellation of the buildings caught pockets of snow, creating a shimmering ice palace.

Rise up, wise up, open your fucking eyes up.

Hundreds of feet marched towards the gravel courtyard outside Carnforth Hall. The event had taken significant planning, but Jane had urged the group to focus on aesthetics rather than logistics. The stories they'd scrolled through – those testimonials that seemed to reach through the screen – had jolted their approach. More had arrived over the holidays, adding to the darkness they were beginning to understand, helping them realise they needed to be unequivocal.

Serena could still sense heat in her fingers, still smell that flimsy wood burning in her parents' fireplace.

Rise up, wise up, open your fucking eyes up.

There was no stage this time. No speaker system hooked up to mounted microphones. No flyers. Jane had advised that something memorable was needed, had encouraged them to land on a symbol to tether their demands. Dean had scrabbled in his rucksack for a well-thumbed paperback – *The Society of the Spectacle* – in agreement. One phrase rose over and again from their conversations. *Turn a blind eye.* Their indictment of the university's intentionally averted gaze. *A blind eye.* So, smeared across their eyelids was the bright red lipstick Zara had applied straight from the bullet.

Score after score of self-bloodied eyes matched theirs. The horror that emanated from the aqua pages of that website had spread across campus, no longer contained in the digital but present in the physical world, its permeating power clear in the number of gruesome, blinded faces. Zara's lipstick smelled like vanilla and made Serena's eyelids stick when they blinked.

Darkness began to descend. The mud they walked across was rigid and their breath fogged the air with every word of the chant.

Rise up, wise up, open your fucking eyes up.

As they marched past the fountain in the centre of the courtyard, Serena stopped. The water had frozen as it fell, shrouding the stone in ice, making it impossible to tell which creature was carved there. The spout at its palm still flowed, continually thickening the ice streams. From a few steps away, it looked like dripping candle wax but, as she leaned in, Serena saw it sparkle, faceted and twinkling like crystal.

Rise up, wise up, open your fucking eyes up.

Serena had never heard so many voices raised together. A few were made mechanical by megaphones, but all sounded furious. The stories on that site made it impossible to ignore the pain that silently circled the campus, impossible to defend the university's dismissive stance.

Jane had asserted, in their planning meeting days before, the need to disrupt the flow, to challenge the platitudes the university sent out. It was the first time she'd offered them clear direction.

'We need to spur people into action,' Dean had instantly agreed. 'We pay so much to be here it makes us passive consumers.'

Her grey eyes sharp, Jane had told them about Act Up, a grassroots campaign she'd researched that had used radical action to highlight the hypocrisy surrounding the AIDS epidemic. Protestors had staged 'die-ins', crumpling to the ground as mock-corpses outside official buildings, streaked with fake blood, feigning mass death to shock governments and industrial bodies into addressing their lethal inertia. Hearing it in Jane's words sent electricity through Serena.

'Similar tactics were used in protests against Vietnam and for the Civil Rights Movement.' She'd never spoken so vehemently in their meetings. 'It's become a mainstay of environmental campaigns. When words don't cut it, and no one's listening, only a violent image matches the urgency of the situation. We need something just as brutal.'

So, a mass of savaged eyes gazed upwards at that Leysham building. A crowd gathered nearby, capturing the grisly sight on their phones: students who hadn't heard about the plan, sixth-formers scoping out facilities for next year, bemused visitors. Large banners spelled out the group's demands. Keira had sketched each letter for the others to fill with black and red paint. The words weren't as catchy as Zara had pushed for, but Dean urged accuracy over pithiness. *Improved campus security. Behavioural codes of conduct. Mandatory consent training.* They'd agreed to focus on Leysham itself, with plans to expand across other universities. The demands felt small to Serena. Their bloodied eyes captured something of the terror, but those calm banners were still too polite.

Rise up, wise up, open your fucking eyes up.

At least the anger had dialled up. The feet that stamped alongside Serena's seemed to mean it. They marched on the spot, a static army, each boot hitting the frozen gravel with fury. They stared at the golden walls of Carnforth Hall, its lit windows glowing magnificent in the half-light, its notches laden with ice. They called to the building as if it was sentient. As if the faces of those carved women could hear them. As if its buttresses could soften, its arches acquiesce, and the thick stone capitulate to their demands.

Serena stamped in that crowd of matching faces, knowing an ability sat within her none of them could comprehend. Almost knowing. Knowing. There was no other way to explain what had happened on Christmas Eve.

Luke's feet crunched gravel at the same tempo as Serena's. It reminded her of the music in the Student Union. The drums somewhere back in the crowd made her chest thrum the same way. Did he think of it too? He was mere steps away. The cigarette he'd rolled had broken to pieces in her pocket, but she'd kept the remnants, sealing them in a zip lock bag, inhaling their trapped scent three or four times a day. That sweet dark smell was so much kinder than its lit equivalent. He'd sent a handful of texts since New Year and she'd made herself pause before replying to each.

She turned to look and, as he noticed her, Serena felt that familiar grip in her stomach, that tension like the cusp of a roller-coaster. His hair was lost under a thick woollen beanie hat, his eyes pale in the dusk. Serena stamped towards him, weaved through the crowd, then tapped the arm of his coat with her gloved hand. She and Luke had spent hours alone together. They'd seen every part of each other. He'd wanted to meet her again.

He turned. 'Hey.' He lifted his head in greeting but didn't stop chanting.

Rise up, wise up, open your fucking eyes up.

The chant's awkward rhythm began to jar Serena's ears.

'Hey. Hi. How was your Christmas?'

He paused. 'Yeah, great, thanks.' He didn't return the question. He'd sent her messages from his parents' sofa, when he was alone in his childhood bed.

Serena didn't know which words to try next.

'Sorry, um, it's just . . .' He gestured to the crowd around them, then added his voice back to the endless chant. Was he so dedicated that a few seconds' pause was unthinkable? When she opened her mouth to speak, he looked down, pulled away.

Serena turned before he could see her face change, let the crowd jostle her back to Keira, who frowned at her, curious. Was his look down a cringe of embarrassment? After minutes of rigidly facing away, still stamping on the spot, Serena cast a swift look back and saw he was no longer chanting, no longer alone. Zara was laughing, tidying the lipstick smudges around his eyes, her fingers on the soft of his sockets. Her words caught on the breeze.

'You can't go there in this weather!'

Serena felt the shame throb through her. She'd asked so little of him. He'd been eager in the dark of his room, but not in that chanting crowd. Her face flashed hot in the cold air, humiliated by how easily he'd lured her. It felt physically painful. How gauche she'd been, how keen. No cool. No poise. Had his coursemates laughed about her, cruel names tripping off their tongues? Other girls would have held back, deft at plying his interest. She forced a breath. He shouldn't have the power to make her feel this bad.

Rise up, wise up, open your fucking eyes up.

The cold scorched Serena's lungs. The longer that clumsy chant continued, the more her rage flamed: at how he'd lingered in her, at how much she wanted him to like her. Now, she wanted to punish him. She wanted him to suffer like she was suffering. An image flashed unprompted. *Luke's face.* Serena's fingers stung. *Luke's face too pale, his lips too dark.* She wanted him to plead for forgiveness. The image was clear. *Luke's glassy eyes.* The details came easily, crisp, without her trying. *Luke's lips, nearly purple.* The anger would not abate. The images would not stop.

Zara's eyes were not simply lipstick-smeared but glittered. Of course she'd set herself apart. Serena tried to focus on her cousin, to clear her brain of anything else. Zara broke away from Luke and climbed the steps to Carnforth Hall alone. When she reached the top, she faced the crowd, and the chanting and drumming stilled. Everyone knew she was in charge. That power was palpable.

So many lacerated eyes staring at her must have been chilling. From that distance, they'd look like real wounds, weeping and sore, open to infection. Those people would look like souls raised from the earth. Zara spoke no words, but removed her fluffy coat to reveal the tight white dress below. She draped it on the wooden sign that displayed the hall's name in gold letters. The cold must have smacked, but she didn't flinch. Serena watched Zara's eyes scan the crowd, then settle. She followed the gaze to Jane, standing to one side of the crowd, who nodded firmly. On that cue, Zara leaned over to pick up a bucket placed on the top step and, without hesitation, upended it over her head. Its contents were blood red, the lipstick on their eyes made fluid. It clogged in her thick hair and covered her face Her dress turned instantly into a soiled bandage. Crimson liquid flowed down the stone steps, covering two or three before puddling to a halt. Phone cameras flashed in the gloom.

Zara paused to let the image land, but before she could head back down the steps, the doors to Carnforth Hall opened. Was this the concession they'd hoped for, Serena wondered? Had the university listened, taken their words on board and agreed to bring about real action? But no administrative officials stepped over the threshold. It was instead a group of young men in purple cloaks. For a second, Serena assumed they'd interrupted a graduation ceremony, then she understood. The

Carnforth Club with their hallmark capes. They walked out with rigid backs and tilted chins, an impression of ancient noblemen, rather than the vicious, grasping teenagers they were. Suppressed scuffles in the crowd, a few boos. Serena scanned to find the boy from the Gilly Sampson Bash. They looked so similar, with matching brows and ruddy cheeks, it was impossible to discern him.

Zara stood at the top of the staircase, dripping with red. One of the boys lunged forward and grabbed her arm as if to escort her away. She yelped in either pain or shock.

'Get out of our way, you ridiculous bitch.'

Shaking free of his grip, before anyone could react, Zara skipped down the stairs, stopping halfway to turn and face him. 'I'm not the one in the fucking cape, dickhead.'

The crowd parted for her now, some applauding. She walked straight to Jane, who didn't recoil for a second from the red mess that covered Zara, but reached out to touch her streaming face in pride. Serena knew how it felt to have those hands on her, to capture Jane's focus.

Knowing they were outnumbered, the purple-cloaked boys left together, their identical features contorted in disgust as they glanced back at the stained stonework, the sea of smeared faces.

15

Zara's actions on the steps had quietened Serena's mind for a
moment, but as she began the walk back to her room across
the campus's icy intersecting paths, the images slammed.
Luke's mouth gasping for air. Luke's body in freezing water. There
was no logic, only stuttering glimpses of scenes she couldn't
string together. The campus was dark, the luminous sign of
the small supermarket a neon beacon in the blackness. The
snow was smudging to brown and clogging every gutter. As
Serena walked, Luke's face, over and over, was lifeless in her
mind.

It might mean nothing. She must have seen Zara's trophy
sitting precariously on the mantelpiece on Christmas Eve. The
tiles of that poolside were always dangerous. Someone had to
win every race. But even as she dismissed it, Serena knew the
burn in her fingers was real. After Niko's words had begun
to fail, her own had taken over and that unwavering heat had

coursed through her as she imagined for herself. It had traced an electric route around her body when Zara's trophy fell.

Serena had assumed that power had been left in the water. Her fall by the poolside had shattered so much more than her patella, leaving her too broken to feel any escape, claim any strength. Now, she couldn't stop these words, these images. *Luke's feet running. Luke's body rigid.* His face again, mouth hanging open, eyes glassy. Serena had seen what water could do to a body. She wanted the image to leave her brain, urged the words in her head to stop speaking, gripped her hands into fists to stop them from feeling anything.

Serena needed her mind to be occupied. The library was quiet at that time of day, people abandoning books to seek solace from the dark evening. Serena ignored the librarian's gape at her reddened eyes. The building stretched to three open storeys, every step sending echoes from its chequered marble floor. Books were dwarfed in that place, tiny in comparison to the endless columns, the tier after tier of ornamental cast-iron balconies. Serena's laptop was back in her room and she had nothing to write with, so she pulled a book off the shelf, vaguely related to her course. Every desk had a burnished brass lamp, but the light did little to help. The words on the page blurred and Luke still nagged at her. The image, once formed, seemed unshakeable. *Luke's face.* Serena sat in her coat and scarf. Term was young, and warmth would take days to reach the towering ceiling. Chill from the gravel had seeped into her bones, making her weary. She wiped the lipstick from her face with a tissue, leaving dark pink smears like bruises. Her eyes slipped, and he was all she could see. *Luke's face. Luke's eyes closed. Luke's purple lips.* Heat moved up her hand. Raised letters on a gold plaque sat over every entrance to the library. *I pledge to injure no volume and kindle no flame.* Serena wished the flames that licked inside her veins had never been kindled.

The images were vivid every time her eyes blinked. *His face pale, eyes unfocused, lips wrong.* Static shots began to move. He wasn't at the river. This water tasted different. *Luke's feet stumble, the alcohol in his veins making each step wobble.* Serena had only seen the beach once, from the car window. It was disappointing, nothing like the glittering places she'd marvelled at as a child, just a small cove with a cluster of trees above. Had she heard him mention going there? Is this what he'd laughed about with Zara? Serena knew about the legendary five-step dare students issued, goading each other to wade into the freezing sea. *Luke's feet sinking into the sand.* The beach had looked hollow, with no pier, promenade, pavilion, no faded Georgian glory. No twinkling, glitzy slot machines. Nothing but the grey of sea and sky, a handful of rusting warning signs. *The water lapping Luke's ankles.* The images were like flashes of film, like the reels Zara created, a few bright seconds each. *The water reaches over his knees.*

The silence of the library offered no distraction. *Luke's hands grasp the air as he's swept rapidly away from shore.* The words had the same urgency as those Niko used by the pool-side. *The water drags him out.* Serena screwed her eyes, alarmed by how real it felt. The images were finding an order, growing into a full story.

Luke's feet stumble, the alcohol in his veins making each step wobble, toes sinking into the sand. He enters the freezing water in one deliberate pace. His mouth gapes as the water laps his ankles. Friends from the beach laugh, but don't join him. He strides in further, calling to them, counting. The water reaches over his knees, buoying him slightly. Whatever he's drunk has numbed him enough to bear the temperature. A moment of joy. Then, a tug. Another. His body is not his own. Luke's hands grasp the air as he's swept rapidly away from the shore. He moves faster than swimming could ever take him. A swift river formed in the heart of breaking waves drags him straight out to sea. The cold is smothering. He does what instinct demands, tries to swim, to fight the flow, but the cold makes him gasp, inhale the water. His addled arms can't muster the strength. The trashing panic exhausts him. The beach is distant, his friends invisible. He can do nothing but battle the foam. Luke disappears below the surface, rising above for a second, then back below.

Serena stood abruptly, screeching her library chair backwards. She couldn't stay in that cavernous room with those raging thoughts, the heat searing further up her arm, down her spine. These unchosen images were too strong to subdue. They were daydreams, surely, vengeful fantasies. Luke was not the sort to be reckless. But the insistence of the images terrified her. She left the building and walked, forcing a rhythm on her body. The images were not simply inventions. They'd all been warned about the notorious local beaches. Everyone knew the foolish games students devised. The cove half a mile from the campus's west edge was treacherous. Serena had read everything she could find about it, intrigued by the strange place that was now her home.

She walked those long footpaths across the grass, passing building after building, chanting numbers in her head to keep it busy. The numbers reached absurd heights. *Two thousand three hundred and sixty-four. Two thousand three hundred and sixty-five.* People must have walked near her, but Serena didn't register anyone. Luke's face wouldn't leave her. *His skin pale, his lips dark.* The broad bay, minutes' walk away, was mythically unpredictable. Deceptive in its stillness, it concealed freak tides and quicksand. Stories were told of cars and horses swallowed whole by the beach. Nothing in that cove stayed still, with sands shifting, channels swerving at will. It couldn't be trusted. Shallow waves lapped at the sand like kittens, luring paddlers in, but could turn in seconds. Its surface hid rip currents that could drag people out and fling them against the rocks.

Two thousand four hundred and thirty-eight. Serena's mind had been trained in laser focus and was not easily distracted. *Luke's feet stumble, the alcohol in his veins making each step wobble.* The image it fixated on, over and again, was not Luke's struggle in the ocean, but its aftermath. *His face pale, his lips dark.*

The electric light in Serena's room shone so brightly it added its own chill. The radiator creaked, emitting only feeble warmth. Serena couldn't knock on Keira's door with her mind in such a state. Those same boxes lined the room. She lifted a jumper from one, slid it onto a hanger. Her hands needed to be full. She'd spent the rest of the holiday keeping her distance from Kelly. What grew inside her sister – the swell of her middle already pronounced beneath layers of mohair – was too precious to risk. All of Christmas week, Serena had forced her mind to skip over thoughts like stones on the surface of a lake, too scared to dwell on anything.

She ripped the contents from the dry cardboard boxes. Anything to keep busy. Heaving armloads of clothes, she piled them on the bed, wrestling with a clanging tangle of hangers. She washed and dried every plate and cup in her tiny ensuite sink. She shoved every book she'd packed onto shelves with no logic, no order. Covers bent back, spines scuffed. She kept going. Her imagination was too powerful to trust. Opening Spotify on her phone, she hummed along to anything that played, turning the volume as high as it would go. Lyrics were all she'd let herself consider. Every time she reminded herself not to think of Luke's face, his face was all she could see.

@zarakarmic • 212k followers

I know I look horrifying with this fake blood, all in my hair and down my new dress, but – trust me – it's for the best possible cause.

We heard your stories and we're going to stand up for what we know to be right.

I believe we can manifest good things. Manifestation works as a kind of collaboration with the universe, and the universe can awaken mighty change if we ask.

We will not be quiet. We will attract the things we believe in. Our energy will triumph.

16

Serena woke earlier than she ever had in that bed. The two tablets she'd taken – left over from the stash of painkillers she'd once relied upon – had sent her to a sleep with no dreams, but couldn't keep her there. Her phone lived inches from where she slept now. Every morning, before her eyes focused, she reached for it. Her thumbs had grown nimble. That day, as so often, the little box showed a message from Keira. The words looked wrong. Serena held the phone closer. The message was in capitals. *HAVE YOU HEARD?* Her muscles stiffened and she fired back a question mark. It might be nothing. Keira always inclined towards the dramatic.

The reply came in less a minute. *Our beloved soy boy was bloody lucky.* Before Serena could let herself react, Keira had sent a link to a local news story. The headline showed in the message. *University student rescued from cove.*

Serena dropped the phone. She sat up in the bed, unable

to breathe. Forcing her thumb to click the link, she read the words, though she knew exactly what they'd say.

> A student is recovering in hospital after being swept away by a rip current while paddling in Lunesdale Bay. The 19-year-old was rescued shortly after 10pm yesterday after getting into difficulty. RNLI lifeguards arrived at the scene swiftly and pulled the young man from the water. He was taken to the Royal Infirmary, suffering from hypothermia, and it is understood he is due be discharged today. A police spokesperson said: 'The young man was fortunate that friends were able to raise the alarm in time. This is a timely reminder to anyone enjoying the beach to remember the dangers of the tide and of open water.'

Serena's fingers were swift. His feeds were full, messages that read like condolences. Pictures of Luke with arms around his neck. *Thinking about you. Get better, mate.* Some risked being jovial. *Taking the Jeff Buckley tribute a bit far there, Lukey.* He hadn't replied to any of them. Serena imagined him propped up in a hospital bed. His face too pale, his lips too dark.

Swiping the phone shut, a single blink released tears onto her cheeks. Her throat throbbed with nausea. Their reactions were wrong. Luke could have died. Luke whose skin she'd tasted, whose arms she'd lain in. Their jokes were hideous, Keira's message horribly glib. Luke could have been dragged out by the freezing water pulled under until his lungs couldn't gasp. Luke could have died at nineteen. They seemed to think it was a foolish prank, but Serena had seen the horror.

How close had her vision been? She could simply have blurred the memory of Tanya with what she'd read about the cove. Luke wasn't the sort to rise to dares. She hadn't chosen those pictures, hadn't summoned them. They were beyond her control. The relentless imagining had been against her will. It couldn't be her fault.

Standing under the shower spray, the words haunted her. *The cold is smothering.* He was safe in hospital, but her imagination hadn't calmed. *The trashing panic exhausts him.* She'd seen him go under and not come back. *Luke disappears below the surface.*

As shampoo suds flowed down her body, Serena jolted. She understood the beach only vaguely, but she knew water. She knew how seditious water could be. Pool safety training, when they'd cupped each other beneath the chin in simulations of rescue, had touched upon secondary drowning. Her memory was fuzzy, but a rapid Google search – hair dripping over the carpet tiles – gave basic information. Rumours had circled at the pool about children who'd been pulled from deep ends by lifeguards but then died days later. Water could lurk in their lungs, ready to attack. Luke's face had been lifeless in her mind. Parts of that ocean might still be within him, enough to choke him, to prevent his blood from filling with oxygen. Someone needed to watch him, alert for signs of lethargy, in case his breath struggled, in case he coughed, in case his forehead burned in a fever.

Serena knew which bar he was at. Plans as well as memories were public property. Luke had been discharged after only one night in the hospital and was celebrating his homecoming with gusto. Standing in the freezing queue for half an hour, Serena realised no one else was there alone. She craved Keira's support, but this had to be stealthy. Flicking through her phone, she watched as Luke's friends uploaded group shots, looped videos where drinks were lifted then lowered, lifted then lowered. They were inside the bar, only steps away from her. Serena pinched the screen outwards to zoom in on Luke's face. The bar's lighting made his natural pallor more pronounced. The pink rims of his eyes might be no more than stubborn lipstick from the protest. He shouldn't be there, as if nothing had happened. It was too soon.

That afternoon, the shop had been crowded, but Serena hadn't hesitated, buying the first dress she tried on – red, strappy, triangles cut to show her torso – wiping out her money for the month. It was worth the bus journey into town, worth the cost. She knew the effect required, had studied other girls long enough to mimic them. Her body was curved now, not the androgynous machine of her teens. She was growing accustomed to what it could do.

Zara's pile of products was intact, but Serena was left to fathom their order, their roles, how to paint a face that could

seduce him. She'd smudged glitter over her eyelids and cheekbones, like armour or scales, a dab on the end of her nose.
Without Zara's tricks, she'd been heavy-handed, but it might
work. He had to look at her and submit. There was no time
for hesitation.

The bouncer nodded another group through. That room
would once have terrified Serena; now she only feared what her
mind might have done. At the bar, her voice was loud. *Gin and
tonic.* The woman she needed to be that night wouldn't wince
at the tang of quinine. In the dim light, her glass shone blue.

His friends clinked their bottles together with every new
drink. Serena realised with relief that Dean wasn't there, as
she stood out of sight, watching their corner. She wanted to
turn, walk back out, but sipped, hoping the tonic would earn
its name, work with the alcohol as an elixir to buoy her. For
over an hour, she watched Luke. As he laughed and drank it
seemed impossible he'd come so close to death. Eventually,
he broke from the group, heading to the toilets.

When he emerged, his feet were unsure, stumbling on the
black tiled floor. He'd been bought so many drinks. *The alcohol
in his veins makes each step wobble.* Her breaths shallow, Serena
steered herself into his path. If he brushed her off, she couldn't
keep him safe, couldn't undo what she might have done. The
sheen she'd smudged, the waves in her hair, the bra that forced
her breasts high all needed to work their sorcery.

He clocked her immediately. Walking over, his eyes lingered. 'Hey.' He didn't say anything else, just leaned in.

He kissed her in front of his friends, but Serena didn't let herself taste the victory. She needed to get him out of the bar. He'd already drunk more than might be safe. His kisses were insistent, his hands on the edges of her dress.

She guided him to the cab rank, remembering his address as they clambered in.

Luke pressed against her. 'You're fucking lovely, aren't you?' The smoke in his hair smelled sweet.

There was no coffee in his room this time, no cigarettes out of the window. She'd intended to get him to safety and watch over him, but he kept kissing her. She wanted him to keep kissing her. When he lifted the dress over her head, his fingers somehow dexterous with its straps, she felt a thrill. This was one way to make sure he was fully alive. Sex was surely the opposite of death.

It was different this second time, as if the dress and make-up had sunk into her skin and through her bones to make her bold. Their bodies remembered each other, like a dance they'd both rehearsed. Serena was no longer inert but certain. Her body was her own. It was fluent, and she hid no part of it. His eyes should see the places her swimming costumes had once covered. With her weight on him, her limbs were able to manoeuvre, could flip their positions if she wanted. She let her body soften to the pleasure, let herself focus on him. The crosshatched texture of his skin, the pale stretch of neck where stubble receded, the darkness near his pelvis. He was alive. Her fingers through the sparse hairs of his chest. He was alive, and she could make this as perfect as her stroke.

17

As it rained, condensation sent water streaming down both sides of the window. Serena's eyes became accustomed to the dark of his room. Luke had been asleep for hours. She stared at him. Those resting features could so easily be lifeless. Face too pale, lips too dark.

He was younger than her, a teenager for a few more months. Asleep, he looked vulnerable. Serena imagined those sleeping features contorting in fear that moment the current had clutched. He'd been so close to death. If she breathed into his neck, she could catch the scent of horror that had grabbed him, of the vicious salty water that might still be trapped inside. Serena held a finger over his wrists, to count the beats that throbbed.

In his calm, dark room, Serena chose what she saw. The fleshy tendrils of his lungs reaching out like leaves. If her mind could see them, it could heal them. *His lungs grow stronger.* Warmth blossomed in Serena's fingers, moving through her as she lay next to him. Her mind was clear, and she could control it. These weren't unbeckoned images, but exactly what she wanted. Staring at the pale hairs across his chest, she focused on what lay beneath. *The charred fragments of his lungs turn pink again. Every breath of smoke he's ever taken is erased; each strand of tobacco lifted.* It was working. Blood filled his lungs, drinking every drop of oxygen. The seawater hidden there was evaporating, leaving his body as a fine briny mist. It couldn't choke him. Nothing could hurt him.

Luke roused slightly from his sleep, and Serena stiffened. He coughed once, twice, lifting from the mattress. Serena didn't exhale. Had she failed? Was this the moment she'd dreaded? But no, he calmed and rolled further into his pillow. She knew she'd succeeded. His lungs were red and perfect. His breaths were rich and full. Serena kissed his forehead, pulled her dress back on and left.

He was safe. She'd made him safe. That power was within her. Whatever Niko had taught her at the pool could reach further. It could do more than vanquish opponents, more than win medals. As she walked those long paths, the campus looked beautiful for the first time. The buildings gleamed rather than loomed. Their crenellations and buttresses looked like icing on a magnificent cake. Those empty hours of the night were nothing to fear. No eyes lurked in shadows. The dark was not theirs to inhabit, to make terrifying. It was hers. No imagined predator crept between those ancient buildings, no ghosts of long-dead killers. The freezing temperature woke her up, and Serena yelled out, her whoop shattering the stillness. She flung her arms outward in a mime of triumph, to see how it felt. That power was hers now, and she wasn't afraid.

Victories in the pool had never landed as this pure, unsullied glee. No smack of hands against the pad had ever made her want to leap so high. Now, Serena couldn't stay still. She bounced on the balls of her feet, her hands loose in their sockets. In that dark, her body knew what to do. Dropping her bag, she removed her sandals, kicked one foot a little, then trusted her hands to hit the ground – one after the other – as she threw her weight. Her legs took flight in a circle above her, the air holding her like water. The cartwheel was perfect. Straight-legged, firm-handed, immaculate. As she landed, her chest and head lifted, arms aloft in a gymnastic salute.

The sky was clear. Clouds had fogged for months, but now it was bright. The longer she looked, the more stars made themselves known. Layer after layer, further and further away. If Serena concentrated, her mind could reach up and make them move. One swipe of her hand could send them scattering.

She knew where to go. The light was rising and it would soon be open. The one place on campus she'd avoided since she'd arrived, walking wide arcs across the grass to keep it from her eyeline. The thrum of the sports centre's mechanisms resounded. Serena's body knew it. The pool was where she would understand. Doors parted: aside from a uniformed boy on the front desk, no one was around. The university squad clearly didn't have her former discipline. Serena flashed her student card, left her shoes on the changing-room floor, then walked to the poolside in her short red dress. The sharp taste of chlorine. That catch at the back of the throat.

Sitting on the bench, she stared at the water. Man-made, chemically altered and safe. She knew that water well, knew how it would feel on her skin, knew its triumphs and disasters. She'd imagined it more times than she'd touched it. For years, her visualisations had been right. It was always right.

They'd all used the same technique. Each girl who lined up at the starting blocks did the same thing, but it worked better for Serena. It went beyond mental rehearsal. Zara talked about manifestation, beckoning something tangible through the power of attraction. Sports psychologists trumpeted the creation of neural patterns, but it could be so much more than that.

Serena remembered the etching in Jane's office. Four women's bodies, luscious and potent, winding together, sharing some secret. Was she like those women? Inhaling deeply, Serena let the chemicals fill her chest. Moving to the edge of the pool, she let her feet feel the water. She knew that temperature. For a second, in that environment, everything made sense. It wasn't her body she'd trained all those years, but her mind.

The wall ran along the edge of the river. The same patch of river where Tanya had fallen months before, where women had been murdered hundreds of years ago. Serena's steps took her there instinctively. It was a few feet wide, with space to stand but no more. On one side was shingle; on the other, the river raged. Plastic barriers had been positioned to keep people from danger, but Serena slipped easily between them. No one could see her. It was daylight, but too early for students to have roused. Serena knew the risk. After a stretch, the wall widened, but for thirty or forty steps, it was treacherous. The cold made it slippery as well as narrow. It was madness to try, but she had to know. She had to prove it to herself.

Leaning against the ancient, blackened stone, Serena focused. The noise of the churning water dampened everything else. She felt how each step would land, the texture against the skin of her feet. Her voice spoke in her mind. *You walk, not slowly, not cautiously.* The images were clean. Heat prickled through her hands, then the muscles of her arms.

Each step is perfect. You reach the end. You are safe.

Hoisting herself onto the wall, she scrambled to standing. In last night's red dress, she looked ahead at where the wall thickened. Breathing, she stepped out. Her bare feet danced over the stone, never pausing to root. She didn't wobble. Step after step until she reached the end. No lingering in glory, but a leap to the ground, landing so nimbly her knee didn't feel it. Serena looked back at the wall. It was under her control. Her words had described it perfectly. If it mattered, she could do it.

Blood was glorious in her veins. Her body was spectacular. Images were swifter now, no need to strain. Heat eased through her bones. *You walk out and not a single car comes near.* The road between the river and campus wasn't busy, but vehicles came at speed, heading to town from the nearest motorway. People on their way to jobs and schools. *Your steps are not rushed.* Her eyes glazed and she walked. Calm, even steps, exactly as she'd imagined. Barefoot on the tarmac. The breeze of the cars rushing by, never close enough to graze her. No wheels screeched. No brakes slammed. Serena reached the kerb, and stopped, arms thrown high and wide.

As Serena's knife slid, her plate flooded with pink, blood meeting redcurrant jus. She'd never eaten venison before, never eaten in a room so grand, but Keira had cajoled her into attending the History Faculty formal dinner. The meat's deep, musky pungency clogged her mouth and nose, taking her mind to the ballerina necks of the roe deer on the parkland beyond the university.

'You alright?' Keira moved closer. That hall of long wooden tables was lit only by candles in curved brass holders and their conversation felt private.

Serena tilted her head, unsure of Keira's concern.

'Luke.'

She didn't reply.

'I just thought,' Keira continued. 'This week's been so much. It must have been fucking horrific to read about. And I wondered if you'd hoped something might start properly with him this term. No?'

The image of Luke's face was still potent. Face pale, lips dark. The death that brushed so close. The deep flesh of the organs she'd imagined.

They'd stood behind carved wooden chairs on arrival, both wearing the demurest dresses Keira owned. They'd stood as ten faculty members swept down the aisles to the high table. The black gown over Jane's dress lifted in the wake of her stride, floating behind her like wings. Keira had risked a wave, but Jane's eyes were fixed ahead. In that room, her simplicity translated to confidence. She was every one of her thirty-two years. Her impressive list of appointments and publications was tangible in her posture.

Serena turned to Keira. 'I suppose I did.' She remembered the fury that had surged through her at Luke's dismissive look. It seemed like months ago. She knew he couldn't evoke that feeling in her now.

'Situationships can be tough.' Keira was locked into a series of recurring liaisons with a third-year Physics student she'd met at a house party, both of them reluctant to assign a shape or name to whatever they were.

'I think I was hurt that he seemed so insensitive about it.'

'He totally was. They're twats at this age, right? It sucks that we're left to hold out for them to grow up.'

A jolt had been sent through the room, eventually, by a man striking the head table with a wooden gavel. Everyone had looked down and Serena followed. Latin words were spoken, a rhythmic incantation she couldn't penetrate. *Oculi omnium aspiciunt*. She listened as the words rumbled around the tables, their meanings shrouded but the solemnity clear. Jane would know what every syllable signified. When the words ceased, it was safe to sit.

Serena had never seen Jane with colleagues, never seen her so assured. On the high table, set on a raised platform, her every move was visible. Turning to a man around her own age, she grew serious, brow puckered. With a senior female lecturer, she sparkled, head thrown back in delight at whatever joke had landed. Serena wished she could watch her all night.

'I reckon it's a uni thing.' Keira took a bread roll from the basket between them and ripped into it. 'He probably doesn't want to sign up to anything too intense here.'

The food was served by staff their own age. Serena prickled as she thanked them, stiff at the assumed superiority. Silver cloches were lifted from their plates with exaggerated flourish. Portraits of long-dead men stared as they ate, judging those below, their paint dense with a history Serena didn't want to know.

'I'm sure you're right.' Serena had never imagined being intense with Luke. Quite the opposite: she'd wanted to be blithe and chilled, going with his flow, learning how to be straightforward.

'You watch, he'll come running back when he realises how lucky he got.'

That wasn't going to be possible. Serena could never be the

girl he wanted. No amount of pennies pushed into a woman's stone mouth could change that. She couldn't be a regular girl for him. She wasn't built that way. Something inside her insisted on being extraordinary.

18

Jane had never called them to her office before. In the scuffles as they settled, the others checked on Luke.

'You alright, mate?' Dean slapped him on the back, too hard for Luke's delicate frame.

Keira hugged him. 'Don't you ever do anything like that again, you utter, utter twat!'

Luke looked paler, somehow much older than before he was pulled from the water, as if some fragment of youth had been left in the brine.

'I won't. I won't.' His hands in front of his chest, spread to stop any future event in its tracks. 'I was a fucking idiot.'

'You really were.'

'Trust me, the lesson is learned.' He bowed his head. Sheepish, or basking in the attention.

When he looked up, Serena let him catch her eye, returned his smile. She was proud of every breath he took. As his jumper rose, the air reached his lungs without impediment. His eyes didn't leave her. Was he thinking of their bodies together? The skin of her face glowed.

Jane had printed the email she and Zara had received from the University Proctors, the reason she'd summoned them all. She held it so tight the paper stiffened and, as she read aloud, her voice took on its flint. The confidence she'd emitted in that candlelit hall was edgier now. Limbs rigid, she perched on the daybed.

'While both staff and students hold the right to protest, events intended to take place on University property must be referred to the Proctors.'

Zara nodded. That permission had been granted for previous rallies.

'And this right does not extend to any damage to, or defacement of, University property. The actions of last week caused irreparable harm to the exterior of Carnforth Hall.'

'Harm?' Keira's eyes narrowed.

Jane broke character. 'The steps.'

That moment Zara had gone from white to red. The pictures that covered the front pages of student newspapers, that had filled Zara's timeline.

'It's a Grade Two listed building, and apparently those steps mean more than the students who use them.'

That mock-blood had seeped into the porous stone, staining it beyond repair. No amount of scrubbing could lift that wound. Zara's marks were always indelible.

Jane resumed her impression of the Proctors. 'While this will be noted on both of your records, it has been decided in this instance not to involve the disciplinary board.'

The room seemed to exhale, that ornate space relaxing.

Pausing, Jane shook her head, then continued in the same brittle tone. 'As members of the University, you have agreed to adhere to its code of conduct, which prohibits any behaviour that has potential to damage the University's reputation or makes defamatory statements about members of the University community.'

As Luke sighed, Serena remembered his advice that they should vet website submissions. He'd always thought they were being too reckless.

'The Rise Up website contravenes both prohibitions, featuring a large number of unsubstantiated claims against named members of staff and the student body. This risks creating a legal liability for the University and constitutes serious misconduct.'

'What the actual fuck?' Keira's tone was flat. Dean's hands pressed together in front of his lips.

'Any complaints against the institution need to come through official channels. We request that the website is terminated.' The irony drained from Jane's voice. 'If this request is not adhered to, it will be deemed an intentional breach of regulation and we will be forced to pursue disciplinary action.'

'What do they mean by disciplinary action?' Zara was unusually quiet.

'They're not messing around. From what I've gleaned, it could be hefty fines or even suspension. My funding could be at stake.'

'Fuck.'

'Yes.'

Zara grew louder. 'This is such bullshit! It's totally unreasonable to make so much out of so little. They can't handle valid criticism. We didn't set out to damage their reputation or their property.'

'You're right.' Dean nodded. 'But we probably shouldn't have used such public channels. It's drawn attention we didn't need.'

'Absolutely not.' Jane didn't hesitate. 'Zara's profile is necessary. We couldn't have done it otherwise. We'd have had no impact.' Serena was struck by her force. Jane stood with her hands on the back of Zara's chair.

'We could have taken more control over the content, though.' Luke aimed his words at Jane. 'We should have been more careful.'

'Can't we move the site elsewhere?' Keira asked.

'The answer is, of course we can,' Jane replied. 'But it would be counterproductive. We'd risk creating an endless cat-and-mouse that doesn't respect those stories, but uses them as bait.' Jane had thought it through.

'You know the rumours going round?' Keira tapped the dark wood of Jane's desk. 'Apparently those Carnforth tossers complained about us. They have some weird ceremony where they place purple carnations by the big painting of the Earl, in those ridiculous capes. His birthday or death day, or something. Anyway, we got in their way, and they didn't like it.'

'That's putting it lightly,' Dean said. 'Zara was basically attacked.'

Serena imagined those thick-set boys with their pink cheeks, placing white carnations in purple ink, waiting for the flower to drink the venom.

'They might have heard they were named on the website,' Luke added.

'I'm not sure dickheads like that care about being named and shamed. It's probably a badge of honour.'

Scores of stories had centred on them. The way they moved around the campus as if they owned it, taking up space that wasn't theirs. The names they called people, the liberties they took. Some stories tended darker, telling of physical altercations, unwanted advances.

'They're so fucking gross. We've all heard the stories from the eighties, when they did unhinged things with dead animals. This lot are just a tribute band, but they're gaining traction.' Keira smacked the desk.

'Yes! What they did to me was horrible, but what we heard described at the rally was clearly sexual assault. No question.' Zara straightened. 'And the university never does anything to stop them. Everything they do is ignored. It's like the uni are on their side.'

'Report has it they encourage them.' Keira stood up, her anger making her restless. 'People reckon that Dr Peregrine Something, senior guy in the History Faculty, came here as an undergrad back in the day and used to be in the Carnforth Club.' She paced now 'Their whole thing is about forming an impenetrable unit, you know, having each other's backs. These guys will be getting each other out of shit for life.'

Dean matched her disdain. 'The stories you hear are grim, not only drinking full bottles of single malt, then eating pigs' snouts or some crap, but paying girls to dress up as foxes and chasing them around the quads after dark. They're always making a mess and it's always getting cleared up.'

'Jesus Christ. Are we going be silent and let some throw-back drinking society get away with whatever they want?' Luke asked.

Serena wanted to speak and, this time, didn't stop herself. 'We can't be silent. People told us those stories for a reason. We have a responsibility.' The echo of her voice in that tiny room surprised her. 'The pain of those people was real.'

Jane's stillness snapped to tension, her fingers clawing on the wooden chair. 'It was. It was very real. There is a fucking rancid stream of horror flowing through this place.' Serena had never heard her swear. Her energy altered, the cool poise replaced. 'And they are refusing to see it, refusing to admit the problems and their culpability.'

As Jane spoke, she walked to the door, and Serena glimpsed

the etched image of the four witches behind her. For a moment, Jane became the fifth of their circle.

'They're doing what every institution does, protecting their own interests even when it damages others. Protecting those who've always been protected. It's not only unfair, it's deliberate. For some people to rise to the top, everyone else has to be trampled.'

Energy thrummed from Jane as she spoke.

'They're assuming we'll follow other groups they've silenced – back away, glad we weren't punished more severely.'

Slivers of light cut through the gaps between the print and the window, illuminating Jane from behind.

'We have to stand firm. Refuse to disappear.'

She looked resplendent.

Serena knew what to expect. She'd never been inside Zara's room, but she knew her cousin, and had grasped details from her videos. Zara had been determined to gain the full Leysham experience. Her building wasn't municipal but imposing, the same ornate stone as the prospectus shots, with a twisting staircase leading to heavy wooden doors. Once inside, there was a dramatic fireplace and arched windows looking over the campus. From that leaded glass, Zara was a warrior princess surveying her battlements. She created most of her content in that coveted room, and the aesthetic was honed. Every mug, every pen, every book on display nailed the colour palette. That rich wash of pastels –

gold, teal, peach – like a constant sunset. Fairy lights draped from every post.

Framed images filled the walls: pictures that must have been sent by her fans, some drawn in pencil, smudged in charcoal, some in full watercolour. Each one depicted Zara's body: the soft, sweet ripples of her stomach, the sway of her breasts. She was near-naked in each. All had the same words written across the top or scribbled along the bottom. *Love Your Body.*

'Thanks for coming, lovely.' Zara's hugs lasted seconds too long.

Her text had arrived half an hour earlier. *I'd love to see you.*

'Do you mind sitting with me while I take a bath? My shoulders are knots from the cold, and I don't have much spare time today.'

Serena nodded. It wasn't easy to say no to Zara.

'You're such a gem.'

That housing block was notoriously expensive, with generous ensuites. The bathtub was plain, but Zara could transform anything. There were tea lights around the edge, prohibited in student rooms, but no smoke detector would dare to interrupt her. She clicked twenty or thirty pictures on her phone's camera before she climbed in. Serena stared at the sink while her cousin stood naked.

Her back against the wall, Serena sat on the floor. Zara's body was blanketed by bubbles, but it still felt too intimate. Only her head and feet were visible, an occasional hand reaching for her drink. Serena held her own glass and sipped the wine Zara had poured even though it was a mid-week afternoon. It tasted cold and sharp. Zara opened a bag of jelly sweets, green and red caterpillars, biting them between her teeth and pulling, extending the creature until it snapped.

She'd never asked to see Serena alone before. Did she sense something new thrumming through her cousin? Could power recognise power?

Turning to rest her head on the bath's edge, Zara spoke. 'You used to be in the water all the time, didn't you? Do you miss it?'

No one ever asked. Serena paused. 'Sometimes. Not often.' She'd never said the words out loud. 'I think if you love some-thing so much, you can come to hate it eventually.'

'You were incredible, though.' The past tense would once have slayed Serena. 'I mean, almost no one's ever been as good at anything as you were at that.'

Serena bit her lower lip. 'I don't think it matters any more.'

'Of course it does!' Zara's voice echoed against the tiles. 'I saw you swim a few times, and you were amazing.' Serena remembered Zara at the side of that pool. Zara sighed. 'I'd love to have a talent like that.'

Her talent was present whenever she walked into a room. 'I don't know how you coped with that being ripped away. You must have been devastated.'

'Yeah. It was very sudden.' Serena's knee twinged at the thought. 'But it would have ended at some point.' There was no one she could tell the truth to, that she'd beckoned her own swift demise.

'You're allowed to miss it.'

'Yeah. It's a kind of grief, I suppose. It takes time.'

Zara shifted until she was sitting, her shoulders out of the bathwater, arms over the side. 'When we were little, I hated my body so much and yours could do such incredible things.' She paused. 'I was so jealous of you. Everything you did turned to gold.'

The acidic wine left Serena's mouth dry.

'I loathed everything about my body.' Zara sank back a little in the water. 'I stopped eating, you know, in my early teens.' She didn't look at Serena any more, but faced the wall behind the bath taps. 'You'd never have noticed. You were storming then. I used to be in awe of you, too scared to speak at Christmas. I used to look at you, with those muscles and that height and leanness you have. I'd have done anything to have a body like yours.'

Serena looked down at her body, still long, still lean, but so different.

'I was this chubby little bug. My mum constantly urged me to diet but disguised it as empowerment, and my dad didn't bother with me much.' Zara swallowed. 'I was really fucked up, you know. I used to count each bite, write down every calorie, the whole deal. For years, it was me in a battle with my body, and everyone around encouraging me. The truth is, I wasn't any good at it. My greed always won out. It wasn't because anyone did anything responsible to save me from something full-blown. I was just lucky.' She smiled. 'I loved food more than I hated the way I looked.'

'Shit.' Serena looked at Zara. 'I didn't know.'

'It's what makes me so loud about it. I can't stomach the idea of some other girl sitting out there loathing her thighs like I loathed mine. It breaks my fucking heart.' Zara's skin was turning pink in the heat of the water. 'I want to help them fight that negativity.' She hesitated. 'Do you want to know something else?'

Serena made a noise of assent.

'Do you know the first time I felt good about my body? I was about thirteen, maybe fourteen, and I was in town, around Covent Garden and this man, much older, at least in his mid-twenties – good-looking, a suit, the works – stopped me to ask the time. I remember thinking, who the hell doesn't have a phone? Then I saw he was wearing a watch.'

Zara stared as if into the distance. 'I can remember how it felt when he looked at me. I know how twisted this sounds, but I was so young, and it made me feel like I sparkled. It felt like my body might not actually be terrible. He was clearly a knob, and if I saw some guy do that now I'd fucking kill them. But it totally changed how I saw myself.' She paused. 'Probably also hooked me on the attention.'

The bubbles diminished, becoming islands in the water. The swell of Zara's breasts was beginning to show. Her thighs breached the surface. Those thighs she'd once hated. It was outrageous that a body so admired hadn't felt good to live in.

'I'm gutted about those steps, you know. Like I've ruined everyone's plans.'

The red stain on pale stone, marking the university as her own.

'That wasn't your fault.' Serena shook her head 'They'd have found some reason to stop us; this is just what they've seized on.'

'Yeah. And it wasn't my idea. It was all Jane.' Zara lifted one leg so it rose from the water and rested on the tiled wall above her. 'She's incredible, isn't she? So different to anyone else I've ever known. She's her total self. There's nothing fake with her. Nothing forced. She doesn't give a shit what anyone thinks.'

Heat from the bath seemed to dial up, making the steam too dense. Serena wanted to throw the window open, gulp fresh, cold air from outside, but didn't move. Zara could sense Jane's magic too, could see what Serena saw. Had something more sparked between them? Zara studied Sociology, so would never be taught by Jane, but anything intimate would surely be forbidden.

'I think spending time with her will be good for me.'

The bubbles clung to Zara's skin, their refracted light making iridescent patterns, shimmers in the same pastel tones as her belongings. Serena stared at the colours dancing on her cousin's thighs and tried not to take in any more of her flesh, tried not to imagine Jane looking at those parts of her.

★   ★   ★

As she left the warm rainbow of that room and stepped into the cold, Serena checked her phone, tilting it in her pocket. *4 missed calls.* Her throat constricted. *1 new message.* The missed calls were from her parents' house phone, the text message from her father's mobile. *Hello love. Call when you can. Dad.* Serena's hands scrabbled to tap the screen. If her mother hadn't sent the message, it was serious.

She had to rely on Google. Serena didn't know what a foetus looked like at thirty-six weeks. It took too many minutes of scrolling to find pictures of placenta that weren't medical sketches. When she found an image of that slab of veined meat, she drilled her mind into it.

Kelly had been struck by an intense headache, blurred vision. A call to the doctor became a rush to the hospital. They knew she was struggling with pre-eclampsia, her heart thumping with too much force. The pain might mean nothing, or might indicate potential disruption to foetal oxygen supply. Kelly's body was being scanned, her heart assessed. They may have to induce labour.

Serena didn't leave her room that day. She knew what was needed. Tapping through Kelly's social media, she pinched each picture, making it as large as possible. Switching from phone to laptop gave the images more space. There was no time to waste. Zooming in on Kelly's stomach might work. Kelly's stomach bare in a bikini. Kelly's stomach peeking out under a halter top. The wedding shots were best: Kelly was pregnant that day. Pushing Dan out of the frame, Serena homed in. Deep under that embroidered ivory bodice, beneath those individually sewn crystals, a blob of cells grew. Serena zoomed so far it was a blur, and stared at the fuzzy image of Kelly's middle. She bored into it, imagining burning through layers of silk and crystal and tulle and skin, muscle, gristle, bone, marrow, to where that little smudge thrashed.

Hundreds of miles of motorway separated them, but Serena knew she could do it. Her own voice spoke in her head. It had never mattered more. *Kelly's heart slows. Blood flows easily to the baby and nourishes her.* That little body, weeks away from readiness. *If she's delivered, it is easy and peaceful.* That creature snug in her nest, coddled in the cradle of Kelly's pelvis. Safe from everything the world might throw. Protected by her mother, by the force of her aunt's will.

Serena felt warmth through her hands and arms, she was sure. She imagined the baby once born. Tiny eyelashes and fingernails. A girl she'd one day love. For hours, she pictured the inside of her sister. She forced the heat down her spine and legs. If it mattered, she could do it. Serena strained each tendon, pushed beyond any pain, desperate for that burning. *If she's delivered, it is easy and peaceful.* Her body screamed with the effort, but Serena always swam to the next wall. Pain had to be her ally.

When the phone rang in the early hours of the morning, Serena didn't give herself time to dread. Her father's voice wavered, but he didn't pause.

'Delilah's with us and she's perfect.'

Serena flopped back on her bed.

'Kelly's doing great, and Dan's with them both.'

The exhaustion felt like the result of rigorous training sets. The throb in her muscles was the same, the weakness in her limbs. The clarity of her mind.

@zarakarmic • 211k followers

You know, I'm sure water is my element. Especially water surrounded by candles and filled with bubbles.

Today, I'm soaking muscles that I've pushed to their limits. With Vernal home workouts, I've learned to move my body for fun, not for results. It is not punishment, but pure bliss.

I don't need my body to change, I need it to feel good and sweaty.

Let me tell you, exercise hits different when you don't hate it. These endorphins are utterly delicious.

19

'This is Delilah.' Kelly's face was round with pride. She looked different now, not only tired but knowing, gazing back from the other side of a chasm.

Serena had headed home a few days after her father's call. They'd settled in Kelly's house, with its hoovered carpets and soft, grey fabrics, and let the baby dictate the flow of each day. That child whose tiny body was at risk so few hours ago, was now real and bright and solid. Born a smudge over six pounds, she had been allowed home after twenty-four hours. They all stared at that tiny creature, every writhe, every whimper seeming miraculous. Serena looked into Delilah's dark, unfocused eyes. It was as if she recognised her.

The smack of chlorine hit as it always had. Serena hadn't been back since her injury. The sports centre's fug was heavy as soon as the automatic doors parted. She had to buy a ticket now, feed it into the turnstile. Her pulse didn't race as she'd expected. It seemed such a long time ago.

As she walked across those bobbled tiles, the chemical cleanness clawed the back of her throat; her eyes blinked at its bleach. The water was no different, always captured and waiting. Serena heard Niko's voice before she saw him, demanding the junior squad kept to their lines.

'You've got to concentrate, guys.'

Those long, drawn-out vowels she'd heard in her mind so many times. She'd recalled his voice more than she'd listened to it. There was time to watch him before he noticed her. The pool was busy, and he held that same red clipboard as he paced its length.

One of the junior girls was out of the water. Niko leaned over her, demonstrating how to alter the curve of her back. She looked about fourteen. From the way he twisted her, she must be a butterfly swimmer. There had been another butterfly swimmer with a tattoo emblazoned on the top of her thigh. One of Niko's hands was on the girl's hip, the other on the dip at the base of her spine. She wore nothing but a thin layer of Lycra. Serena could feel those hands on her, on her breasts, her inner thighs, her face. Niko had touched her years before any other man. Serena watched him manipulate the girl's body. Under any other circumstances what he was doing would be unthinkable.

When the girl returned to the water, Serena walked over. Niko didn't notice her until she was almost next to him. They were the same height. He'd surely always towered over her.

'Oh my God!' When he recognised her, he shouted. It was a performance for the teenagers in the water. 'Serena! My champ!'

Those words would have stung months before, but Serena played along, knowing how impressed she'd been by his previous mentees. She saw the wet faces near her feet, those strange fish in goggle and caps. They would know her name.

Niko swept her into a hug, and Serena sensed the muscles beneath his shirt, smelled his aftershave. That sharp, lemony scent sent it rushing back – her elation at his praise, the horror of his disappointment – but, holding him in that embrace, he wasn't as broad as she recalled. The span of his shoulders felt reduced. She could see the top of his head, the gleam of scalp that shone through his hair. When they pulled back, his face looked tired, skin weathered by those hours at the poolside, the stress of every race his students swam. It never ended for him. The circle of silver rested on his chest, that metal image of Saint Sebastian, prone and bleeding from so many arrow wounds, holding on through agony until it was hopeless.

With his arms around her middle, Serena knew her body would feel different to him, but she felt proud of that. This man's voice should never have been in her head, twisting her thoughts. It was cruel and unnatural. She had her own power now, heard her own words. The urge to whisper into his ear that she'd brought on her own downfall was almost too strong to resist.

The girls in that pool were taut, as firm and honed as she'd

233

ever been. Muscles with no purpose. She couldn't bear to see what was being trained into them, to glimpse the damage it was inflicting on their bodies and minds, to think of how it would gnarl the lives ahead. She didn't let her gaze linger long enough to assess their form as they swam up and down in that sterile box of water, turning endlessly, going nowhere.

Although she'd passed her test three years before, Serena hadn't used the car. She'd lacked confidence at first, too aware of the one and a half tonnes of death that sat in her hands. Those fears had gone. Nothing could happen to her; she didn't even need to visualise.

Elizabeth had driven them to the sports centre and waited in the café. She now sat in the passenger seat Serena had occupied so many times. Facing forwards, they couldn't see each other's eyes. It was late afternoon, late February and nearing dusk. It had been dark so long that sunlight would feel alarming. Serena dipped the clutch to pull into second gear. The mechanics of the car felt alien after so many months.

Her mother cleared her throat. 'You smell of chlorine.'

Serena didn't reply. It was true.

There was comfort in the rhythm of those pedals, the flow of the gear stick. It felt good to focus on physical actions.

Elizabeth tried again. 'Do you miss it?'

Serena wasn't sure what answer her mother wanted. 'Not any more.' She indicated left, swung the car away from the route home.

'This isn't the right way.'

'I feel like a bit of a drive.' Serena followed the loop until they reached the slip road. The engine of that old Volvo estate whined, so she bumped the gearstick to lower its note.

Her hands were looser on the wheel. She eased into the middle lane, enjoying how simple it was to overtake.

Elizabeth spoke quietly. 'Did you hate it?'

Serena knew what it took for her to ask the question. Those medals had been cleared away at Christmas. Serena had left their twisted metal hooks on the carpet, splinters of wood sticking out, but when she went upstairs to bed, steeling herself for the carnage, they were gone. Two holes remained in the wallpaper where the rack had been wrenched loose, but someone had smoothed the ragged edge of the wall, picked shards from the carpet, cleared the detritus. The handfuls of medals were gone too. Serena imagined her mother folding their ripped ribbons.

'I wouldn't say hate.' Serena could never confess what had happened in her mind before that fall.

'But you don't miss it?'

Serena's eyes didn't leave the road. 'I miss having that purpose. I miss how winning felt. Everything else, no.' She pressed the accelerator and reassessed. 'I missed it at first.' She no longer yearned for the person she'd been when she swam. She didn't need that girl any more.

It was remarkable how the slightest movement of her

right foot made a machine move faster. One tiny nudge and the car lurched forwards. Serena looked at the dial. Sixty-five, seventy.

'Do *you* miss it?' A few raindrops spattered the windscreen, blurring to nothing. She flicked on the wipers, their swish giving the car a pulse.

'It was wonderful.' Elizabeth swallowed. 'It was the most wonderful thing.'

Serena's foot pressed further. Her mother only saw the glory. She'd also been carved into someone who thought a particular way, willingly contorting their family's life for those medals. It would be so simple to push the pedal to the floor. It would offer a release, somewhere for that pent-up energy to flow. Her mother never saw the pain, never understood the sacrifice. She'd competed at county level as a gymnast, but had never reached the stage where pressure bit.

Serena swerved the car into the outside lane. A rattle from the boot: the can of antifreeze that lived there year-round. They sailed past bigger cars, cars with men at the wheel. The wipers thwacked, clearing raindrops as soon as they landed.

'You know, I only ever wanted to encourage you.'

Staring at the road ahead, Serena tightened her hands on the wheel.

'I didn't get that kind of encouragement when I was younger.' 'I was prevented from becoming what I could have been.' Serena had heard those words before. 'They said it would take too much to pursue it. Too much time, too much money.' She'd seen the pictures of her mother in a leotard, hair severe, face bright. 'I've never fully forgiven them for doing that. I never wanted you to feel like you hadn't done all you could.'

The rain was heavier now, the sky a grey sheet of solid water.

'I kept the leotards.'

The swimming medals would be wherever those thirty-five-year-old costumes lived. They'd pushed past eighty now. Other cars were simply lights: red flickers ahead when they braked, white blurs behind them. It was faster than Serena had ever driven. She knew they were safe. Elizabeth's handbag was in her lap to stop it rolling in the footwell, but she wouldn't want Serena to slow. Her own driving was always at speed. Her father stayed at a constant sixty in the inside lane, but Elizabeth sought any opportunity to outflank other cars.

'I'm sorry you had to give that up,' Serena said. Her mother carried her own distress, had her own story to tell.

'We all have to give things up.' The rain pounded, wipers fighting to keep pace.

Serena sighed. 'I don't miss swimming, but I do miss seeing you every day.'

Elizabeth said nothing, but placed her bag back down onto the mat.

Easing her foot from the accelerator, Serena let the car slow.

★   ★   ★

Elizabeth rarely put Delilah down. Cross-legged on the grey carpet, the sinews in her legs were strong. Those thighs had once propelled her into the air so high she had time to flip and contort before landing. Those arms had held her weight so easily she could swing in full circles. Her body was still tight and capable, but as she curled with her tiny granddaughter, there was a softness Serena had never seen.

In that jerking, new-born way, Delilah stretched her left foot. Elizabeth laughed and looked at Kelly.

'With that extension, she'll be a ballerina!'

Serena wanted to beg them to stop, to invent no illustrious future for Delilah, to let her be whatever mundane thing she desired.

As Elizabeth held the baby, the muscles in her arms showed. Ambition was the steel core that ran through her. Serena knew the same blood flowed in her own body. Being ordinary had never been an option.

Serena placed a hand on her mother's shoulder. 'I think you're wrong.'

Elizabeth twisted, a frown forming.

'With that kick, it's going to be martial arts.'

The gums of Elizabeth's mouth showed as she smiled, pink grooves where the roots of her teeth lay. 'You might be right—'

'Well . . .' Kelly's voice cut through the air. When her mother and sister turned, she raised her eyebrows, adopting a sing-song tone, suitable around the baby. 'As long as it's not fucking swimming.'

★   ★   ★

In her arms, the baby was bigger than Serena expected. No Tiny Tears doll, but a thrashing, shouting ball of muscle. At a little over six pounds, it took strength to hold her.

Delilah might not be able to lift her head, and Kelly had explained about the patch on the top of her skull that hadn't yet toughened, but she wasn't delicate. When she slept, her face was gentle, but became solid red when she screamed. The transition was almost instant. If anything troubled her, she hadn't learned to stoically accept, so she roared. A few whimpers were the only warning. Every time, Kelly fussed and shushed her, jiggled up and down as she walked, rocked her from side to side.

There was magnificence to that honesty. The baby bucked in her arms, and Serena was impressed. Even the soft brushed cotton of her yellow onesie couldn't disguise her might. This was the body Serena had imagined, straining her mind so oxygen could reach these thundering lungs. How long would it be before that girl was silenced? Before she had her own story to add to the litany of horror, before she learned to loathe her own flesh? It was too awful to imagine. Nothing should ever dampen her. Delilah's cries were rhythmic and intense. She didn't need to be fed or changed, was simply furious with the world. Serena understood. That scream was timeless, the yell of every mouth ever born. She looked at her niece's tiny face and let her holler.

20

It was as if Jane expected her. No surprise crossed her face as the door opened. Serena had never been alone to that office with its thick scent and rich colours. The velvet throws of the daybed were rumpled. Jane clicked the kettle on and prepared cups, her actions neat and sharp. Being together in the dense, textured space felt intimate.

Serena let her gaze run across Jane's shelves. So many books winked out their gold titles, books Jane knew the secrets of. Her mind must be so full, so faceted. In between volumes were small stone sculptures, ceramic vases, objects of meaning for Jane, curated from her journeys. One photograph in a simple frame. Jane, but not as she was now. She looked in her late teens, the clear openness of youth intact. The girl next to her was striking: dark skin and thick hair that filled half the image. So much like Zara's hair, Serena had to look closer. The girl's red lips were wide with delight.

'That's Nylah.' Jane said nothing else.

'She's beautiful.'

'She was.' Serena clocked the past tense. 'A force of nature.'

Jane stared at her own younger face.

'What does she do now?' Someone as vivid as Nylah must have a formidable life.

The look on Jane's face startled Serena. A flash of distress. 'I don't know.'

Before Serena could respond, Jane flicked the lights off.

Her tone was bright. 'You have immaculate timing, you know. There's a planetary conjunction tonight. Mars and Saturn. Not one of the most intense, but we should be able to see something.'

Pushing the daybed to the window, Jane placed a cushion on its curled iron bars so that they could rest their heads, peer into the darkness. The building's sash windows opened wide.

'It'll take about half an hour for your eyes to adjust, but there's so little light pollution out here we might be lucky.'

Serena climbed on the metal-framed couch next to Jane, their bodies so close she could feel the warmth. Had Jane lain here with Zara? Their proximity in that academic office at night must cross a boundary, but Jane lay calmly, so Serena followed.

The moon was too bright to see the sky. Serena waited, listening to Jane's even breaths. Slowly, the night came into focus. The black of the sky showed shades of blue, paler patches, specks of light all over. The longer she looked, the more stars made themselves known. Layer after layer, further and further away, no clouds to block their view.

Finally, Jane pointed. 'Can you see the reddish star over by that cluster? That's Mars.' Her voice was low, as if she feared spooking the planets.

Serena wished she could. 'Not really, no.'

Jane moved closer, so her eyes could see what Serena's saw.

'You have to focus on Vega, the bright one next to that rectangle. That's the Lyra constellation; follow it and you should see the red star. Saturn's about thirty degrees to the right and looks sort of yellow-gold. They don't flicker like stars. Their light's constant.'

Jane's temple against her own, Serena stared at the sky.

After a minute, Jane spoke in a whisper. 'In astrology, conjunctions are believed to combine the powers of two planets. I don't believe that, of course, but it's an enduring myth. These two are tricky together. Mars is about strength, energy, even anger. Saturn's wisdom, discipline, or ambition. They're apparently combative in conjunction.'

Eventually, Serena's eyes tuned in, and she could make out the stars that didn't sparkle, one that shone red and one golden. They stared until their vision blurred. For those minutes, they might have been the only people on the planet.

'It makes you feel small, doesn't it?'

'Sort of.' Serena swallowed. 'Or maybe part of something bigger.'

She heard Jane exhale. 'I prefer that.'

'That's why I came here.' She let the words flow. 'What you told us about in that first lecture, months ago, has lived with me. The women who drowned. The priests who turned on them. It's haunted me. The absolute horror. I can't look around this place without seeing it. That's what's been missing in what we've done. If we can't talk about what's happening now, we should talk about what happened before. It all connects. Us and those women.'

Serena knew it was garbled. Jane said nothing at first. Staring into that dark seemed to detach Serena's body from the ground. Her hands gripped the daybed to keep anchored. The stars were too close, the planets loomed too large. She spun with the strange vertigo of looking at something enormous.

The silence broke. 'It runs deep with you, doesn't it?'

As they walked, Serena felt her heartbeat in her throat. It thumped like another set of steps behind them in the dark. She and Zara had met Jane at the west gate of the campus and followed her down a narrow road. They entered the woodland through a small gap. It wasn't a forest, but a clutch of trees barely thick enough to hide the waves. Beyond them was the beach. The beach so treacherous it could kill.

Those woods smelled like fire and salt, like the tea Jane brewed in her office. The moon was hidden by clouds, and the dark made everything monochrome. The only colour came from the glow of Jane's torch, a slick Maglite that could focus to a single, sharp beam. Jane's neat elegance appeared urban, but she knew those woods as if she'd grown up there, learned their cambers and twists as a child. Each step of hers was sure.

As their pace picked up, Zara stumbled on a rock, her ankle rolling out of her purple canvas shoes. 'Shit. Sorry, keep going. I'm good.'

Zara had to be there. They needed her on board.

In a clearing, Jane stopped, rotating the torch so its pale light diffused. Serena settled on the leaves, and Zara lay on her front, palms supporting her head, no concern about the cold or the muck beneath.

Jane crossed her legs. 'I thought it best to bring you here. It makes what I'm about to tell you more real.' Her hands moved in that measured way.

A crack of twigs made Zara yelp.

Jane smiled. 'Animals. They won't come too near, but watch this.'

She picked up the torch, casting them into darkness, flashing its fuzzy light in a circle, swift and skilled, fast enough to see, but not to startle.

'Do you see them?'

Two green circles had shone out from the trees nearby, a foot or so off the ground. They looked electronic at first, like computer LEDs, but this wasn't Zara's world of circuits and filters; those bright green orbs were part of the woodland.

'She's close.' Jane's voice was barely audible.

'She?'

Jane propped the torch up. 'Fox.'

Shifting to sit, Zara exclaimed. 'Wow!'

'It's eyeshine. Like red-eye in a photograph. With animals it's more distinct. Different animals show different colours. Green tends to be small mammals, and by the height, you can tell she's a fox. Rodents and birds flash red. Deer a sort of yellowy-green, and apparently bears are orange, but I've never seen one.'

'That's incredible.' Serena hadn't spent time in forests – years had gone by where she'd scarcely been outdoors – but those trees felt familiar.

'Woodlands, even little patches of woodland like this, are teeming with creatures. They're all around if you know where to look.'

The trees seemed to creak with life.

'Some women can smell foxes, you know. A musky, yeasty smell. As much a taste as a smell. Men don't detect it so easily.'

Had the fox stayed, breathing next to them, silently watching the other mammals in her domain, or fled away to safety? Wild creatures must spend their lives in fear, Serena realised. Something was always creeping closer; they were always quarry.

Zara shivered. Her furred jacket and light trainers wouldn't keep in the heat, and the temperature was plummeting.

'Does it scare you?' Jane reached to rub the soft arm of Zara's coat.

'More like a thrill.' Zara's voice clanged in the dark.

Serena wasn't scared; she was mesmerised by those swaying branches.

'I brought you out here to tell you more about Gilly Sampson.' Jane's voice was quiet. Over the rustles and mutterings of the woodland, Serena strained to catch her words.

'Gilly Sampson was a local woman accused of witchcraft, roughly four hundred years ago. There's no documented evidence she did anything that could be deemed ungodly, but Gilly was known as a healer. She created poultices with flowers and herbs, and people recovered speedily from illnesses that would otherwise have ended them. This was considered suspicious. Gilly was thought of as a troublemaker. Records from vestry meetings show several disputes with men of the parish.'

The hard *g* of the woman's name made Serena think of fish in the seawater beyond them.

'She was accused, tried in the usual way, and drowned in the river which now runs along the campus. Bodies were believed to flow down to the sea.' She gestured to the other side of the trees. 'Gilly was different, though. Legends from this area have it that she didn't go so easily.'

A pause let the silence deepen.

'You can imagine how the myths crept out. All island cultures have similar legends – selkies and kelpies in Scotland, nixies in Scandinavia, ningyo in Japan – water spirits, usually female in form or energy, that emerge from the sea to cause havoc.'

Zara leaned close to Jane, her body taut. Serena could smell her heady floral perfume. That enhanced nature felt at odds with their surroundings.

'Stories were told around here that Gilly survived the rocks and lived on in the sea. That she managed to transform her body to breathe underwater and started a new life. They believed she rose from the waves occasionally to seek her vengeance. Men were found injured, horses bolted, sermons calling for the punishment of women were discovered burned or torn. Anything unusual was attributed to her. It was even thought she lured men, standing naked on the shore to captivate passing riders. She would apparently seduce them, then lead them into the water, where they'd drown.'

As Jane spoke, Serena could hardly move. She'd forgotten the cold.

'Gilly is remembered here as a myth, a story. She's remembered in a fancy-dress party for freshers, and apparently a sugary blue cocktail to represent the sea.' Serena was sure Zara had sipped that traitorous drink.

Jane continued. 'She's not understood. She's essentially a joke. But Gilly had good reason to want revenge.'

The torch lit Jane's face from below, casting deep shadows. Her tone was not that of her lecture. She didn't treat them as students, but something far closer. This was conspiratorial.

'The main hall of this university is named after the Earl of Carnforth. As in the Carnforth Club. People say that name here every day, with no sense of the man behind it. The most prominent painting in that room – you know the one – is of Richard Pelham, the third Earl, who once owned most of the land around here. That face stares out at anyone who enters the university, and presides over everyone who graduates from it. He's from a little after my period of study, but I've done the reading.'

Jane's voice stayed slow and calm, but the harder edges of her accent crept in. 'Richard Pelham married a much younger woman and had two children, both boys. When they were twelve and fourteen, the boys went riding in the woods. They didn't return and, the following day, were found dead on a mud path, their horses fled. The Countess sank into a deep grief, and the Earl, unwilling to believe they'd simply fallen, sought retribution. He decided the boys must have been cursed, or their horses bewitched, and in his fervour, accused twelve local women of witchcraft. One of those women was Gilly Sampson.'

Blood thumped in Serena's ears.

'These women had no connection to the boys but were picked one by one and charged on the most tenuous grounds. They were taken from their homes, sleep-deprived, starved and tortured until they confessed, not only to hexing the boys but also to every count of devil worship you can imagine, including seeing visions and having the power to dictate events around them. They were killed for it. All twelve of them.'

The breath left Serena's body. How much did she and Gilly have in common? She also saw visions; she'd worked to heal injured bodies. Was her power the same power women had wielded for centuries? Was the strange, shifting energy that crackled through her ancient?

'They were each drowned in the river we know well. Every time one was murdered, evidence came to light of another conspirator, so she was also dispatched. It took two years for him to kill them all.'

Serena's fingers burned. Men like him had destroyed women like her. Women who had done what she could do.

'Twelve women were tortured and killed at the behest of this man. There may have been more. These women were poor, for the most part, often illiterate, and unable to defend themselves.'

Serena couldn't stay silent. 'This is what we have to talk about.'

'I agree.' Jane nodded. 'Our enemies are no longer kings and bishops, but they're every bit as seditious. Seeing that man's face gaze over us is nothing but an insult. The university wasn't founded until nearly a hundred years after his death, but his family made donations large enough that they could dictate which image sits above us. They donated the hall itself. Carnforth Hall was once the seat of the Pelhams. They lived here before the building became part of the institution. That darkness sits in its bones. Keeping the name, writing it in gold leaf on the sign outside, displaying his image so prominently – lit up and sanctified – doesn't tell history as fact but as propaganda.' The words flowed from her at speed. 'It tells us what to think, holding him as a man to be revered, not a petulant murderer. That risible drinking society rejoices in his name. Having his portrait there is not only insulting, but it makes real change impossible. They can tweak gender pay gap figures, promote one or two women to high-profile roles, but while an image this diabolical hangs, we're seen as expendable. Every story that was shared is insulted.'

Zara put her hand on Jane's shoulder. Serena's fists clenched, rankled by the action. Jane didn't need to be soothed. Jane's anger was necessary. What she told them was urgent. Despite the hundreds of years between them, Gilly was a woman no less real than if she was sitting there, the same earth beneath her limbs, the same sea roaring in her ears. Jane had brought them to that woodland for a reason, as if she could sense what was alive within Serena. Jane could understand Zara's power; Serena's may be just as visible to her.

'I'm not sure how we go about it,' Jane continued. 'But this is the topic we need to tackle.'

Serena agreed. 'Without question. It gets to the heart of everything that's wrong here.'

Jane didn't miss a beat. 'Those women can't be left as footnotes in the history of brutal men.'

Zara made a noise close to a cough. 'Do you think people will care about stories from so long ago?' It was as if she hadn't been listening.

Jane turned to her. 'Zara, you're speaking to two historians.' Serena felt the flutter inside as Jane spoke of them in the same breath.

'No, I'm sure they will, but it's quite a leap from talking about student safety on campus.'

'They will.' Serena barely recognised her voice as her own. 'We have to make it real for them. The actions of the Carnforth Club show that this hasn't stayed in the past. They show the same arrogance. The same abuses of power remain. The same kind of men are doing whatever they want and getting away with it.'

'Zara, are you on board with this?' Jane's voice swooped lower. 'We need you at the helm again.'

The same trees were above their heads as had existed hundreds of years ago, the same salt on the air.

'Are you up for it?'

Zara's eyes were wide. If a torch had been swung in a circle, they would have shone out like beacons.

@zarakarmic • 208k followers

I'm out here among the trees and it is magical.

The Japanese have a term – shinrin-yoku – which means forest bathing. I think that's beautiful.

It means absorbing the energy and atmosphere of the woodland and the creatures that live within it.

It's so vital to take the time to immerse ourselves in nature.

I don't know about you, but it's where I remember what's most important.

21

The glow was clear for over a mile. A square of flickering light in the dark night. To get there, the group headed north of the campus, along paths that skirted several fields, deep into the cut-off mainland. Students walked in clutches, surely gaining a thrill from the oddness, in this strange corner of coast so far from where most had grown up. Ostara was rarely cele-brated in its raw form. The tradition persisted in that small northern nook, marking the moment when day and night reach equilibrium. Serena had grasped sketchy details. Local farmers pledged the last sheaf from their harvest. This stash was preserved, then soaked, bundled and woven into an intri-cate corn dolly, known as Lady Corn. She was propped up for days so that children could garland her with flower crowns.

The fairground was like a false dawn. Hours raced back-wards as they stepped into that neon throb. The lights jarred with their surroundings. It wasn't that kind of coastline; it was dank with history, not glitzy and sparkling. As they entered the throng, taking in the food stalls and mechanical rides, Serena was thrown. She'd expected something weirder, more archaic. This was every fairground she'd ever visited, with shrieks from the Ferris wheel, ghost train, dodgems. A transatlantic twang through loudspeakers, urging them to scream. *Slide to the end and squash your friend*. Caramelised onions and candyfloss making the air sticky. Pop songs dialled to unrecognisable bassy notes.

That bright square of activity forced their bodies into a state of exhilaration, drilled their heart to its rhythm. Serena could taste sugar and smoke. Everything fizzed. Zara and Keira knew the song playing and shouted the words to each other, pouting and posing like a music video. University could seem like a holding pattern for childhood, keeping them just this side of adult expectations. It let the teenager in each of them rule for a moment longer. Even Dean walked with a bounce.

Zara corralled the group towards a ride decorated as a kraken, each of its glittering tentacles gripping a metal-barred seat. The others joined the queue, but Serena shook her head. Adrenalin felt toxic now. Her veins had already pulsed a lifetime's dose. With Keira's rucksack on one shoulder, Zara's crossbody on the other, she watched.

Jane joined her, cradling a polystyrene carton of chips. 'I've only ever been on rides like this once.' She paused. 'It's not fear – I never saw the point.'

Even in the muddy, crowded field, Jane's long black coat

looked sleek. She didn't use the wooden fork, but lifted each chip with her fingers, licking salt and sauce off as she spoke. It was somehow precise.

'Nylah loved this sort of thing. It made more sense with her.'

Serena clocked Nylah's name. 'What . . . ?' She tightened her core to ask the question. 'What happened with Nylah?' She didn't know if Jane would reply.

'I knew her at Oxford, as an undergrad. We met on the first day and . . .' Jane exhaled sharply. 'It sounds dramatic, but I felt like my life had started.'

'That's intense.'

The others waved from the queue, trepidation and excitement building as they waited.

Jane took a few deliberate breaths, then spoke rapidly over the noise of the crowd. 'I knew I liked girls, but until that moment it had been a distant longing for members of the netball team. I'd never been bold enough to aim that pent-up affection at anyone. But Nylah was unafraid. We'd kissed by the end of freshers' week.' She turned to face Serena. 'No one had ever kissed me before.'

It felt like Jane understood, like she saw something familiar when she looked at Serena. Like she could confide in her. Jane tilted the trough of chips in an offer, and their hands touched as Serena picked one from the edge.

'If I ever have a year better than that, I'll be dazzled. I didn't think a life like mine could hold something so perfect.' Jane's lips stretched in a smile that made her look years younger. 'It wasn't that she was beautiful – although she was – it's that she was simply the most alive person I've ever known.'

Zara settled into the ride's seat, that thick, dark hair splayed across its metal and plastic. Did Jane look at her and see someone else? The loudspeaker voice urged people to join the ride, performing a live cost-benefit analysis before activating. *Take a seat for the ride of your life.* Keira and Dean saluted, strapped firmly by the seat's black bars, their legs dangling. *Can you tame the kraken? Can you handle the beast? Come on up and join the ride.*

Jane's story kept flowing. 'Nylah was openly ambitious in ways I'd been taught to hide. And she was endlessly inspiring. Her essays sparkled; I used to read them in awe, not fathoming how someone my age could possibly have such confidence. She was in a band. They played the kind of music I'd never listened to before, but it was captivating. I'd stand and watch her sing on those stages, her hair whipping through the air, her voice so powerful, dazzled that she'd picked me out of everyone who clearly adored her.'

Serena noticed Jane's cheeks becoming pinker under the lights.

'She stood uncontested to become JCR Vice President. Every other member of that committee was a white man from considerable privilege – so much like the Carnforth Club – but Nylah was there with her South London accent and no-bullshit attitude. She stood in their seats of power.'

Jane's eyes were not quite focused, lost to memories in that noise.

'Everything was blissful for this precious moment of time.' Her free hand seemed to hold it in the air. 'But the thing with bubbles is you don't know they're about to burst.'

She paused. 'There was a knock at my door in the early hours. They'd had some kind of committee night out, a posh dinner thing. She'd worn this beautiful midnight-blue strappy dress. It was the dress I noticed when I opened the door. Then I saw she was sobbing.'

The ride began to move, and Zara's excited squeal reached them. The kraken heaved its seats slowly at first, from one side of its base to the other, tentacles intersecting.

'The dress was ripped at the neckline; her hair was everywhere. She couldn't get the words out and I'm not sure I ever knew what happened that night. Whatever it was, it was awful.'

Serena didn't speak.

'I saw enough, though. Her bloodied lip, her torn dress, the look on her face. She wouldn't tell me what they'd done. She didn't like men that way – she would never have encouraged them.'

Serena moved closer to hear Jane over the music. The trough was half full, but the chips had grown cold.

'She didn't want me to report it to the college, but I did anyway. I don't know if that was a betrayal. I couldn't stay quiet. Their response was horrific. Without a statement from

Nylah, they refused to do anything. I tell a lie, they offered to move her to a different room in the building. But no repercussions, no punishments.'

Jane's voice was firm, the memories clearly raw. 'The committee secretary was this little weasel, Felix. He'd been there that night, and he'd seen what happened. He was an acolyte, the sort who follows brasher, better boys and loves being at the centre of everything. His best friend was the JCR president. He was a boastful creep, always reminding us that *Felix* means "lucky". I knew him – he was my tutorial partner – so I went to him, and I begged. I begged him to tell me what he knew, to tell the college. But he wouldn't. The little shit kept quiet. Men like him always watch their backs.' The anger shimmered from Jane, rising through the fug of lights and music.

'The college brushed the whole thing off. With no hard evidence, they vanished it, carried on as if nothing had happened. But Nylah was crushed. I always thought of her as so robust, but she just shattered. It was a few missed essays at first – radically out of character – then, utter despair. I'll never forget the look on her mum's face when she came to pack her things.'

Jane's voice sank lower, heavy with a decade of emotion. 'She thought I could have protected Nylah, but there was nothing I could do. Not then, not at that age.' She was fierce for a second. 'Now, I'd destroy them.'

The ride was in full flow, lurching each tentacle one way,

then halting, pausing for full seconds before reversing as rapidly. Faces dashed towards Jane and Serena. Zara's mouth wide, in focus for a flash, zooming towards them, then gone.

'All I could do was watch as she crumpled. I haven't seen her since that Christmas. She wouldn't return calls or letters. She must have thought I'd abandoned her. We didn't have the language then. I didn't have the strength.'

Jane sighed, her whole body shuddering. 'I can't bring myself to google her name. I don't want to know how she is, in case she's not okay. I should have done more. I'll never regret anything as much.'

'That's the most terrible thing. I'm so sorry.' Serena reached out to touch Jane's arm.

Jane nodded, her lips pressed.

The ride lifted dramatically, adding an extra dimension to its careening seats. As the body rose, the hydraulics of the beast were revealed. Dark pistons and cylinders, the mechanics of the mythical giant that would upturn ships and devour their crew.

'I've never known anyone like Nylah, and I failed her.'

Jane didn't watch the ride, couldn't see the blurs of colour as their friends sped by.

'That's not true.' Serena dipped her head to meet Jane's eyes. 'Nothing that happened was your fault. You know what people like that are willing to do.'

The kraken tilted perilously, sending some cars high, swooping others to the ground, working with then against gravity. That mechanism had been bolted together only days before. It was both mighty and precarious.

@zarakarmic • 203k followers

I'm not sure if you can hear, I'll have to shout over the music, but I bloody love a carnival.

My inner child is having an absolute ball. The colours, the lights, the candyfloss, everything.

This gypsy soul is fed by adrenalin, and there's nothing better than being flung around on a fairground ride.

Scream if you wanna go faster!

In a beat, the energy of the crowd altered. Without any announcement, they surged towards the dark field, away from loudspeakers and painted wood and blinking cabochon bulbs. Serena moved with them, stepping off the fairground's plastic flooring onto mud that sank beneath her trainers. After minutes of walking, the music became nothing but tinny pops on the air. The centre of the field was the main event. There was Lady Corn, larger than any human woman, propped upright with her head lolling. Her dress was made from bulky bound sheaves, but her face was a fan of the softest corn, marked to show eyes and mouth.

She was languid, her limbs relaxed. She can't have known what was coming.

Lady Corn watched through blank eyes – representing abundant fertility through no will of her own – as a group of men gathered nearby. They lit rags tied to the ends of thick wooden sticks. The flames gave their features the sheen of something ancient, they were not modern men, but were cast in bronze, carved from wood. Men from an older, fiercer time, carrying their torches with intent.

Serena tried to catch Jane's eye, but Jane was listening to Zara chattering about the kraken. She stared alone as the men walked towards Lady Corn. An urge seized her. She wanted to rush from the crowd and place herself – arms outstretched – between the corn woman and these men bent on destruction, to make them go through her first. There wasn't time to focus her mind on stopping them, but it was too awful to witness. The ritual apparently signified the cyclical cleansing of the land, necessary to bring in fresh life, but that felt like bullshit. Serena held back a scream as they placed their torches against the stiff woven stalks of the corn woman's skirts. That corn, harvested months ago, was brittle and took to flames in a heartbeat. The tassels of Lady Corn's face remained serene, placid in the sight of horror. She didn't flinch as her skirt, then her breasts, then neck and hair set light. A cheer swelled from the crowd. Children waved miniature corn dollies. It took no time for her devastation to be complete.

A group of women gathered, the way Serena knew women

always have, to sluice away the carnage caused by men. They tied skirts over their jeans and leggings, sending themselves back centuries, their actions smooth with practice. Each of the six women held an identical wooden-clad bucket filled with seawater. Someone must have gone to the shore, lugged those heavy tubs back. It displayed the coastal community's protection of its crops. Walking in a ragged line, they smiled in the embarrassed delight of being watched.

Smears of modern make-up made no difference: they were the same women who'd always lived here, who'd always trodden this earth, tended these fields, harnessed this water. They knew what happened to women on this land. Did they participate in relief that it wasn't them being burned? One by one, they threw their buckets of salt water into the blaze, altering nothing. A rubber hose attacked the fire from behind, hidden from the crowd, until the flames guttered.

Parts of Lady Corn had somehow survived. Her skirts had perished, but her limbs remained intact, their bright yellow gloss charred. As the smoke lifted, her impassive smile was calm in the dark.

The music behind Serena still thumped, rides still lurched wildly into the air. Children were pulled back from the smouldering mound for their own safety. Everything smelled of smoke and salt.

Why did this ritual require the brutal annihilation of a woman? She'd been formed with such skill and care, women's hands gently weaving each part of her, flower garlands placed on her head with reverence. Yet no one cared that she'd been wrecked.

The men who'd lit the fire whooped in exhilaration at what they'd done. Serena felt heat, not from the quenched flames, but inside her, clawing at her blood. The rest of her group were lost to the crowd; there was no one to understand her despair. Another woman had been destroyed in full sight while people smiled and explained it was the way things had always been. The men clapped each other's backs in celebration. The tallest of them was the loudest, shouting his delight to the night. Serena couldn't save Lady Corn, that damage was done. But she could avenge her.

She wanted that man to understand fear for a moment. The heat already flowed. *He falls to the ground.* Her own words in her ear. *He can't get back up.* Serena stared at the man from across the field, his features contorted in terrible happiness. Could her slippery ability encompass this? *He falls so hard he's hurt.* She'd never deliberately visualised someone's pain. The fury that surged down every vein, every muscle, was visceral, a darkness she'd never known. Maybe they were right about the women who'd lived on this land. Maybe they had consorted with the devil, jigged with him until daylight, shocked him with their shadowy powers. Serena stared at the man as her words continued. *He falls. He falls. He falls.*

Heat and anger coursing through her, Serena watched as the man lost control of his feet on the rough scrub, faltered, then fell. The landing was messy and hard. His guttural cry reached her. She was in control. She'd made his body do her bidding. He fell with some force and stayed there. The wind had been knocked from him, leaving him breathless and useless on the muddy land. Serena smiled. He'd easily recover, but for one pure moment he could feel it. He'd seen a flash of the horror those women knew. Lady Corn, Nylah, Tanya, Gilly Sampson. All targeted by men like him. For a second, they had reprisal. His body was not his own. Staring at the charred, salted corpse of the corn goddess on the pyre, Serena knew exactly what they needed to do next.

22

@zarakarmic • 191k followers

As you know, I love to chart the waxing and waning of our lunar goddess. She rules over us in all her phases, whether she's a tiny fingernail in the sky or a full luscious orb.

According to my moon almanac – which is the most gorgeous book, look at these illustrations – Saturday night will welcome a full Pink Moon, named after springtime wildflowers. It's also known as the Awakening Moon, and should be bigger and brighter than any other time this year.

If you identify as a woman, join us by the sea. It's time to get serious. Now we take back control.

Electricity didn't reach the beach. There was no microphone, no lights; nothing felt authorised. Thirty or more girls had arrived in small groups, walking the half-mile from campus along the woodland and onto the moonlit beach. Zara had been right about the moon. It was so massive it looked artificial. She'd made clear this event – the first of the new term – was for those who identified as women, those who sensed the pull of that tide. Serena associated seawater with Luke but was glad he wasn't there. They needed to high-light the women who'd perished, and the boys understood to duck out.

The beach was charged that night, as if fish had swum too close to the shore, as if animals crouched in the scrub-land. Seagulls cawed their deathly croaks, hidden by the dark. Everything prickled. Those shimmering green eyes reflected in the forest might be all around. A pile of logs was being gathered in the middle of the sand, someone carrying the ones dry enough to burn from the woodland. A girl Serena didn't know flicked a lighter grate over and over to ignite the bark.

'We need tinder and kindling for that to work.' Keira pushed her hair back with a band as she took charge of building the fire.

Zara joined her within moments. 'What can we use?'

'Anything that'll burn easily. Paper or leaves are usually good, then twigs to keep it going.' Serena watched as a stack of small branches was collected and layered.

'I can help with the tinder.' Zara pulled a handful of

tampons from her bag: eco-friendly, organic cotton lozenges. As soon as the lighter was held near, they whipped into flames and the fire took hold, twigs coaxing the logs to burn.

The fire raged, sending out harsh new warmth. Flames so close to the ocean were thrilling, as if the elements might do battle. The skin of Serena's face stung in the heat. Did no one else remember the fire from the fairground? Did the crackle of Lady Corn's flaming skirts hiss in no other ears?

Serena turned to the water. It was here Luke had nearly died. It was here Gilly had lived on. She tasted salt on her lips. Dark shapes moved against the sky, shadows visible when they blocked a star, seabirds flying in the night, or bats swooping for insects. The moon was unfeasibly large. Serena kicked off her trainers, paying no heed to where they landed, and let the seawater cover her feet. The cold was soothing. The clocks had recently gone forward, and there was a spark of spring in the air. She took another step to feel the water on her ankles, then another. The same bold steps Luke had taken. The chill thrummed through her. The sea was nothing like the swimming pool. It was old and cruel and had killed. The water she knew was sterile, hollow. This water was real.

This water stretched thousands of miles. It reached women all over the world, women who faced far worse dangers. Distance didn't matter in this water. Time didn't matter. It turned stone and glass into sand, made everything tempo-rary. Gilly Sampson had stood on this same shore. As the tide raged in and out of the bay, it might be on their side. It might keep the bones of those women safe. Serena reached down, forming her hands into scoops to hold the water for a moment. It could be gentle as well as destructive.

Turning back, she watched the bodies on the beach. Sparks from the flames danced like they had volition. Those figures lit by the fire were less than a mile from that hallowed campus, but it could be a hundred. If you took away their phones and trainers and hairstyles, that gathered group of university girls was no different from the destroyed women Jane had told them about. On that beach, in that darkness, it all connected.

Light from the burgeoning fire cast twisting shadows. From a distance, Zara's hair moved of its own accord. Her silhouette writhed as Serena watched her head towards Jane. They spoke, words shielded by their cuffs. Jane's fingers tangled in the dark of Zara's hair.

Walking further up the beach, Serena's damp feet sank into the sand. The fire caught in her lungs, burning her throat. When she looked again their heads were touching. Their mouths were hidden behind cupped hands, and it was impossible to tell if they were talking or kissing. Were Zara's lips on Jane's? Serena couldn't see clearly in the flickering dark, didn't know if anyone else was watching. Was Zara's deep berry stain on Jane's pale mouth? Jane who had taught them so much. Was Jane willing to risk her job? Was she thinking of Nylah? Whether Zara's mouth touched Jane's or not, it was Serena who Jane confided in.

Whatever had happened behind those fingers seemed to feed Zara's energy, and she strode forward as they stepped apart. She held a megaphone, a clumsy grey cone with a strap that wrapped around her wrist, pressing its button, readying it to boom out her mechanised voice. But, before she could speak, Jane held her arm, stopping her actions. Serena saw her cousin's forehead crease, her mouth slacken. Jane lifted the device from her hands. Zara's face contorted further, but Jane gave a single firm nod. Without turning, Jane seemed to know where Serena was, and paced towards her.

Serena understood what was happening. She didn't look at Zara, didn't want to see her eyes. Jane handed her the megaphone like an offering.

Blood beat in Serena's ears, behind her eyes, under the skin of her face. She pressed the button she'd seen Zara press. Her voice was instantly epic.

'We came to this beach because they wouldn't listen. We asked for almost nothing, only to be safe.' Her words clattered through the mechanism. 'To be safe from being drugged and killed, from stumbling to our deaths in a place we pay thousands to call home. We didn't demand much, and we were punished for it. We told our stories, and we were silenced.'

Dozens of women had gathered on that beach. They stood, listening.

'We came to this beach because this is where murdered women once washed up.' Serena registered shock in their faces. They hadn't all heard Jane's lecture. 'This land we walk on has a bloody history. Horrific acts took place and so many women were killed.'

The sea rumbled, urging her on. She knew its tides had her back. The moon that gazed over them was benevolent.

'Women were tried as witches at Leysham, on our beautiful campus grounds. They were found guilty and were destroyed for it.'

Serena remembered how she'd felt when Jane first told these stories. She raised her voice even louder.

'These women were not only killed but tortured first. Screws were tightened on their thumbs, iron cases heated on their legs, slabs pressed on their chests, until they confessed, until they accused and denounced each other. These trials were not about truth, but power.'

Serena couldn't keep her words as measured as Jane's had been. It was too personal. 'Then they were killed – sometimes hanged or burned, but around here they were drowned. They were dragged, wrenched by the hair until they were bloody, then thrown into the freezing river. The water we walk by. That raging stretch of river by Bowland Gate. Tell me you haven't sensed it?'

Serena looked out to the women. Jane's eyes were fixed on her, undeviating. 'They were held in that black water so long their lungs seared, so long they had no choice but to gulp. If they didn't die quickly enough, more elaborate deaths were created. There was no escape. There has never been any escape.' Her amplified words boomed in the dark.

'Their bodies would end up here.' She pointed to the water behind her. 'These women did nothing we don't do. Which of us wouldn't be deemed troublesome or immoral? Which of us doesn't step out of line? We're all here chasing an education that was unthinkable even a hundred years ago. We all conduct ourselves in ways that would have been deemed wanton. Our freedoms are so new, and they still want to rip them away. It's precarious, and we can't take it for granted. The reasons they concocted then are the same reasons we're treated terribly now, the same reasons we're dismissed by men who think they should decide how we behave. They still think we're less than they are, that we don't deserve autonomy. We are the most advantaged women in history. But, even with our abundant privilege, we are still attacked, still frightened, still belittled. And every one of us fights it every day. We are no different from them. Which of us would not be called witch?'

Those women centuries ago were no different from them. Serena knew they'd have looked in wonder at the brightness of the moon, cupped their hands to catch the ocean. The fire would have tugged their lungs too.

'But these women weren't murdered. They were convicted and legally executed. They haven't been pardoned in most places. They died criminals and remain so to this day. Where are the memorials to these women? Where are the apologies?' Serena's breath shook.

'There is a painting in Carnforth Hall of a man who destroyed at least a dozen women. Twelve women no less alive than any of us. No less scared, no less wonderful and no less real. Dead by his command. It is an offence to everyone who walks past that image. We stare into the face of an oppressor, and it lessens us all. It tells predatory men they'll not only be tolerated, they'll be praised. This man killed Gilly Sampson. Gilly Sampson, who we party in the name of. A disgusting group of Leysham men call themselves after him and act in his memory. We know who they are. We know what they do and what they get away with because they have money and prestige on their side. We should stand against them. We should preserve Gilly's legacy, avenge her murder.'

The group around Serena clapped, the smack of their hands lifting into the dark air.

'This is no time to be polite. We don't need to be liked. We don't need to gain followers.' It sounded harsher than Serena had intended. 'We know we're on the right side of history. If those women were witches, then we all are. We fight for them and for ourselves.'

The heat moved through Serena, from her hands to every part of her. 'They'll tell us we're being irrational, but it's not their destruction being celebrated.'

Niko's words were in her ear, this time welcome. *You are so powerful.* They formed in her mouth.

'You are so powerful. We are so powerful.'

She shouted into the grey cone, knowing her words would blast. The sea roared behind her, adding its applause. Did Gilly cheer along from its depths?

'What is a witch but a woman with power?'

Heat surged through Serena's core. No images accompanied it. She didn't need them; there was nothing she'd change. Her power was magnified on that sand. No longer hemmed in by the sterile lines of the pool, looking out at those waves she was indestructible. Her body had once cut through water, faster than anyone. This felt better. No fear, no stomach plunge. She was part of the earth, not just coinciding with the ebbs of the moon, but dragged by them.

The bottom of Serena's jeans clogged with sand. She removed them in one fluid motion, her legs bare to the breeze. Her hand grazed her calves. The ritual of shaving each inch twice over was gone. She stroked against the grain, enjoying the prickles that grew there, the mammalian soft-ness of them. It was impossible to stay still, so she let her body move. With no music, the waves gave their own beat. Other women watched as her feet stamped, her arms reached upwards. Her body had been controlled by her mind for so long. Now, it led.

Keira was steps away, staring at Serena. Her eyes looked alert, as if she could tell what her friend was thinking. Serena's feet pounded the sand as she moved up the beach. Slowly,

Keira followed her movements. By the fire, Serena's jumper and coat were stifling. She shed both, unsure where they fell. In underwear, her skin was exposed to the heat and the wind and the salt.

Keira unwound her scarf, pulled her jumper over her head, yanked the band from her hair and began to dance the way Serena was dancing. More girls moved with them. This was not the calculated strut of a nightclub, but something primal. It was not about how they looked, but how they felt. Serena leaned back and whooped, the sound coming from her stomach. She'd never made a noise so loud. The sound, like an animal cry, echoed. Keira joined her, howling into the dark. Others followed, filling the air with their yells. Yells of rage or freedom or strength or glee. These women were invincible. This is what men were frightened of. They were absolutely right to be frightened.

The beautiful, righteous rage was no longer stuck in Serena's body; it infiltrated them all. Everything built up inside was released. She was surrounded by women who'd been judged for every action, touched in ways they dreaded, told their bodies were not their own, made to fear when they should be bold, sold the idea of empowerment so they'd buy more things, diminished in a thousand tiny ways every day. Even those gilded girls had been called every name they could imagine. Slut, slag, whore, cunt, bitch, witch. In other parts of the world were women with struggles Serena could barely comprehend. They were bound by something dark. It lived in the inky mulch of them, the deep peaty richness they shared. The horrors they knew. Their combined feet found a rhythm. Arms whirled. Not frenzy but unity. Women were so often pitted against each other, safer isolated as rivals. When they pushed in the same direction, it was overwhelming.

They moved together, drumming the sand flat. That beat was ancient. Had women performed this same ritual for millennia, somewhere between the earthly and the divine? Serena glimpsed Keira, bright green bra and pants against her dark skin. Final items of underwear were removed as they danced around the fire, like the women who'd trodden that land centuries before, like the etching on Jane's door. That prestigious university couldn't ignore them, couldn't contain them. Their flesh was hallowed. Their power indisputable.

Suddenly, Zara. Not dancing, but hurrying to take off her dress and tights. Alarm in her eyes. She was no longer in control. Serena didn't stop, but moved to the other side of the bonfire, arms snaking. She hardly knew those dancing girls. Zara had earned their attention, but they followed Serena. Every one of them looked to her. As Serena danced, leading the other women, she whipped her head to find Jane. Jane stood to the side, fully dressed and unmoving, but staring at Serena with a growing smile.

23

Jane handed Serena a segment of tangerine. Just one, between her thumb and forefinger, furred white like a tiny animal. Serena didn't want to eat it, just cosset it in her palm, but Jane offered, so she placed it in her mouth, where it popped. They'd been walking for over an hour.

When Jane had called, she'd made no mention of Zara, and Serena knew they'd set off alone. She still wasn't sure what she'd seen between those two on the beach. She and Jane walked in silence, leaving the campus immediately on tracks Jane knew by heart, with no maps or apps to guide the way. Jane set the pace. Serena's legs were longer, but she fought to keep up. Jane didn't slow for her; she'd seen some of what Serena was capable of.

Their breaths became synchronised, their muscles strained in the same rhythm. According to her timetable, Serena should have been in a lecture, sitting next to Keira, tapping notes into her laptop, but this felt so much more important.

Stopping, eventually, on a cluster of smooth rocks, Jane pulled a Thermos from her rucksack, poured dark brown liquid into the cap and handed it to Serena. Bracing herself for the bitterness of coffee, her mouth flooded with salt.

'Bone broth, great for hiking.' Jane sipped from the neck of the flask.

The broth was deeply savoury, as rich as blood as it flowed down Serena's gullet, warming her from the marrow out. On that brisk day, Jane was at one with the elements. Her clothes were immaculate, but her nose and cheeks were whipped red, stark against her pale skin.

'How's research going?' Serena tried to keep up with Jane's work.

Rearranging her wiry frame on a stone slab, Jane nodded. 'Not bad. I've won a small grant to spend some time back in Scotland. Outside Aberdeen, there are kirks and chapels with handwritten sermons well preserved. They have significantly better archival resources there, and it will round out my monograph.'

'That's fantastic.'

'Yes. It's coming together for my submission date, but it's near-impossible to focus. My contract ends in the summer, and it's horribly precarious. With so few early career jobs, everything I do has to be leveraged: teaching, conference papers, publications. Nothing exists organically. It's draining.' Jane tilted her Thermos to drink more. 'And there's so much competition it becomes vicious.'

Serena watched Jane's throat ripple as she swallowed, the tiny hairs on her skin golden in the light. 'Really?'

'Academia shrouds itself in high-mindedness, but I've never seen such a den of vipers.' Her voice wasn't quiet in the open field. She spoke from deep in her chest. 'It's simply one of the most hierarchical, misogynistic spaces it's possible to enter. Of course Leysham loves the Carnforth Club. Keira was right about Peregrine Carnegie: he was a former member, and does anything he can to encourage them, even though it's all terribly hush-hush. He makes sure they have keys to whichever rooms they like, can buy those absurd capes at university-approved shops, makes sure any problems are cleared up. They love the glamour of it, the Oxbridge sheen. Every rumour about those boys drinking port from the skull of a wild boar just adds to it.'

She paused. 'Aesthetically, this place is chasms from high finance, but the energy's not far off. I hadn't realised how much I'd have to watch my back.'

Serena rested the lid on her knee. 'Anyone specific?'

Jane sighed. 'Yes, one new colleague. Nicholas. Dr Matthews. Are you taking any of his classes this term?'

Relieved, Serena shook her head.

'He's my age but a research fellow, so more senior and more secure. He's maddeningly unassuming. Tweed and brown brogues, couldn't ask for a nicer guy. But he's wary of me and always slyly critical of my research.'

A slight underbite pushed her lips into a downturn, a

perpetual petulant frown. 'He finds these subtle ways to imply my work is reductive, that I'm forcing an agenda rather than uncovering historical truth. He focuses on the same period, but, as you can imagine, from an entirely imperial perspective.' Her voice carried on the air. 'The machinations of kings are apparently more robust than the persecutions of women.'

Did Jane think of how they'd danced on that beach, of what Serena had unlocked?

Jane looked into the wind. 'He was a peer reviewer of a journal I submitted to recently, and essentially rejected the piece by giving so many queries it was impossible to salvage. He understands how important these things are for academic CVs. The submissions are anonymised, but he knows my research interests well enough to recognise my work in a second.' Her anger was palpable. Serena felt her blood heat at the idea of someone hurting Jane.

Jane turned back to Serena. 'You were magnificent, by the way.' She did think of it. 'I need to channel that fierceness.'

His faculty webpage was easy to find. Dr Nicholas Matthews. A posed picture in front of a bookcase, tweed jacket, open-necked shirt. His face looked no older than Jane's, but his clothes belonged to a retiree. His expression was neutral, a half-smile like an actor's headshot. Alongside the picture was a dull paragraph listing his research interests – *Political Unrest in Jacobean London, English Constitutional Conflicts of the Seventeenth Century.*

His face was almost handsome, could be mistaken for it in the right light. When you looked closer, you saw the tension in his mouth, the skin too tight across his cheekbones. There was cruelty in those brittle features. Serena could see the character Jane had described, the cost of his public school present in the planes of his face, the ruthless gloss it had gifted him. The speed with which she disliked this man she'd never met took Serena aback.

The images came swiftly. It was no longer a strain. She was in control, could tap into the energy that had flowed on the beach. She hadn't gathered enough detail to conjure a specific cause, so focused instead on his response, on the delicious horror as it landed.

Outrage flashes across that genial face. People like him didn't face setbacks. *A brief snarl on thin lips.* Heat flowed through Serena's arms immediately, as she'd expected. From her fingertips to her skull to torso to waist to knees to toes. *His brow creases right down the middle.* Serena didn't need to know what had triggered his indignation. *His fists clench against the wood of his desk.* The images were bright in her mind. *He tries to maintain a dignified stance, but the paper in his hand ruckles under the force.* Serena sensed his seething rage, as if the picture onscreen grew sentient. He barely restrained himself from tipping the desk. She smiled. Whatever had sparked his response was significant.

The phone's beep woke Serena. She'd set up a Google alert with his name. Academics engender little news, so she'd expected nothing for days, but here he was. The inbox link took her straight to the Times Higher Education website. His name was in the first paragraph. *Dr Nicholas Matthews.* The same picture Serena had stared at. Taut lips, blank eyes.

It was an allegation of plagiarism from two postgraduate students, claiming he'd lifted substantial parts of their work for a journal article and his upcoming monograph. It constituted academic misconduct. So, that's what had tripped his fury. Serena grasped elements of the story. The pressure it outlined matched Jane's description: a brutal environment with the need to produce high-level papers at impossible speed. Nicholas had fathomed how to slicken his route. Men like him got away with so much, but this time was different. The university was reserving judgement while they assessed the case, but it could devastate his career. It had to. This man would not hinder Jane again.

Serena ran her fingers across her laptop. She took her class notes methodically now, not typing random clutches of words. She stroked each bevelled key. Hurrying into the classroom, Keira placed a takeaway cup of hot chocolate next to her. Serena had come to accept her love of its sweetly unsophisticated taste, rejecting the need to punish herself with bitterness. Smiling her thanks for the drink, Serena stopped. Keira's eyes were off kilter, asking a question she didn't want to utter.

'What is it?' Serena didn't care if the rest of the class heard.

Keira's face stayed twisted as she fumbled in her pocket, swiped her phone twice and handed it over.

The image was too fuzzy to see without squinting. Pale shapes against dark. A spray of orange. It took a moment for Serena's eyes to adjust. The beach. Two weeks ago. Bodies moving around the fire. Limbs at odd angles. Shadows and colours more than people. Only Serena was in focus, open mouth, wild eyes, skin where there would usually be clothes. Her hair, caught in mid-air, was longer than she'd realised. She stared at the bold, bright O of her nipples. Her breasts had grown heavy now she allowed herself to eat.

It should feel invasive to be exposed, shown naked to the world. It should feel cruel, but Serena marvelled at the shape she formed on that phone's screen. The image might not look pretty, but it did look glorious. It looked how she'd felt, her skin radiant in the firelight. There was no doubting her conviction. It reminded her of pictures taken as she swam, mid-race, with her face set, her hands in prayer. The energy of the dance was somehow palpable in that static photograph. The beautiful fury and hope were alive in its pixels. No wonder they'd stared.

'You understand we have to take action over this.'

The female Proctor wore a necklace of large, bright plastic orbs strung together, the pattern of each blended like the glass of a marble.

'Students have the right to protest, but as you know, this must be sanctioned ahead of time.'

Her dress was soft grey jersey, but her jacket sat rigid. She spoke words they'd read in the previous letter.

'We understand our students are adults, but you are still within the jurisdiction of the university, and you have agreed to the code of conduct.'

A narrow man sat beside her, the second Proctor. He was unmoving except for the occasional worrying of his beard with his fingertips.

Neither Serena nor Zara spoke.

The first Proctor continued. 'From what other participants have told us, you two were at the centre of this event, along with Dr Sinclair. Is that correct?' Her mouth was a pinch of cerise lipstick.

Someone must have relayed the details of Zara's invitation, of how Serena had danced. Surely the same person who'd uploaded that image and scattered it across campus. The morning after Serena had seen it, she'd received the email ordering her and Zara to attend a meeting.

She'd stared at the picture – screen-grabbed by Keira – for hours. Her arms and legs at angles she'd never imagined, as if she was taking flight. Her hair soaring, no part of her touching the ground. The image was assumed to be provocative. The women pictured were read as seductive, but that was wrong. There had been no audience, just their brilliant bodies learning how to move from instinct, fathoming how to connect with themselves, with each other. Serena could scarcely comprehend that anyone had stopped that night, in that charged moment, taken their phone from their bag and snapped a photograph, but she was delighted. She hoped the picture had reached Luke's phone. She hoped he'd zoomed in, his fingers stretching outward on the screen, her skin in close-up. That body he'd known, now magnificent. The image lighting the dark of his room before he slept.

Serena saw Zara nod.

The Proctor cleared her throat, the spheres of her necklace clattering. 'Not only do we have a duty of care to protect the wellbeing and safety of our students, but we have to act against anything that can discredit the university. The actions depicted in this image qualify as indecent and, even though they occurred off campus, they constitute a breach, especially given the attention they've generated.'

The male Proctor stroked his beard, still silent.

They'd tapped into some ancient force on that beach. The image caught some flicker of it in twelve megapixels. The reprimand was absurd. Serena tried to keep herself calm. Their challenge to the university was to protect others. They should never have to apologise. This institution let the Carnforth Club run riot. The website testimonials were clear. They knew what was going on and did nothing, their minds on donations that might flow in twenty years' time, from people with names in the worst of high places.

Zara's voice rang out, loud and too fast. 'You have to understand, we didn't think anything like that would happen. It wasn't a protest as such, but a small gathering of a few friends on the beach. We're sorry how it ended. It got out of control.' She gasped at the end of the utterance.

Serena breathed in through her nose, letting her belly rise as she filled her lungs, then out through her mouth, calming herself the way she'd been taught. Anything to cool her blood. Was Zara foisting the blame onto her, agreeing that their behaviour was unacceptable?

'Okay, thank you.' The cerise of the Proctor's mouth relaxed. 'I understand these things can take on a life of their own, but you should have sought permission beforehand. This will not only be noted in both of your records but will be logged as a serious breach. If any other incidents occur, your places at Leysham will be at risk. Having said that, we will not put anything forward to the board of discipline if you agree not to distribute the image further.'

Zara sighed, her shoulders sinking lower in the chair.

Serena felt no relief at their supposed leniency. As the Proctor spoke on, Serena pushed her nail beneath a loose flake of paint on the wall beside her until she felt a spear of pain. She pushed harder. Pain distracted her, calmed the flames in her fingers. Some part of pain was pure. *Pain is the fire in which you forge yourself.* If she focused, could Serena force Leysham to acknowledge the truth? No. It wasn't hers to do alone. Pushing to the point where her teeth had to grit, Serena leveraged a large shard of the thick, metallic emulsion until it peeled away in the shape of some unearthly monster.

*   *   *

Something in Jane's face was wrong. Serena saw it as the door opened.

'They've suspended me.'

The words were simple, but Jane's lips were white. Serena had feared this. They'd withheld punishment for her and Zara, but savaged Jane.

'I've been suspended from teaching pending further investigation. They're convinced I led you all astray, that I can't be trusted around undergraduates.' Her breaths came too frequently, each phrase ragged. 'They won't reach a final decision until the committee convenes next term, which means I'm stuck in this situation until after my contract ends.'

It was Serena's flesh naked in that picture. If her clothes had stayed on, the incident might not have garnered attention.

'My classes have been given to someone else in the faculty. The classes I planned and prepared and have been running. I have to leave this office in a few weeks.'

Serena clocked the boxes filling one corner, books stacked in jagged piles. She didn't know where Jane would take them, didn't know where she lived outside of that dense room.

Jane paced as she talked, back and forth along the length of her rug. The kettle rumbled its way to boiling, clotting the room with steam.

Serena pushed the gnawing remorse away. Whatever had crackled through her on that beach had been essential.

'Academic careers are so unstable, and this effectively ends mine. They won't extend my contract here and no one else will touch me.'

She scooped two dark spoons of those pungent tea leaves. 'I can continue working on my monograph, but the Fielding Grant to go to Scotland has been put on hold. I can't complete my research without those manuscripts.'

As the water poured, black smoky shards danced in their strainers. 'I need to examine them close up. I need to see how that ink was pressed into the page. I need to see what state those men were in when they wrote those evil words. A scan won't do. I've already extended my deadline by three months and the publishers are pushing me for a final draft.'

Serena had never seen Jane like this.

'Gossip abounds in academic circles, and so much is based on reputation. This shreds mine. People will assume I'm not capable, or that my behaviour has been heinous. Not that I stood for a valid cause.' Jane sat on the messy daybed with her cup. 'Writing anything feels futile.' She sipped, though the tea was scalding.

Serena seized the pause to speak. 'It's a moment in time. They'll see the truth, and you'll be vindicated. There's no question.'

'It seems wholly unreasonable. They're punishing me for challenging historical dogma. That's my job. It's what I'm here for. A university is a critical institution or it's nothing.' Her voice lowered. 'I knew it would rile them, but I didn't think they'd go this far.'

Her shoulders rolled, anger fading into exhaustion, her

fingers twirled the silver ring on her right hand. 'And you remember I told you about Nicholas? You know he was suspended?'

A flash of his tight, furious face in Serena's mind.

'He's back.'

Serena's spine stiffened.

'The university supported him through every step and the accusation was dropped. There was so much evidence, but he shrugged it off immediately. He's just been named as one of the university's "New Generation Minds".'

Serena couldn't move her face. That wasn't what she'd imagined. She'd seen his anger at the destruction of his career. It had to have worked. He was ruined. She'd seen it.

'Wherever I look, they're celebrating him but I'm disregarded.' Jane sighed and her frame seemed to deflate.

'You saw what happened on the beach.' Serena thought of the picture, so powerful it burst from Keira's phone. 'You felt that energy. It was real. They can punish you, but they can't change what we witnessed. They're frightened of it, frightened of you and what you can spark.' Serena kept her voice to a whisper because otherwise she'd shout. 'You can't let this defeat you. You have to keep challenging.'

As Jane turned, there was a new curl to her mouth, a glint of fierceness. 'You're right. I can't let them win.'

@zarakarmic • 177k followers

*How many of you consult the cards when you face
big decisions? Tarot gives me such clarity, especially in
complicated times.*

*This is a simple spread, showing past, present and future
influences. I'll analyse their meanings as best I can.*

*The past is the Hanged Man, this upside-down figure with
the beams emitting from his head. He can represent trials
and sacrifice, so I see it as our connection to the women of
the past.*

*The present is Justice, the monarch on their elaborate
throne, which is surely the truth we can see and have to
fight for.*

*The future is Death, the skeleton knight on a white stallion.
Now, that sounds incredibly bleak, but this card is amazing.
It's about newness, beckoning in a whole new way of being.
Let's hope it stands for the mighty change we so desperately
need.*

24

Five books were heavy enough to dent the flesh of Serena's arm. She joined the library queue snaking around the marble floor. A few desks were still occupied that late on a Friday, heads bent, brass lamps dim. The thud of the librarian's inky stamp echoed to the distant ceiling, catching in the whorls of each iron balcony. Serena gripped the pile of books. Her blood hadn't calmed.

After long minutes of waiting, she sensed a light pressure on her back and turned. Standing behind her, hair longer than when she'd last seen him, was Luke.

'Hi.' He mouthed the word. That cavernous room amplified any sound.

He was close enough to smell and Serena felt a ripple swell through her. Unlike the heat she'd grown used to, this tingled rather than burned. She'd once sat in that grand library with Luke's face horrific in her mind. His face pale, his lips dark.

'What you did at the beach was excellent.' He risked a whisper.

He'd seen the picture that showed her body as only he knew it. Did he feel a kind of ownership? Could he sense the new power throbbing beneath her skin?

'Thank you.' Serena let her nose bump his cheek. Their faces were close, too close. It would take so little to breach the gap.

'You looked incredibly . . . confident.'

He didn't know her at all. He'd only remember an awkward girl choking on her first cigarette.

'I felt it.'

'You looked . . . you looked amazing.' His words were slow. Their faces froze for a second, and Serena's books were suddenly too heavy in her arms.

'Sorry.' He smiled, looked down, seeming embarrassed to have been so candid.

Serena's right hand found his palm. They faced forward and spoke no more, their tangled fingers hidden from anyone else in the queue.

Light flooded in after two dark terms. The brightness caught motes of dust in Zara's room, made the smudges on every surface glaring. Serena tried to take it in. That space was always immaculate, styled to impossible coordination. More had changed than the unfiltered daylight; the surfaces were littered with boxes and packages, their dead, unrecyclable polythene skins lying in sad piles.

Zara looked different too. Her skin's constant gloss had faded and her eyes were bloodshot as she stared at her phone.

'You okay, Zee?' Serena rarely used that nickname. This looked like more than the ravages of a night out.

'Yeah, yeah.' Her fingers scrolled incessantly. 'Checking in with the haters!' Her voice was glassy.

'Haters?'

'Haters gonna hate.' She sang the words in a tune Serena didn't recognise echoing the last word five times. By the final repetition, her eyes were full.

'Hey, what is it?' Serena knew far more of the inside of Jane's mind than she did of her cousin's.

'It's constant now.'

'What do you mean?'

'Every day I get hate messages.'

Serena's muscles tensed. 'People say things to you?'

'Not in person. Never to my face.' Zara sighed in a long quaver. 'But online. Every morning I wake up to so many notifications – direct messages, comments on my posts.'

She seemed to take up less space than before, slumped on her usually pristine bed. Her responses were always extreme, Serena reminded herself. Nothing hit Zara subtly.

After a faltering breath, she continued. 'There've always been trolls, people who take delight in calling me a fat cow and telling me that I'm promoting obesity, that I'll die young. They've been around for years and they're easy to ignore. I

HAZEL BARKWORTH

don't give a shit about them. I never check the burn sites. But this is from my fans.' She paused. 'My former fans.'

Serena sat on the edge of the bed, leaning across a pile of cushions to put her arm around her cousin's shoulders.

'That's awful.' She didn't know if she should ask. 'What do they say?'

'That I don't represent them any more. That I've become obsessed with campaigning for other things, lost sight of what I stand for.'

'That's ridiculous. It's up to you what you talk about.'

'I know. But they needed me. A lot of girls struggle with body stuff, and I was a bit of a lifeline for some. They say I've lost weight, which isn't even true.'

Serena tightened her grip on Zara.

'I know these years are supposed to be tough.' Zara wrapped her arms around her own middle as if to soothe herself. 'No one says otherwise, but this feels too hard. It's my fault for showing so much.'

'That's not your fault. Absolutely not. You did that so other people would feel better.' Serena sat back to see her cousin clearly. Did Jane ever witness this side of her?

'Maybe, but also so I'd feel better. It was amazing, so many people wanting to see what I was doing. I lived for that praise. For that delicious dopamine hit.' Tears flowed and she did nothing to stem them. 'I've exposed everything.'

'You don't share too much. Nothing to do with your personal life.'

Jane remained on the edges of Zara's feed. Despite the plethora of images of women, Zara's followers could assume she was drawn to boys.

'No. But my body's personal enough. They've seen all of me so often, they think they own it. I used to love that my life was big enough to share. People wanted to be like me. Who wouldn't want that kind of power?'

Serena's palm twitched.

As Zara tilted her head to look at the ceiling, tears spilled in rivulets down the sides of her face. 'I've lost so much. I had a big opportunity coming up.'

Serena pressed her tongue against her teeth as Zara spoke. An image was forming in her mind. More than an image this time. It came with sensations.

'It was a column in an online magazine, about body image and how young women experience the world.'

There were no words. Only fire. Not the fire of the beach, but equally untamed. This fire was not warming, but destructive. Not a joyful blaze for dancing, and burning more than kindling. She'd been waiting for something unbidden. This was it.

'It would've been amazing, would have given me a much wider audience and meant I could make a real difference. They emailed yesterday saying they've reconsidered. I've never wanted a management team, but it means there's no one to support me. I know they've dropped me because of the comments. They think I've lost focus too. I've muddied my brand.' Zara's tears soaked into the pillow. 'People saw me as their representative. My body isn't really mine any more. It's become a symbol. It's all I'm allowed to be.' She hugged her knees to her chest. 'I've fucked up the one thing I was good at.'

Serena tried to soothe her cousin, but the fire in her mind blazed. She could almost smell it over the distilled flowers of Zara's perfume.

Serena scrolled back through Zara's posts, her fingers uncovering months in their swipes. She'd never read the comments before. Videos and images from the previous year were radiant. Zara shone with confidence, her body plush and curved. Comments tumbled compliments upon her. *You are iconic. I nearly dropped my phone . . . Spectacular. Why r u so exquisite? . . . This is perfection . . . What the hell. A goddess. I want this picture on my wall forever.* The fire emoji, a face with hearts for eyes, explosions, rainbows, fireworks. Some comments shared more. *Honestly, you're such a role model in my life . . . Your posts inspire me to love my body.*

Then, a change. Imperceptible at first, growing more pronounced. *Who does she think she is these days? We follow her for body posi stuff and fashion.* They were unconvinced by her recent content. It had flipped from a pastel aesthetic to something darker. *I used to live for her posts, now she preaches hippy nonsense . . . She's being used for someone else's agenda, it's inauthentic. She's lost everything that made her special . . . This witch crap feels like propaganda.*

Her follower numbers were tens of thousands lower. Zara wasn't recruiting them to the cause, wasn't sparking a generation of activists. She irritated them. *For fuck's sake, most of us aren't even at uni.* Serena scrolled upwards, through the lattice of posts. Sponsored images still featured – Zara's hands striped with lipstick shades – but they jarred. She posted every few days rather than every few hours, and corporate patrons were losing interest. *Why would we care about what happens on some random campus in the north?*

You look thinner. What's happening? The comments became a conversation. *Where's our thicc queen? She doesn't even look healthy any more . . . She's making money off body positivity. She was never exactly Fat Lib. It's always been about how she feels, never anything systemic . . . It's not like she's even that big, barely a small fat . . . She's clearly miserable. It's because she's got wrapped in that protest stuff . . . I used to look up to her.*

The instinct to help flared in Serena, but it felt impossible. There was nowhere to focus. This wasn't Luke's lungs or Kelly's placenta, or even Jane's nemesis. It was disparate: comments came from scores of accounts. Serena knew she'd contributed to her cousin's fragility. That moment she lifted the grey plastic megaphone from Jane's hands. In those seconds, it had felt wonderful. Now it seemed cruel. Serena thought of her cousin, but the fire didn't stop. It raged in her head, its smoke spiralling upwards, leaping and twisting, acrid with things that shouldn't burn.

The once-labyrinthine paths through campus were now well trodden, and Serena walked them without thinking. Those buildings had stopped registering as magnificent. The marvels of their struts and spires, their complex twisting curves, had grown familiar. The campus felt smaller, its hemmed-in edges creeping nearer. Nine thousand people the same age crammed into three hundred acres could be stifling. The campus was almost an island, with water on all sides, and there was no easy escape from that place.

On the way to the lecture hall, Serena sensed something she'd nearly forgotten. The prickle of eyes on her. It had once been second nature to be watched. She'd walked onto so many pool-sides; her name had been called over endless loudspeakers. The muscle memory hadn't left, and she felt her back straighten, her stride lengthen. She was no longer anonymous.

Turning as subtly as possible, Serena saw a group of three students she knew vaguely clustered beneath a black lantern lamppost, their hair all dyed in vibrant colours; purple-dipped ends, a shock of blue above shaved sides.

'Hey,' one called, jerking their head in invitation.

Serena paused, then walked over.

'You're Serena Roberts, right?' The cropped top they wore exposed inches of hairless stomach, a pin striped in pale pink and blue sat on their lapel. They knew her name.

Serena nodded slowly. 'I am.'

What had happened on the beach had spread through those honey-gold buildings, sped along their sinuous corridors. Serena had become someone people knew. She'd scarcely recognise the blank, hobbling girl of freshers' week.

'It's fucking epic, what you're doing. The picture from the beach is amazing, we love it.'

That picture, sent out by someone who'd aimed to humiliate her, had done the opposite.

People had stared at her naked body, dancing unhindered, and seen its glory. Could these people sense her power, a faint buzz thickening the air round them?

One of them pushed her hair back. 'It's great you're standing for all that. I'm a third-year, and we've put up with this crap for too long. Two girls from my year left after a couple of terms because some guy on their course was a complete bastard, but no one seemed to care—'

Another interrupted. 'And I love the witchy stuff. Very Stevie.' She lifted an arm to let a wide chiffon cuff flow. 'Have you seen what's happening at the river?'

'The river?'

'You should go and see. And people have been wearing these.' She dug into her neon patterned tote bag and pulled out a badge. Printed on it was the simple outline of seaweed. Serena reached out to hold it.

'It's to show, you know, solidarity. Against how the uni reacted.'

'And support for what you're talking about.'

Serena didn't know how her words had been repeated, but these people had listened. She turned the smooth plastic edges of the badge over in her hands, flicked its pin back and forth.

The student with purple hair spoke. 'I've heard people are

boycotting lectures. I don't know if it's true, but people say that if the curriculum doesn't tell the whole truth, or appears patriarchal, they walk out.'

Serena felt a flush through her body, as if the heat from her fingers had sunk into the bones. The fire rose in her mind. It flamed away, abstract and wild.

'Is it true Zara Carmichael is your cousin?' Their eyebrows were raised in question.

'She is.' Serena nodded. 'Did you see her rallies last year?' It felt right to credit her.

'That's so weird.'

'Who's Zara Carmichael?' One of the girls frowned.

'You know Zara. The influencer.'

'Nope.'

'You do. Zarakarmic.' A gesture around their own head. 'The one with the hair. Pretty. Always hawking some new eyeshadow or chocolate. Always in pink.'

The *k*-sound landed harshly in their mouth.

The river looked no different. The dark stretch of water that raged beyond the Bowland Gate would have looked the same four hundred years ago. Only the garish safety barriers were new, decorated now with ribbons, flowers strewn on the ground.

Serena crouched to see clearly. Messages were written on cards. *To the women who lived here before and were killed. We're sorry.* Handwritten, then slipped into plastic document folders so the rain couldn't reach them. *We see you. We know you.* Dozens of messages, placed at the spot where women were lawfully destroyed all those years before. *We're all witches now.* The stories Jane had told – that Serena had repeated on the beach – had resonated with such force people felt compelled to respond. *What is a witch but a woman with power?* Wildflowers picked from the woodland, cellophane-wrapped clusters of roses bought from supermarkets. *I'm a PhD Student, and I'm so proud to see younger women speaking out.* Chunks of quartz, potions in stoppered bottles, tarot packs. It looked like a shrine. Over and over, the outline of fronds of seaweed reaching upwards.

We're the granddaughters of the witches they couldn't drown. Some of it jarred. Statistically, more of them were likely to be descendants of the men who had slaughtered the accused. When she'd spoken of witches, Serena hadn't meant the pretty crystals and cards of Zara's feed, but the people who'd left trinkets meant well.

A flash. So bright, Serena closed her eyes, making it only more vivid. When the images summoned themselves, they were searing. Something visible through the flames. She could finally see what was burning in her mind. Wood, but no twigs or branches. Carved wood, ceremonial wood. Words drawn upon it. *Carnforth.* Serena felt the energy surge through her, almost painful in its vehemence. Fingertips to arms to skull to torso to waist to knees to toes. She lowered herself to the ground, to the mud she'd once clambered on. Every flame made the gold-and-black paint of the letters blister. It was glorious. Peaceful protest had come to nothing. They had to act. With support building across the campus, they needed to do something irrevocable.

@zarakarmic • 172k followers

Tiger's Eye was used by the women before us as a powerful amulet to ward off curses.

This particular chunk, with its beautiful layers of honey and gold and flint, was gifted to me by the wonderful souls at Aquarian Heart.

I'm so grateful, and I call upon its protection to beckon in the strength and confidence I need to flourish.

I won't permit anything to squash my spirit or keep me small.

25

'I have an idea.' Serena forced herself to speak calmly. 'I think we need to capitalise on the support we've gained. We need to do something they can't brush away.'

'Carry on.'

The breeze from Jane's window made her heavy velvet curtains billow, brushing against the stack of packed boxes. It was always too warm inside that room. Zara was curled on the daybed, eating from a package of pastel-toned macarons stamped with a beauty company logo.

'We can ask politely for the university to listen, or we can do something they can't ignore.' Serena knew her words came too fast. 'The sign outside Carnforth Hall, the huge wooden one with gilt lettering, that sets his name up as something impressive. Well . . .' She swallowed. 'Wood is flammable.'

Jane's face altered. It was as if light shone from her, a radiant nimbus like medieval paintings of saints. 'You have remarkable instincts.'

Serena's jaw clenched with delight. 'I know it will cause damage, but I think it's worth it.'

'It is worth it. But we can go further.'

'Further?' Zara looked up.

Jane's smile stayed neat, but her eyes gave her away. 'I think it might be time. Historically, protest has always ended in direct action – why not hasten it? I don't have much to lose right now.' She leaned closer. 'What if we burned something else?' Jane stared beyond them both. 'Why not go straight to the source?'

Instantly, the image in Serena's head morphed. The flames shimmered, and something new emerged behind them. Richard Pelham's face. It was as if Jane had spoken into her mind, but not like Niko once had. This was collaborative. Serena could see the painting of the Earl of Carnforth; arms crossed, lips thin, eyes glaring forward, pallid cheeks pinched and judgemental, each feature created by brushstrokes. The edges of the canvas were already curling.

'The painting?'

'Absolutely. It would draw real attention.'

They could reduce this villain to ashes. Serena let the images flow, enjoying each scorching second. The bubbles that formed over his skin, his eyes distorting, the boils rising hideously along his painted limbs. Flames made the canvas warp and bend and fray. Black stains darkened everything.

Zara nibbled on a pale green macaron. 'The painting? That's crazy. Think of the repercussions.'

A flash across Jane's face as she registered dissent. 'It will absolutely have repercussions. But that can be positive. Others will be empowered. You've seen the river. People want action. Suffragettes had to smash windows before they were taken seriously.'

Serena could imagine Jane in long skirts, toffee hammer in hand.

'I'm sure you've heard of the *Rokeby Venus*.' Jane always assumed their knowledge. 'One suffragette, Mary Richardson, took a meat cleaver into the National Gallery and slashed the naked back and thighs of that painting. She was quite clear that if people were outraged at the destruction of a piece of art, they should be more outraged at the treatment of real women.' She smiled. 'Our action would practically be a homage.'

Jane spoke as if it was inevitable. The flames in Serena's mind would soon be real, that canvas soon charred and blistered.

Twisting the blue gem that severed her nose, Zara frowned. 'No. It's too much. We'll be thrown out. You heard what the Proctor said.'

'That won't happen.' Jane's mouth was tense. She'd already faced such punishment.

'It feels like a risk.'

'It is. But you're not afraid of taking risks. We'll only be hurting property, not people.' Jane looked at Zara. 'You do want to be involved, don't you?'

Jane moved closer to Zara. Serena knew how it felt when Jane turned the full beam of her attention on you; like being lit with infinite candlepower. Zara might know that light far better than she did. 'Yes, of course I do, but this goes too far.'

Serena jumped in. 'Maybe that's exactly far enough. We've been too safe.'

'It's time for us to do something significant. You saw the energy on the beach, and what it's spawned. We can't ignore that.' Jane touched Zara's hair lightly, her hands becoming combs for a second. Serena wondered if she'd done the same to Nylah.

Zara's face didn't soften. 'People listened when we ran approved rallies too.' Her eyes were sharp. 'They put their stories on the website and got on board then, when we didn't do anything extreme. They put lipstick on their eyes and marched with us. We reached them. It still mattered.'

'Yes, and the university made us stop, made us take it down.' Serena's voice was loud. 'We can be as polite and safe as we like, but they'll diminish us. We need to do something they can't revoke. It needs to be permanent. Not just for us and for the women who died here, but for the people who'll attend this university in the future. They should be freed from that image and what it stands for.'

'But what are we willing to sacrifice?'

'Whatever it takes.' Serena couldn't stay calm with her mind on fire. The heat from those flames scorched her body; no water could cool them. Those same flames had to flicker, burn and destroy that man.

Seaweed soaked through their clothes in minutes, seeping up sleeves and into collars. Serena narrowed her eyes to the breeze, her arms laden. Their bare fingers had recoiled at first from the slimy mass. They'd headed for the rocks, but the fronds had clung too tightly to pick off, so they'd learned to go for piles cast from the water. Clumps that lay like carcasses on the shore.

Some handfuls were a dull, earthy green; others gleamed. Some strands were so long they could be lifted skyward while attached to the ground. Holding those tangles, they looked like creatures from the deep, bellies silty, dragging the sea with them.

Jane tumbled against Serena as they walked along the sand. Her face was pink in the cold. Serena had feared the collection would seem sombre, reminding them of that shore's horrors, but it felt vital. They needed a piece of the ocean with them for this, to be present as they acted for the women who'd died there. They hadn't invited Zara.

'There's something freeing about it, you know.' Jane's voice reached Serena through the wind. 'Losing everything.'

Serena's eyebrows tightened.

'I'm completely untethered. Nothing to bind me, nowhere to fall.' Her words were brave, but Jane's eyes were full, whipped by the wind or whatever she was feeling. 'It's like I could float into the air or swim for ever, dissolve into nature.'

The jumbles of seaweed moved as they walked, covering their faces with each step. They smelled of salt and of some-thing darker, some sourness Serena couldn't name.

'Everything I've poured my life into for so long has come to nothing. Everything I thought I was. It makes me want to scream, so I know I'm still here.'

Serena knew the sensation well. 'So, scream.'

Jane looked to the waves. There was no one else around. She opened her mouth and breathed, but nothing came out.

Serena waited. Then, a noise from Jane. Not the deep shout Serena had prepared herself for. It was reedy, wavering, more of a keening. A wail of grief and despair. Jane dropped her armload of clotted seaweed to the sand, rested her hands on her knees to send the sound out to the ocean. Not fury, but sadness. The waves continued in their constant swell and fade, inching ever closer. Jane surely screamed not for herself but for all of them, for those ravaged women. For everything they'd shared, everything that hurt them. Could she hear Gilly Sampson screaming back to her?

Jane's composure vanished as she howled her pain to the world. Nothing was hidden, and only Serena could see her. Shifting the seaweed to one arm, she held Jane's hand as she wailed.

Jane didn't stop. The noise continued, without breath to pause it. For those moments, Jane was mythical. A harpy thundering her wings, a siren calling ships to the rocks. A woman wronged and terrifying. The flying strands of her hair could so easily morph into snakes. Serena knew, standing on that damp sand, that the bitter, salted smell would never fully leave her.

'You need to make clear demands, otherwise it's just theatre.' Dean's beard was thicker now, smothering his collar, adding a decade to his age.

They'd met the boys with Keira in the social sciences café, around those heavy wooden tables. Sun through the stained-glass windows sent rays like light through water, cast blurred rainbows on every surface. That high-ceilinged space was bustling with students heading to lectures but, with coffees and muffins, their group's conversation was hidden in plain sight. Accessing Carnforth Hall after hours was a challenge, and the boys were necessary.

'We have clear demands.' Jane counted on her fingers. 'Take down the painting, change the name of the hall, issue an apology on Carnforth's behalf to the women killed.'

'What about the policy issues we highlighted before?' Luke asked.

Dean rubbed his bristled upper lip. 'Yeah, absolutely. The welfare provision, disciplinary procedures, consent training? Even the pay gap, ceasing donations from irresponsible insti-tutions? There's so much we could ask for.' He was already speaking of them as a collective again.

Jane didn't pause. 'That's important, but it can come later.

We need to be single-minded. We're taking symbolic action against a symbol of oppression.'

'I don't know if that feels indulgent, though. With real problems and real victims, is this just window dressing?' Luke looked at Jane.

The words wouldn't stay in Serena's mouth. 'Without that man removed, everything else is talk. We can't be free with him staring over us.'

Serena could sense Luke's eyes on her, his concern or disapproval.

'I agree he needs to go, but this level of disruption is extreme and it might not gain us anything concrete.'

'The point of protest is disruption. You know that, Luke.' Jane's voice was tight. 'It's how movements get people to look, to care. It's a valid and essential tactic. It starts conversations. It draws vital attention.'

Zara picked at one of the muffins, crumbling it to pieces on the table's varnished surface but eating nothing.

'I can see that, definitely.' Dean's head bobbed. 'But if that's your aim, you need to make sure you stay symbolic and don't do anything that can be seen as destructive. There can be no damage to property. What they'll see as trespass is bad enough, but I'm sure you've thought of that, Jane.'

The fire soared again in Serena's mind. She didn't speak of the flames, the heat that pushed against her skin. Jane didn't want them to tell the boys.

'Absolutely.' Jane's face gave nothing away. 'We intend to

attach our list of demands to the painting, set the paper alight, let it singe a little to trigger the fire alarms, then leave before the fire brigade arrive. The only damage will be to our own stationery.'

Keira's head jinked upwards. Serena caught her friend's eyes and widened her own. Keira stopped, then eased further back in her chair, but didn't break her gaze.

'Sounds sensible.' Dean's mouth turned down as he nodded.

'It definitely doesn't sound sensible, but if you're very careful it might work.' Luke's fingers drummed lightly on the tabletop. 'I'm dubious, but I appear to be outvoted. Your main problem is how to access Carnforth Hall at night.'

Serena stared at him the way she once had in a nightclub. 'That's where we hoped you might come in.'

Luke pinched the bridge of his nose as Dean answered. 'I think that should be feasible.'

As Serena reached for her backpack, Luke's hand grabbed her wrist. The warmth and pressure were startling.

'Stay here a moment.'

The others headed out, rushing to seminars and classes.

'What's up?' There was an intensity to Luke's eyes Serena wasn't used to.

'I wanted to check in with you.'

'Okay?' Serena didn't know him well enough to read the nuances of his face. That face she'd watched sleep.

'I don't know . . .' He faltered. 'This seems pretty dark.'

'Dark?'

'Everything you've done before has been so positive. You were radiant on the beach.' Serena wondered how often he let that photograph fill his phone's screen. 'You've stood up for people, encouraged them. This isn't like that. I'm not sure it feels like you.'

Serena felt the air leave her lungs too quickly. He didn't know what was her. 'I'm good, thanks.'

He didn't know what she was capable of. He didn't know what burned within her. He saw what he wanted to see: a benign girl happy to acquiesce. That's not who she was. He'd never seen her slice through water.

'Cool, cool. I wanted to make sure—'

She cut him off. 'This was my idea.' It was close to the truth. 'I couldn't be more certain.'

The fire inside her no longer hurt. It fizzed in her veins, made her buoyant. Luke still held her arm, looked at her intently, but Serena tugged herself free. She walked away without turning back.

26

Serena caught up with Keira on the long path back to their rooms. The sky darkening, they kept their pace up to beat the rain.

'Are you okay with this?'

'What do you mean?' Serena hadn't mentioned her conversation with Luke.

'The way Jane openly lied to the boys then. She's asking them to be involved but is clearly deceiving them. That's fucked up. We both know she's going to destroy that painting.'

Serena tensed. 'Don't you agree?'

'I agree it should be taken down, of course. But burning it is insane.'

The blaze inside Serena scorched and sputtered, fuelling her with its energy. They walked side by side along pavements Serena had trodden alone so many times.

'She knows they'd try to stop us if we told them.'

'Exactly! Maybe they'd be right. She's already in so much trouble with the university, she's got nothing to lose. But we have. You and Zara can't see it, you're so blinded by her. You trail after her. I haven't seen you in weeks, not properly. You're either with her or doing her bidding.'

Their route took them past honeyed buildings Serena had once been unable to tell apart. 'We have to burn it.' She missed those long, chatty nights with Keira, but this was too important. Serena wanted to hold her friend's face, look into her eyes and explain what she could see. 'We have to do something real.'

'I don't know if this is real. I loved that moment on the beach when it was this big, brilliant group of women. This feels narrower and nastier.'

'I loved that too, you know I did. But we need a smaller group. Someone there leaked the picture. Someone close to us was clearly a traitor.'

'A traitor! It's so dramatic. Jane's not the queen. It wasn't high treason. It was a properly low thing to do, but . . .' Keira sighed. 'Look, no one hated what happened more than me. I know what it's like to have a picture like that circulated. And you handled it with such fucking grace. But most people there had nothing to do with that. It feels like an excuse to make this whole thing bitter and vile.'

'We're still standing up for others, but we need to be nimble now. We need to call out how the university are behaving. And don't you want to show those Carnforth bastards that they can't get away with it?' That group always fired Keira's outrage.

'Of course! But I don't think burning a painting will do that. It will feed their narrative that we're foolish and disrespectful and unable to engage like grown-ups.'

'That's idiotic.'

Their halls were in sight and Keira slowed. 'I'm not sure, lovely, I'm really not. I don't think this is heading to a good place.'

Keira and Luke didn't understand. The images couldn't be quelled. The fire couldn't be stopped. Serena turned to her friend. 'This is what it's all led to. I know it's frightening, but that's how we know it's worth it. This will be our legacy.' The flames rose along with her voice, filling her to the edges.

Zara arrived at Serena's room soaking. Her trainers were thick with mud, her fur coat sodden.

'I thought it would be sunny today.' Her voice was flat. She paused in the doorway, where she'd usually crash in.

Serena leaned on the cliché. 'We're too far north to make assumptions like that.'

Zara didn't return her smile.

Peeling the dripping pelt from her cousin's shoulders, Serena draped it over the en-suite shower cubicle and tossed a towel for her hair. 'Try to dry off.'

It wasn't cold, despite the rain, but Zara shivered.

Picking Zara's trainers up by their inside heels, Serena lifted down the shower attachment. The mud, thick and tangled with grass, stained the water brown. Had Zara gone to the riverbank? Water alone had little impact, so Serena grabbed a dish scourer.

Zara looked unfocused, her hair hanging in strands.

'Are you okay, Zee?'

The scourer loosened the worst of the muck, sending an earthy smell into the cubicle. The released grass choked the drain.

'Is it the trolls again? Don't listen to those losers – they're not worth your time.'

Zara gazed at the wall.

Once the treads unclogged, the trainers remained tinged with earth. Serena poured bleach straight from the bottle onto their soles. It formed a lavish stream that caught the light like oil and gave the air a new texture. That familiar prickle in Serena's eyes, the clench at the back of her throat. The flames within her were constant now, a burning that never ceased. The crackle and spit of them sat behind everything. She feared how they'd react to the chemical sting of bleach.

Looking up, smiling now, Zara spoke. 'Do you see a lot of her?' Her voice was cold and bright.

Serena dropped the bleach bottle, her hands toxic with its residue. She inhaled to speak, but Zara hadn't finished.

'How much time do you spend together?'

'With who?' Serena knew it sounded false.

No response. Zara's face flattened again.

'Jane?' The word stretched to several phoney syllables in Serena's mouth.

'We used to be so close.'

'You are close. She clearly adores you.'

Serena could never grasp quite what existed between Zara and Jane.

'Oh, I get close to some parts of her, but nothing real.' Zara moved to the bed, curling her legs onto Serena's duvet as if to sleep. 'She doesn't talk to me.'

Serena thought of Jane on the beach, howling against the world. 'Well, she's got a lot going on with work stuff. It's kind of horrific.'

'I wouldn't know. She doesn't tell me about that. She doesn't even look at me any more.'

Zara was pale, with shadows under each eye. Keira had been wrong. Serena didn't follow Jane as Zara did. She and Jane connected. They were allies, equals, partners.

'Of course she does. Everyone wants to look at you.' Serena stated it as fact.

'No. She's bored of me now. I'm bored of me. I'm so tired.' Zara spoke so slowly each word was a sentence of its own. 'No one looks at me. It's you they turn to. Everyone who used to follow me. It's your name they know. It's like I'm not even involved.'

Zara looked at Serena, but her intensity – the heat and light she usually beamed with – had faded.

'It's only because that picture was seen by so many people.' Serena didn't believe her own words.

Zara began to cry, her body convulsing silently. The Zara who'd shone with gold and made Serena feel invisible was gone. 'I've never met anyone like her. Other people are so dull in comparison. She's more alive.' Serena remembered Jane's description of Nylah. 'But she's drifting away.'

Serena placed the clean trainers by the door, their swoosh and tongue both baby blue again, and sat next to Zara. Close up, there was something sour beneath the ylang-ylang, like flowers curdling, browned at the edges and softening to a sludge.

Serena stroked Zara's hair. The hair that had once held such magic.

Serena stared at the image and tried to decipher it. Zara was so hard to grasp. She'd been persuaded – by gifts, by adoration, by money – to show more and more, but had learned how to reveal nothing. Each time she appeared to peel away another layer, the praise heaped higher. The monochrome image of sadness she'd recently posted had scored more likes than her previous ten combined. Bleakness was more beguiling than passion. Zara paused her days so often to capture moments; grasping every opportunity to garner attention. Every encounter, every view, every nugget of joy could be packaged. No wonder she was fractured. Serena's whole life had once been about triumph. Zara had her own lane pads to smack and seemed no less addicted to that feeling. Serena remembered the sickening thud of horror. She knew how it felt to stop winning.

@zarakarmic • 163k followers

I'm sorry to look such a mess here, but I wanted to be honest. Not everything you see on socials is real.

I've been struggling a lot lately.

Thank you to all those who've send your love and support. I stand with everyone who feels low at the moment.

Always remember that loving yourself is an act of rebellion.

27

Looming over them that night, Carnforth Hall didn't look grand, but gauche. A pastiche of something once formidable. As its bricks glowed rosy from angled spotlights, that towering building seemed flimsy, a collection of fripperies. The crenellations and pinnacles were ridiculous. Serena stared at those hollow arches, amazed they'd ever intimidated her. Richard Pelham had once lived in this building. Its flamboyant pageantry had aimed to evoke the sublime, to trigger awe or fear, to make foolish men look powerful. Now, it signified nothing.

Women's faces stared out from the main doorway, but their eyes were dull. Those stone features were bloodless, not real women, but false renderings carved by men. Women as men wanted them to be, smooth and silent. That building didn't expect women to have power. It didn't understand the red stains that still marked its steps. The stone women's gaze fell on the lurid fountain. The Carnforth Club had held its annual dinner that night and, following their forebear's infamous japery, had dyed the water purple. There would be no repercussions; this would never be deemed destructive. Poseidon had no choice but to churn that gaudy liquid over and over.

The group entered the building through a side door as planned and Serena swallowed back a shiver. She'd lived so much of her life in accordance with rules that breaking them now felt exhilarating. The narrow corridor was dark. No bulbs flickered, not even the security lights they'd expected. No foxes hid in those corners, no eyes shone out, but Serena was reminded of the creaking forest.

Only one room was lit, a door on the corridor casting a beam towards them. Dean walked ahead. A cart of cleaning materials sat by the entrance. The logistical conversation happened too far away to hear. Dean shook the hand of an older woman, then spread his fingers wide in gentle persuasion. All he asked was that she lock up with a little less diligence than usual when the maintenance staff left in a few minutes' time. His nod to the group indicated their plan was intact.

As they walked towards the back door, Serena felt invincible. She moved through the dim light of the corridor like she'd once moved through water. An arrow shot through the dark. Nothing restricted her. Her form was impeccable. If Niko could have seen her, he'd have gaped with pride.

By now, fire filled every part of Serena's mind, the images vivid and incessant. The face of that man had to be eliminated.

His skin, his eyes, his lips had to be reduced to char. Those oils had lain dormant for so many centuries; they'd greet flames like an old friend. Oil wanted to be fire. If Richard Pelham, the third Earl of Carnforth, had been alive, Serena knew for certain he'd destroy a woman like her. Obliterating him was necessary.

To reach the main hall, they walked past double doors that led outside. As they neared them, Keira grabbed Serena's arm. All Serena could hear was the drum of her own blood. She didn't want to step into the courtyard and talk; she wanted to keep moving.

The spotlights that scattered the building kept the outside brighter than the corridor. Serena's eyelids showed pink when she blinked. The breeze out there was a balm, but Keira's grip on her arm was hot.

'I'm out.' Keira's face was unnaturally still.

Serena didn't have time for this. 'What do you mean?'

'I'm done. I don't want to be here. I'm going. This isn't right.'

Serena inhaled. 'We need you.'

'No, you don't. It will spiral, and I don't want to be a part of it.'

'Jane knows what she's doing.' Serena kept her voice hushed so that her words didn't penetrate the walls.

Keira's face remained hard. 'That's what concerns me.'

Serena shook her head in reply.

'Whatever Jane wants goes. We know what she intends to do, and how much trouble we could be in.'

'Some trouble is necessary trouble.' The blood was hectic through Serena's veins.

'That's a neat phrase, but she never considers what else that trouble destroys.'

Serena found no solid ground in Keira's words.

'This was always Zara's thing. She was the one who got us involved, and now it's like she doesn't exist.'

'Zara?' The word felt wrong in Serena's mouth. 'Zara's here.'

'No, she genuinely isn't. You must see it. She used to lead everything. It was her voice people came to hear. Nothing could have happened without her.'

'I know—'

Keira didn't let her finish. 'It was amazing to see a woman like her with that kind of influence, with so many people hanging on her words. Now she just sits there.'

'Of course she doesn't.'

'Look at her, Serena: she's gone, she's empty. It's horrible.'

Serena didn't realise anyone else had noticed.

'Everything is Jane's plan. I don't know what the fuck has been going on between those two, but it's not okay. It's manipulative. She used Zara's following. She convinced the boys to get involved. She's determined to light that fire she's obsessed with.'

Serena couldn't explain the coiling flames in her own mind,

the image of that painting curling at its edges, writhing and distorting.

'You're wrong.' It was all she could say.

'Come with me.' Keira's eyes wouldn't leave her. 'Serena, please. I'm scared.'

'No.' Serena stared back at her. 'We need to do this.'

As Keira walked back across the courtyard, Serena watched. Her steps curved around the fountain. Poseidon's muscles bulged as he held his trident, his raised palm pouring violet.

It took seconds for Serena's eyes to adjust back to the dark of the corridor. She wished Keira was still with her. She'd watched her friend until she was lost to the campus footpaths. The corridor wasn't empty. Leaning against the wall, far behind where the others were huddled, was Zara. Serena blinked. She needed to see the expression on Zara's face.

'Hey.'

Zara jumped at Serena's greeting, although the opened door had sent light streaming.

'What are you doing?' Serena's voice stayed low.

'I've lost it.' The wideness of Zara's eyes showed genuine distress. The blankness of their last meeting had vanished; her emotions were pushed again to their brink.

'Lost what?' Serena was eager now to catch up with Jane, to enter the hall.

Zara covered her face with one hand, muffling her words. 'My nose stud. The little blue one.'

Serena was surprised she hadn't noticed the lack of it. 'I know the one. Where did you have it last?'

'On my way here. I remember fiddling with it.' Her voice rose to shrill. As she pulled her hand away, Serena saw the space where it had once glinted.

'We won't find it in this dark, Zee. We'll have to come back.'

'I need to find it. My dad gave it to me.' Zara pressed where the stud had once sat, nothing but flesh between her fingers.

'We'll look for it later.'

Zara seemed younger. Years younger, as if she was again that shy child, that little girl who hid behind her own hair. Keira's words echoed through Serena. *She's empty.*

'We'll find it, I promise.'

'It's not that.'

As Zara slid down the wall, Serena crouched to join her. 'What's wrong?'

Her cousin's eyes were bright again. Too bright. 'It was me, you know.'

Serena didn't answer, didn't understand.

'The picture.'

The only picture Serena could think of showed the face of a wretched man who wouldn't stare much longer.

'On the beach.' Zara smiled, her face soft.

It hit Serena like a slap. The photograph of her dancing,

naked on the sand. The photograph that had risked everything.

'You took it?' Her pitch was higher than expected.

'Yeah.' The word lingered. 'And sent it out.'

Serena wanted to grab her cousin. If anyone knew the
horrors an image like that could provoke it was Zara. She
knew the internet like Serena knew the water. A flash. Zara's
smile across a crowded swimming pool, sweet and seditious,
knowing exactly what she was doing. Zara's hands holding a
black plastic goggles case.

'I wanted to cause so much trouble.' Her voice was light.
It was eerie, the jealous child in her fighting through.

'And it did.' Serena stood up. 'What the fuck? Why on earth
would you do that?'

'You took something from me, so I wanted to take something from you.'

'What did I take? What on earth do you mean?'

'I was so angry with you.' Her words cooed out. 'I wanted
to make you feel as stupid as I felt on that beach when they
forgot I even existed.'

Zara knew the comments a picture like that could engender.
She knew the hatred that flowed from people's fingers. It was
an act of knowing cruelty. She knew what could have sparked
if the image had stayed online for longer. If people had chosen
not to support her. But they had supported her.

'I wanted you to know how it felt.'

Of course she knew how it felt. Her light had so often been obscured by Zara's.

'I couldn't even get that right.' Zara's lips pressed together. 'It made you more popular. Made her think you were even more special.'

Serena remembered the smack of hands on the surface of water. After all those years, she'd come out on top. Serena had always been able to imagine it better than the others. She'd triumphed against Zara. The cousin who'd stolen the oxygen from every room, who'd taken their matching eighth of DNA and used it better. Who'd marked her ownership in every space they'd shared. Serena had won.

'I didn't think that would happen,' Zara said.

Serena was sure Zara hadn't. She'd never seen Serena as a threat. They had far more in common than Zara realised.

Serena stared at her cousin, cowed now, crouched on the floor at her feet, and waited for the thrill of victory to rip through her. Nothing stirred. Perhaps it would land instead as fury. That deliberate callousness deserved anger, deserved for her to scream at Zara, demand an apology. But no rage surged either.

'I even fucked that up.'

Sitting there, Zara seemed small. Her gloss and assurance had faded. Sending that photograph had been a feeble act, a pathetic attempt to grasp something back. Serena couldn't muster the anger. Her impulse was to protect Zara, to shield her. To look at her cousin and not turn away.

But there wasn't time. Jane was at the end of the corridor now, signalling.

Serena held out her hand, pulling Zara to her feet. She stood inches taller, felt decades older.

'Shall we go in together?'

Jane carried twelve white tapered candles. Without acknowledging Keira's absence, she held three herself and handed Serena one extra as she passed them out. She lit each one with Luke's silver Zippo lighter, that lighter with its dedication – To Sarah – to a long-forgotten woman. Serena had been surprised when Luke had arrived with Dean, hands in the pocket of his peacoat.

'We should say their names before we go in.'

'Okay, but let's move to the fire exit. If the candles set off the smoke detectors, we won't be able to do anything.' Dean's mind saw practicalities everywhere.

All five of them stepped to the nearest door, and Dean pressed the bar to let in a crack of light. The candle flames bent towards the outside, hungry for its oxygen.

'I'll start.' Jane's face flickered, lit from either side by the candles. Her black clothes were lost to the dark, leaving her features to float, spectral and impossible. Her eyes didn't blink.

Each candle had a tag tied to its base: a name written in Jane's hand.

'Gilly Sampson.' The pause held in the air. 'Janet Lachlan. Alison Duncan.'

Zara barely let a moment pass. 'Martha Clarke.' Her voice rang along the corridor, nothing like Jane's hushed reverence. Dean urgently gestured for a lower tone. Zara's confidence appeared to have returned to its height. She articulated every syllable as if they were delicious. 'Catherine Simpson.'

She looked at Jane as she said the women's names. Jane looked back.

Luke spoke next. 'Agnes Balfour. Ann Weir.' His hair was tied back from his face.

Dean lifted his candles to read from their tags, sending a halo above them. 'Marion Watson. Elizabeth Waterhouse.'

Serena had memorised the three names on her candles. 'Mallie Grant. Elizabeth Horne. Jean Patterson.' She tried to think of the women as she said their names. Women murdered by the man whose face they'd soon destroy.

Jane blew out her candles, then pressed licked fingers against the wicks to stop them from smoking. The symbolism was important, but couldn't scupper their plans. The others followed suit. Jane handed the bulky silver lighter back to Luke, but Zara snatched it.

'I'll take this.' Her smile was wide, a plastered-on eagerness. Serena knew the planes of that metal lighter would be cool against Zara's palms, but didn't know what stirred deep within her.

Sound travelled differently inside the hall. It echoed high before crashing back down, giving every footstep epic consequences.

The elaborate vaulted ceiling made it feel like being inside the ribs of some terrible beast. Wood panelling along one side gleamed with polish and thick curtains glowed maroon, even in the dark. Row after row of chairs were laid out, facing the stage. An invisible audience, ready to watch them.

Hung in the centre of the back wall, above the raised dais they'd one day collect their degrees upon, was the Earl of Carnforth. All major events staged by the university were watched over by that man. As Serena met his eyes, rage slammed through her bones. This was it. Fingertips to arms to skull to torso to waist to knees to toes. The full line of her body burned. He would have ended a woman like her. As she looked, his face seemed to morph into a third dimension, to push from the canvas, shed its oil and gain consciousness for a second.

Serena smiled. He was dead. All that was left was a thin rendering of what he might have looked like. She wanted to blow him a kiss.

As they reached the painting, Jane upturned the canvas bag she carried. Dean and Luke did the same. The armloads of seaweed they'd gathered on the beach lay in heaps underneath that man. Some of it had grown brittle, its fibres tangled; the rest was pulpy and repulsive. All of it smelled. The sharp saltiness of the beach had given way to something sulphurous and rotting. It felt right. Some part of those women was present. Some part of that horror. Some part of Jane when she'd howled her pain to the elements.

Serena looked around in the dim light. She wanted to catch

Jane's eye, hold her dry hand, steal a moment in that echoing hall. A moment of communion at this place they'd imagined. But Jane was distracted.

Zara dragged a heavy chair, scraping it across lacquered parquet wood. She heaved it onto the raised platform and settled it directly in front of the Earl of Carnforth. Jane didn't hesitate, pulling an A3 page from her backpack. She'd written the demands in something close to calligraphy, swooping curves forming each letter. Serena knew what those words said, but also knew they were irrelevant.

Zara stood on the chair, putting herself within easy reach of the painting, where they'd told the boys the charred paper would be clipped, left to make their point. She flipped Luke's lighter open in one dramatic movement, flicked its wheel with her thumb, grinding the flint to release the flame. In that dark hall, the leap of light was astonishing. Serena stopped breathing. This was the moment she'd thought of so many times.

Dean and Luke moved towards the chair as if drawn to the glow. They watched as Zara held a corner of the paper to that juddering plume of orange. There was no pause. One side of the page was instantly alight. Zara shook it, trying to slow its pace, but was too late. The plan to scorch its edges was gone. The blaze already emitted smoke, coils that shimmied to the high ceiling. The smell was familiar, all Serena had breathed for days. That A3 sheet was over halfway destroyed, its flames creeping closer to Zara's fingers. Standing to her full height, Zara held the page against the painting.

'Be careful! You're way too close.' Dean's voice was lost to the huge room.

Serena prepared to witness the image her mind had played over and over. She knew how delicious it would be. But it became clear in a single second that she was wrong. It was nothing like she'd imagined. Serena didn't know fire. She didn't know how it behaved. That nipped, callous face didn't pucker and bubble into boils. She didn't watch Richard Pelham writhe in agony as the oil that preserved him was eaten away. There was no moment of bliss where his eyes bulged and his mouth seemed to scream. Instead, he vanished. The oil darkened on contact with the flames, wiping him out before Serena could see anything.

Dean was shouting now. Serena could barely make out words, only exclamations of horror. The painting switched steadily from black to red, as if the oil remembered it was combustible. Flames did not reach up like delicate dancers, but were hard and ugly.

Serena realised their chief demand was now irrelevant. Richard Pelham had gone. Nothing about it tasted like victory. He wasn't within that painting. That man had felt no fear or pain, no remorse for his actions. The university wouldn't change its stance. The Carnforth Club wouldn't alter their actions. There was no triumph. The fire Serena had carried in her mind was a fiction.

28

'What the fuck is going on?'

Dean's words were clear, but Serena had no idea how to answer. The painting was ablaze, smoke gathering in the vaulted ceiling, too high to reach them yet, but it wouldn't take long. Serena steeled herself, remembering the siren from freshers' week, when she'd first met Keira.

'We need to go. Now.' Dean's face was a mask of panic.

He looked from Zara to Jane. 'We need to move.'

Zara remained standing on the chair.

'Why the fuck aren't you moving? We need to leave!'

Jane's voice rang out. 'No. Not yet.'

Running a hand down his face, Dean shook his head. 'No, no. Shit, no.'

He looked to Serena, appealing to her. She avoided his gaze, watching the flames instead. They were content for now to gnaw at the canvas.

Dean's whole body lurched as he looked around the hall. He ran to the back corner. Luke was already at the main doors, propping them open, phone to one ear, summoning help.

The fire wouldn't stay contained. Jane must have a plan, some final action, some flourish before they left.

Beckoning Zara from the chair, Jane steered her across the room. Serena followed. She felt the impact in her stomach as she saw what they'd done. This was not a statement, a piece of charred paper. The fire in her mind had been so consuming, she hadn't considered what would remain. Her imagination hadn't encompassed the repercussions.

Jane paused, her brow firm. 'I need a little longer.'

Serena's words tangled. 'Longer? What do you mean? We're done. He's gone. We can't put this out on our own. We need to leave. We need to work out what to say; they won't believe it was an accident.'

'Not yet.' Nothing about her acknowledged the smoke, the flames that still seethed.

In the low light of that room, Serena froze. Everything registered in flashes. Jane and Zara whispering. Dean charging towards them with a fire extinguisher. The streams of foam that seemed to blast out like the tentacles of some terrible cephalopod. The chemical foam mixed with smoke to thicken the air further. The flames didn't die, but Dean dampened them. The damage was not extensive. One painting, some scorched wall panelling. Serena noticed Luke looking at her through the haze. Their expressions matched. By some miracle, the smoke detectors had not yet triggered. They'd already gone too far.

Silence fell. A breath that felt like calm.

Then Jane spoke 'We need to finish the job.'

'What? We need to get out of here.' Serena had never raised her voice to Jane before.

She received no response.

'We destroyed him. He's gone.' Serena pointed at the smouldering canvas. 'We need to leave. It's not safe; the security guys will be here any second.' Her body towered over Jane's, but it made no difference.

Jane's face didn't move. Serena couldn't see her. Not because of the smoke and the foam, but because those features weren't Jane's. They were hard: rigid and unrelenting. As she glared at Serena, there was no light in her eyes, only calculation. Her clothes were severe, her hair stiff, her lips taut.

'I'm not going yet.'

Jane's head turned for a second. It was almost indiscernible, but Serena followed her gaze. The wall near the main doors. As she looked, Serena's stomach contracted. On that wall were twelve framed photographs. Twelve faces. Black and white and glossy, as vaunted as the long-dead men in the paintings. Above them, gilt on wood, the words *New Generation Minds*. Jane's eyes were focused on the one nearest to them. Nicholas Matthews. His tense smile. His tight features. Serena had imagined them in detail. She walked towards the display. Under his image, the same gold lettering in miniature. *Dr Nicholas Felix Matthews.*

Felix. The name that meant 'luck'. The boy Jane had begged to tell what he knew. The boy who'd sealed Nylah's fate. A boy who found a moniker to give him the Oxford gloss he craved, grown into a man who used his full name.

Next to the grid of framed pictures was a poster. *New Generation Minds Inaugural Lecture.* The date was the following day. The venue was Carnforth Hall. The keynote was Felix. Jane had known all along. She was here to destroy Felix every bit as much as Richard Pelham. She was here to destroy the hall, to make sure the words of his lecture would never be spoken. She didn't care what trouble they unleashed, didn't care about the implications. She was willing to endanger them all.

Jane strode over to Felix's larger-than-life-sized face. That half-smile like an actors, that studied neutrality. A glint in her hand. Luke's silver lighter. One strike and the glass splintered into a wild spider's web, severing Felix's face, turning his skin to ragged shards, slicing his flesh from hairline to chin. Serena saw the shine of Jane's eyes, the tears that nearly formed. Jane wasn't thinking of those women who'd been killed, the women cursed by the sermons she studied. Serena was sure. She was thinking of one woman. One woman she hadn't seen for over a decade. A woman who might not even remember her name. She was thinking of her own shredded career. The fire that burned in Jane wasn't justice but vengeance. They were all collateral damage.

Jane walked towards her now. Reaching over, she held Serena's cheek. 'You understand, don't you?' Her hands were rough and hot, and Serena wanted them off her face. 'You always feel it so deeply. I know you understand.'

Finally, the smoke reached the detectors, and a soaring, oscillating siren began to wail. In that sudden noise, a nauseating jolt. Serena felt the past weeks and months come into focus. For Jane, had it only ever been about making amends for her own past?

Then, Zara's voice. 'What now?' Her eyes were wide. She grabbed the lighter from Jane's hands. Did Zara know about Nylah? Had she seen that framed photograph in Jane's office? Did she know her own hair flowed the way another girl's once had?

The siren was more a sensation than a sound, searing down Serena's spine. She shouted over it. 'No. This is not happening. We have to go.'

'I thought you were committed to seeing it through.'

Serena no longer felt the blow of Jane's words. 'You can't do this. We're leaving.' She put as much strength into her voice as she could muster, to reach above the alarm's shrieks. She whipped around, looking to find Dean for support.

'No. This is what we have to do.' Jane snapped her fingers. 'Now. And here.' She gestured to the smoke-blurred room. 'We're already going to face repercussions. We're not done with Leysham yet. Don't you want to make a real statement?'

Shaking her head, Serena said all she could. 'No. Absolutely not.' She felt hollow. No ending to that night could be good.

Zara dragged the heavy chair from the platform across the room.

Serena watched Jane turn. The woman she'd walked so many steps with, whose words had changed who she was. The woman who'd sparked something deep within her. Who'd made her extraordinary again. She looked like a stranger.

'Let's get rid of them all!' Zara shouted over the wavering blare, throwing her arms towards the images that lined the walls. Stony-faced men with positions of power. 'I don't know who these fuckers are, but I know they wouldn't be on our side!'

Zara brandished the lighter with a flourish. She was no longer performing for the camera. There was only one audience member now.

Zara dashed to the shattered picture of Felix and held the flame until it ate beneath the fractured glass, looking at Jane the whole time. Did she know who that man was? Serena saw Jane smile slightly. What satisfaction could she gain from seeing the image of him warp and vanish? It was meaningless. The photograph withering would do nothing to thwart his ambition. His papers would still be published to acclaim. He still hadn't helped Nylah. His name still meant 'luck'.

Zara climbed onto the chair she'd dragged. Dean ran over, trying to haul her off. 'Get down. Come on, Zara.'

She kicked out at him. 'Get the fuck off me – don't touch me!'

Raising her arms above her head, Zara looked like she was dancing. Serena recalled the Gilly Sampson Bash, Zara's hair and the tendrils of her dress flowing, as if underwater.

Zara stared at Jane. 'We have work to do.' Serena knew what Zara was capable of. She was so fragile she'd become brittle. She'd do whatever it took to keep Jane's eyes on her.

Luke stood by the main doors, watching out for the security team, for the fire brigade.

Dean tried one more time. 'Jane, this is insane. We need to get out.' His voice was swallowed by the siren's noise. 'We can't stay here with you. It's not safe. Come on, Luke, we should go.'

Jane spoke slowly. 'This is a protest. Protest is never obedient. We have to take risks.'

'No. This is reckless. You're putting us in danger.' Dean hurried to Luke, pulling him through the main doors.

Before Serena could see Jane's response, Zara flipped the lighter awake and heaved the chair across the room.

'Jane! Jane!' She needed that attention to be unwavering.

This painting showed a man in a crimson academic gown. It was far bigger than Richard Pelham's, showing his entire body. It was out of Zara's grasp, higher than the chair could lift her. She placed her trainers on its arms, but couldn't get to the canvas. The chair teetered, forcing her back on the seat. She tried again, but it was even more precarious than before. Her energy was frenetic, her eyes wild. She craned her head to Jane, flicked the lighter, barely able to reach the red paint at the base. For a few seconds, she held the flame against the canvas, against the velvet drapes next to it. The chair wobbled again, perilously this time, scraping over the wooden floor, dancing as if possessed. Zara's arms flailed, windmilling, nothing to grip. She yelped one high bark, then jumped to the floor, landing awkwardly.

Serena seized the chance. Her muscles took over. It was as natural as cutting through the water. She reached Zara, grabbed her arm and pulled. At first, it worked. Zara stumbled a few steps with her, through the alarm's wail. They got closer to the door. Serena was taller than her cousin, far more muscular. It should have been easy, but determination made Zara strong. Once she'd recovered her footing, no matter how hard Serena tried, Zara was immoveable.

The thick, maroon drapes were engulfed in seconds.

'Shit!' The fire was making inroads into the wooden panelling that covered the wall. Zara shrugged free of Serena's grip, then pulled the chair out of the way as the fire blasted through the velvet, creating a wall of heat from floor to ceiling. This was not the fire Serena had imagined. This fire was their enemy.

She watched as Zara dragged the chair to another painting, tried to light it.

'Zara! No!' Serena's screams didn't make it across the room.

The smoke grew thicker. The endless, thundering alarm vibrated in Serena's throat. Her lungs struggled for air, even so close to the open door. Everything had changed so rapidly. It wasn't a fragment of time but a chasm. The fledgling blaze was now raging, an anarchic force. Loud pops competed with the siren's bleat, as hidden pockets of air in the wood were forced out.

Serena couldn't leave without Zara, but the chairs between them seemed to multiply. The blaze reached one corner of the set-up, smashing through the fabric and foam of each, creeping closer, chair by chair. Serena tried to clear the smoke and noise – that constant, constant noise – away. Despite the chaos, despite Jane's betrayal, she needed to help Zara.

The sound of metal hitting metal. Serena looked up to see Jane ahead of her, trying to push through the chairs, to clatter them apart and reach Zara. Her was mouth open, her words lost. The chairs seemed to battle her, each leg interlocked to the next, forming a shield wall of infantry that kept her at bay. They were impenetrable, but Jane didn't stop. Serena saw her bared teeth, her clawed fingers. She seemed to be fighting for Zara the way she wished she'd fought for Nylah.

Then she stopped. The smoke between them made her indistinct, but Serena saw her pulled backwards and away from the phalanx of chairs. Luke lifted her with strength Serena hadn't known he held. Jane flailed, but had to submit. Then, arms around Serena's waist. Dean's arms, hoisting her from the ground, removing her volition, ignoring her struggles. Making her safe.

29

The hit of cold was like jumping into water. One breath of night air triggered Serena's lungs. She coughed until her body bucked. The hairs on the back of her throat were annihilated and she heaved until she threw up on the magnificent stone steps. The steps stained by Zara's fake blood: part of her, but not her. The smoke and char of the room fought to get free. Serena's body was resourceful. When it had expelled everything she'd eaten, it dug deeper, and strings of bile heaved over the stone. She felt Keira's arms on her shoulders, Keira's hands rubbing her back. The siren had called her friend to return. Serena's eyes and nose streamed as she struggled to take in clean air.

Serena knew what she had to do. Her eyes were too blurred to look around, but she knew Zara wasn't safe. This is what it had all led to. The enormous wooden doors that guarded

Carnforth Hall were ajar, letting a sliver of fire shine through, cutting it into a neat, manageable slice. It couldn't be real. Each flame seemed formed by strokes of paint, colour and nothing more.

Zara was in there. In that burning wood, those oils sending their toxic fumes into her lungs. Serena had imagined it. It was her fault. Zara was alone. The plastic and metal of her phone would have warped in the heat. Even Jane couldn't see her now.

Smoke didn't reach them outside, but the air was thick with noise. The wail of the alarm met with something deeper, the grumble of flames devouring the room. The heat must be unthinkable. Serena longed for the water she knew so well, wished she could summon it, call it from her fingertips. She twisted her head to Poseidon, his fountain feebly tinkling, dyed to shrill violet, a god of water with only a trickle. Serena would have to be the water.

She knew she could control it. All she had to do was see clearly. She knew what water could do, but fire was so different. Its intentions were shadowy: the destruction it could wreak, the strange horror it inflicted upon anything it touched. Fire could morph things, buckle them to nothing. It never stayed still. Even with the flames so close, Serena couldn't capture them in her mind.

She closed her eyes. She couldn't imagine fire, but she could imagine Zara. She tried to fix Zara in her mind, not Zara as she showed herself to the world, but Zara as Serena knew her. The dark of Zara's hair, the soft of Zara's laugh. Zara's lips when the red had smeared off. The ache of her stories. The vulnerability at her core. The tiny gap where her nose gem had once been. It was useless. The image ducked and jittered like flames.

She needed to think of nothing but Zara. The girl who stood firm when others turned away. The brilliant girl so many thousands looked up to. Her sweet, gentle cousin who'd fought to love the body she lived in and had showed others every inch of it so they'd feel better. The hair that flowed over all surfaces. The soft squash of her stomach. Serena knew Zara's body better than she knew her own.

She tried to sense the heat inside of her, not just on her skin, but every breath was a struggle. Her muscles shook as she pushed them until it hurt. She had always been able to continue beyond the moment she wanted to stop. Pain was pure. *Pain is the fire in which you forge yourself.* The mind always gives up before the body. Zara was the black line at the bottom of the pool that she had to focus on. The pain seared along Serena's thighs as she strained. With each exhale, she allowed herself a short, guttural shout, a second of relief.

The heat wouldn't be summoned. Her fingers felt nothing. She tried to smell Zara; that sweet, overwhelming scent of flowers distilled. Nothing. It had to start in her fingers, as if they were cutting through the pool's water, then flow up her arms and down her spine. Nothing. Serena smacked her hand against the stone steps, smashing her fingers until they were bruised and bloody. Anything that might ignite the sensation. She had created that fire. Now, she had to defeat it.

You run back to the building. The others try to hold you back, to keep you safe, but you escape their arms and get to the doors before they catch you. The heat as they open is like a physical blow, but you don't stop. The smoke doesn't block your view. It clears for you. You can see her. She's bent over in the corner, staying low. The fire knows you and keeps away. It knows your strength. It opens a path, bows to your power. Even with its reverence, that heat is a solid thing, a living beast. Your skin and eyes and nostrils scream. Your hair singes. Fear roots her to the ground, but you pull. You find a route through the chairs, through the flames and take her with you. She stumbles, but you hold her up. You pull her onto the steps, away from the heat and the smoke and the blazing wood and velvet. She crumples in the dark, but she's breathing. She is safe.

Serena couldn't discern whose limbs held which parts of her, only that she was trapped. Both Luke and Keira stopped her from running to the doors. She couldn't escape them. Each breath rattled and burned in her chest. Keira sobbed in her ear.

Jane stood to one side of the courtyard, silent and pale. Serena couldn't look at her, couldn't think about her. The doors would open. They would open and Zara would walk out, resplendent, arms in the air, laughing at their concern. She'd snap a picture to record the moment, post it on every feed.

The endless, ebbing whine of the alarm was finally met by something more purposeful. The throb of a fire engine, hurtling towards them. They'd arrive in seconds. Zara would be pulled from the room by trained professionals with boots and hats and hoses. The fire would stand no chance against their efficiency.

People gathered in the courtyard, spilling from the nearby buildings, woken by the noise, but Serena registered them only as vague shapes. She couldn't move. Luke's arms were around her collar, the cage of his bones locking her in. She could see the thatch of hair on his arms, feel the bristles of his chin pressed against one side of her forehead. With her throat raw, Serena couldn't scream her cousin's name, but it shrieked through her body. *Zara. Zara. Zara.* It seared through her muscles and ached the marrow inside her bones. It thumped in whatever part of their blood was the same, the hidden places where their DNA matched. *Zara, Zara, Zara.*

30

Don't ever let yourself be diminished.

You are made of stardust. You are perfect. The universe is miraculous and so are you.

It was September and warm, the remnants of summer refusing to ease their grip. It had been so dry the mud was dust that caught on the breeze now. The trees held their leaves but were bent double as if the wind haunted them. The river didn't seem so far any more. The paths that cut across the grass didn't twist so dramatically. The buildings that towered in the heart of the campus were benign, gentle in their golden prettiness.

Serena had longed for that river for months. Her parents had urged her to take a year off, move back home and recuperate, but she could think of nothing worse than languishing in her childhood bedroom. She needed to be back at Leysham. She wanted to sit silently and read from crisp pages. The stories of people from long ago felt calm after so much noise, even if the past could never be reliable.

It was clear the disciplinary committee should have been harsher. They'd all expected expulsion, but the timing saved them. The inquest only days before had discovered that the fireproofing of the room, notably of the maroon drapes and fabric chair cushions, was perilously out of date. Although the students had started the fire, they weren't to know Carnforth Hall was a tinderbox. It was deemed a terrible accident. After everything that had occurred on campus that year, the institution was eager to sidestep further press coverage. Only Jane was dismissed. Serena hadn't spoken to her since they'd left for the hospital in the early hours of that morning, oxygen masks strapped to their faces. There was nothing Serena wanted to say, nothing she was willing to hear. The others were allowed to continue with their studies, and no one faced criminal charges. It took Serena weeks to feel relieved.

She looked out at the river. The water that had tried to wrench Tanya away a year before. The water where women had gasped their last breaths. It looked tranquil on that mild day. Peaceful. Was it too optimistic to hope fire might cleanse as well as destroy? That something of what they'd done, what they'd illuminated, might ease the way for the women and men who followed? That perpetrators might face fiercer opposition? That whatever potency they'd summoned might have an impact? That Gilly Sampson might rest easy?

The news was reported widely, Zara's face printed on paper as well as shared in the pixels it knew so well. They used her profile picture, cropped so only her head and neck showed. They didn't know the power that lay in the rest of that body. The picture had been taken the summer after sixth form. Before Zara had travelled up the coast to university, before her follower count had reached six figures, before she'd met Jane. Before Serena understood who she was.

Her cousin looked so young in those pages. Her flesh was full, and she seemed to steal the pigment from her pink jumper. It was as if she carried nothing on her shoulders. Her hair shone and her blue nose stud glinted in the sun.

Serena cut the images from the papers, snipping neatly along the edges. She bought every newspaper she could find, found every reference to Zara. She wanted to hold them in her hands, let their print stain her fingers. No report ever grasped it. They didn't know her. She was reduced to Zara Carmichael, social media influencer and first-year student of Sociology at Leysham University, who had died in an accidental fire at the age of nineteen.

The colours on her feed were uniform again. In her final few months, Zara had favoured mythical images, black-and-white shots, protest slogans. She'd muddied her own rainbow. Now it was back to sweet technicolor. Under #zarakarmic, time reversed to the days when her feed was a wash of rich pastels. Her fans, her friends, her admirers mimicked the style, uploading quotes of hers, images with filters that made them beam like an endless sunset. Gold, teal, peach. Anoushka reposted, curating those pictures with skill. Zara would always be alive in that grid. Her face always laughing, the ripples of her stomach always warm, the flesh of her thighs abundant. Everything was positive, everything inspiring, everything beautiful. Nothing could ever hurt her.

The guilt felt feral, and the ache in Serena's core wouldn't ease.

The smack of chlorine hit like a memory. It made Serena's eyes sting and her nose run like so many times before, but there was no adrenalin this time. She took a different route on those familiar bobbled tiles, not to the lanes and Niko's voice but the bath-like warmth of the children's pool. Delilah was solid in her arms. She wore a turquoise costume with ruffles around the middle and a picture of Ariel emblazoned on the front, her red hair suspended in the ocean. Delilah's seriousness didn't suit its frivolity. On one of the shoulder straps was a tiny, sequinned seashell.

Serena cupped her niece's bare feet as the water buoyed her. Delilah didn't protest, didn't giggle, but fixed Serena with those grave eyes. The soles of her feet were like velvet. She was over six months old but seemed brand new to Serena. Kelly would squeeze the plump flesh of Delilah's thighs between her fingers as she tickled her, but the baby was firm and resilient. Delilah could stumble and barely flinch.

Serena's own body was denser, more tightly packed than before. Her flesh was only flesh. It held no more power than that. Her mind stayed in the moment, no different to anyone else's. The feel of the water on her skin remained a balm.

Delilah didn't kick in the water but was composed. She could lie on her front and not fear the waves that lapped her face. She reached her arms out as if she knew how to form a stroke, her body finding its way through nothing but instinct. Serena could let go and those strong limbs would hold her.

Serena had once imagined that body before it was born, longed for it to grow robust. She kept her hand under Delilah's stomach, feeling the muscles that had already developed. This tiny girl would have so much power.

'Gosh, she's a natural, isn't she?' A woman with two small boys smiled at Serena. She wore a black costume with a high racing neckline. Without thinking, Serena scanned her arm muscles, the span of her shoulders.

She smiled back. 'She is.'

Delilah's face dipped peacefully into the water and, for a second, she formed a perfect streamline under the surface. Her eyes were open to the chlorine, but she didn't blink. Her body was fully extended and Serena could see the invisible line flow from her fingertips to her skull to torso to waist to knees to toes. Delilah was an arrow shot through the pool. For that moment of glide, she became part of the water.

ACKNOWLEDGEMENTS

A second novel is a whole new voyage. I am endlessly grateful to everyone who supported me along the way.

Thank you to my inimitable agent, Lucy Morris, for your clear-eyed intelligence, remarkable vision and fierce support. I'm so glad to have you on my side. Thank you enormously to Rosie Pierce for supporting me with such passion, care and skill. Thank you to Anna Weguelin, Liz Dennis, Georgia Williams, and everyone at Curtis Brown for your excellence and hard work.

Thank you to my editor, Frankie Edwards, for being extraordinary. It is an utter joy and privilege to work with you again, and benefit from your passion, insight and luminosity. Thank you to Jessie Goetzinger-Hall for your thoughtful brilliance. To Amy Cox for the exquisite cover, to Ollie Martin and everyone at Headline for being the most spectacular team.

To get under the skin of competitive swimming took some exploration. For the inspiration, thank you to *Swimming Studies* by Leanne Shapton, *Swimmer's World* magazine, *Relentless Spirit* by Missy Franklin, *Beneath the Surface* by Michael Phelps, *Swim* by Lynn Sherr, *Barracuda* by Christos Tsiolkas. And huge thanks to Cressida Brown for sending me a recording of the beautiful *Amphibians*.

I wrote this novel while watching my first go out into the world. I am so thankful for the writing community who buoyed me when we couldn't even walk into bookshops. Thanks to the writers who gave their support so generously, the bloggers who kept the spirit alive, the event organisers, and everyone who tuned in.

This novel took me back to my own university days, so thank you to Anna Beer and Julian Thompson for ensuring it was breathtaking, and to everyone at Regent's Park for haunting me still.

Writing would be so lonely without other writers. I am infinitely inspired by my beloved Unruly Writers.

Talking about writing might be my favourite thing about writing, and I'm so grateful to Shahla Haque, Susie Campbell, Charlotte Turnbull and Sarah Neary for being scintillating.

I am incredibly fortunate to do work that makes the days in between writing just as good. Thanks to the friends I've been lucky enough to work with. Thank you especially to Izzy Pugh for telling me a story I will never forget. To the incredible team at Oxford Outreach and Admissions. To all the CI Babes and everyone at Space Doctors. You make the days fascinating.

I am blessed with friends who offer outrageous spirit and support. Carli Bean, Ruth Brock, Mary Groom, Eiluned Jones, Xavior Roide, Francesca Millar and Jess Parr. I will never be able to thank you enough. Katy John, your sparkling and constant friendship is one of my greatest delights.

Thank you to my family for the joy and love. To Elaine and Andy, and Wendy and John. To Ellen, Nathan, Christopher, Henry and Joshua. To Janet and Norman. To Harry, and to my fantastic in-laws, Muriel, Bill, William, Sarah and Jasmine. To my parents, Linda and Glen, for your wonderful conversation, love and encouragement.

To Paul. For being there for every word. For holding my hand through every step of our strange and beautiful adventure.